ETERNAL TIME
―――――――――――――

THE PARALLEL WEAVE

DRAVEN NIGHTSHADE

Copyright © 2025 by Draven Nightshade

All rights reserved.

No part of this book may be reproduced in any form or by any electronic or mechanical means, including information storage and retrieval systems, without written permission from the author, except for the use of brief quotations in a book review.

*For those who find their balance in chaos.
Of those treading the thin line that separates light from darkness.
And that takes guts: facing the unknown.
This is for you, in turn.*

*To stand watch over the watchmen.
The rebels who challenge,
And the witnesses that speak the truth—
May connectivity bring strength to you.
Understanding with hope.
And in destiny, cross fates in harmony.*

To the dreamers, who envision bridges instead of walls. And to the authors who brought harmony amidst turmoil— That is testimony to an unconquerable spirit.

PREFACE

Eternal Time: The Parallel Weave, Book2 of the series.

In the river of time, a few stories rise to mere recounting, becoming witnesses to the birth of a civilization. That is an epic woven of threads of hope and chasm, shadows and light, demise and rebirth.

Long, long ago, humanity saw the Abyss as a foreboding presence that invited taming, attempting to dominate the unknown with mere force alone. But sometimes, reality prefers to seek refuge in the most unlikely of locations: oftentimes, it is precisely that about which one most fears that one must work hardest to understand in a quest for survival.

The epic tells the legend of seven protectors: El, Prophecy Child; Seline, Guardian of Life; Monica, Warrior of Blood Crystal; Victor, Shadow Walker; Count, Keeper of the Eternal Ring; and Miller, Keeper of Wisdom. All of them arrive at a critical point in fate, when they realize that purpose runs deeper and grander than any one of them could ever have dreamed.

In this epic, an awakening will occur through dimensions, an odyssey that redefines even the most basic of light and shadow. As seals shatter through ages, threads of prophecy intertwine, and the Eternal Ring melts into starlight, a new beginning takes shape.

Not an epic of discord, but an allegory of reconciliation and awareness, a new city arises out of the ashes of the City of Hope. And when, at long, long last, first light begins to break through smoke, when source energy spills down in a waterfall of gold, then, and then alone, will we realize: every demise foretells a new beginning, and each fall tends to nurture rebirth.

Let us follow in the path of these guardians through mists of fate, and behold a world changing from discord to harmony, mastery to understanding, and fear to hope.

We find, at the edge of the narrative, that conquest's greatest power is not in conquest, but in listening; that mastery's greatest strength is not in dominating, but in comprehension; and disunion's greatest enemy is not disunion, but in its acceptance, in its embracing of unity.

The narrative will have no conclusion, for with each age, a new one will start to break. In the heart of the City of Hope, radiating its glory, stands the Tree of Light, a quiet guard to an unending line of new tales as they unfold.

INTRODUCTION

At the crossroads of reality and legend, when shadows and light become one, a journey begins that tests our very understanding of fate. "Eternal Time: The Parallel Weave" invites readers into a reality in which ancient prophecies become intertwined with modern thinking, a reality in which shadows protect deepest hope and brightest aspirations.

The journey begins in the Abyssal City, a city shrouded in deep and paradoxical mystery. For centuries, this gargantuan city dominated humanity's tireless quest to encircle and understand powers in and out of the Abyss. Maintaining a tenuous peace between harmony and discord, between knowing and not knowing, were the Seven-Star Guardians, fated and forged through circumstance.

But below the thin veneer of painstakingly constructed equilibrium, revolution simmered, inches below, ready to boil over. In its midst, in its heart, lay the Eternal Ring, an artifact of unimaginable power and even deeper mystery, whose sound, heard not for a thousand years, began to resonate through the ages. Behind its motives, calculated to rend reality's very cloth, lay the Shadow Council, long seen to guard ancient lore.

Our journey threads together a single tapestry out of seven extraordinary lives:

El, whose prophecies sew threads of gold into life's cloth, guiding searchers who falter in search of a path.

Seline, life's bearer, whose healing touch carries creation and destruction's burden.

Monica, a wise strategist, whose integration of age-old traditions with modern awareness brings disparate threads of thinking together in harmony.

Victor, a shadow walker, intimately familiar with mortality, in search of life's essence.

Count, protector of the Eternal Ring, whose unselfish sacrifice would echo through eternity's corridors.

Miller, unrelenting in search of fact, whose quest for knowledge could reveal secrets strong enough to save and forever change their reality.

Together, they face a challenge that extends beyond the simple dualism of good and evil. Their journey invites us to redefine our most basic understandings of power, information, and reality itself.

Introduction

This five-part epic journey takes shape in five phases: initial awakening, realignment of cosmology, encounter, restoration at dawn, and transformation at its peak. With each, a new level of consciousness is revealed, and what long lay in apparent reality turns out to have a deeper reality residing in its shadow.

Here, between these covers, you will not simply witness a battle and its resolution. Instead, you will witness an investigation of transformation, a price for knowing, and an enduring power in hope. As ally and enemy become one, long-standing enemies become reconciled, and reality's purpose is rewritten, we realize that sometimes, transformation happens not through fighting shadows, but through embracing them.

Not a journey through space and time, "Eternal Time: The Parallel Weave" enters into topology of possibility. It is a reminder that in each closing, a new beginning waits, and in each shadow, a glint of its counterpart, light, longs to reveal its presence.

Join me in a universe in which fate is not a foreseen path, but a garden of forking paths, each one an invitation to explore.

PART I

THE AWAKENING ABYSS: TREMORS OF THE ETERNAL RING

With the last seal broken, a pulse beat outwards from the Abyss, and ripples ran across the world. It wasn't just the stillness of a vacuum; it was the wake-up call of a gigantic, slumbering being that had lain asleep since time immemorial. Standing at the edge of the Abyss, Seline felt the regular energy waves, like a pulse.

For the first time, she heard the whisper of the Abyss-an ancient, wise voice. They stood there at the edge and looked down into the seething vortex of energy. There and then, in perfect clarity, they finally realized that their very, very ancient mission had been fundamentally misconceived. It was about listening, not suppression; it was about understanding, not about control.

El's eyes, at that instant, shone a bright, golden glare.

. . .

And the bloodline of the Child of Prophecy quickened, rivulets of higher-dimensional awareness coursing through his soul like some heavenly river. Monica's armor of silver Blood Crystal began to vibrate in harmony, its brilliant surface etched with fine, pulsating patterns of energy as if in answer to some call from the Abyss. Victor's dark energy, once a jarring note, now wove in and out of the scene with ease, an integral part of this glorious tableau.

The Eternal Ring flared with bright light under the command of Count, breaking through the dimensional crack, scattering the ancient wisdom like golden raindrops. Miller's Book of Life appeared in the air and its pages turned, blown by some invisible wind, writing down this historic moment. When the dust finally settled, the Third Power quietly appeared-also not aligning with light, nor with darkness, simply a power of transcendence.

1

AN ACCIDENTAL ALLY

Golden dawn sunlight streamed over the jutting spires of the Abyssal City, casting long shadows in through the great council chamber. From outside its door came the sound of scurrying feet; the guards were coming. Commander Chris strode into the great hall, his footsteps purposeful.

My lords," he said with steadiness, though his tone was urgent. "Victor, former head of the Shadow Council, wishes to speak.

The room fell silent; the faces all told different stories. Count Roland's eyes narrowed, his fingers tracing outlines of the Eternal Ring absent-mindedly. Instinctively, Seline's hand closed a little tighter over her Sacred Artifact, until she saw that the Life Map spread before her was pulsating in a very regular rhythm. El looked toward the door, a reflective expression on his face.

. . .

Victor entered alone; his figure seemed more attenuated beneath the flowing black robes than they had remembered it. He came to the center of the room and looked around on the faces present with a piercing glance, his eyes gleaming bright without hostility or meekness but with something else.

"I know my coming here is unforeseen," Victor said in a hoarse and even voice. "But after the great explosion, there are things I needed to explain personally.

Monica, in her quivering silver armor of Blood Crystal, replied, "The upheaval you mentioned-are you referring to the resonance between the Eternal Ring and the Heart of the Abyss?

"It goes beyond that," Victor said, stepping forward in a very deliberate manner. "At that moment, I felt something much deeper. It was like..." He stopped and tried to find his words. "...like I'd passed through some threshold.

"How interesting," Roland breathed almost inaudibly, "do go on."

Victor's gaze fixed intently on Roland. "For years, I was convinced I stood firmly on the side of truth. Yet, on that day, it became clear to me—truth has never been merely a question of black and white."

"The Book of Life contains accounts of such phenomena, indeed," said Miller, opening an ancient tome. "It says herein that when true transformation occurs, the opposing forces often unite on a higher plane of understanding.

As he finished, it seemed the room's nature changed subliminally, the pulsing within the Heart of the Abyss beating out a strange cadence. That sent a ripple across its energy field, disturbing somehow.

"Wait—" exclaimed Seline, the sudden clarity cutting into the atmosphere. "This is telling me the Life Map of Victor's energy pattern has wholly changed. This isn't a disguise; this is something deeper.

El's eyes went wide, crystal clear. "Like the dawn of the Third Power.

Victor nodded thoughtfully. "Precisely. And that turbulence unmasked a larger vision before me. The past conflicts were but different faces of the same truth.

. . .

Commander Chris interrupted, the patience wearing thin on him. "My lord, are you saying—?"

"I've come to propose an alliance," Victor declared, his gaze unwavering as he looked directly at Roland. "Not for gain, but for a shared awakening."

There was a moment of tense silence in the room. A soft 'ding' escaped Monica's armor; its pitch synchronized with Victor's energy field.

"How interesting," Roland mused, getting to his feet in a slow motion. "It would seem this was set even by the Eternal Ring long ago."

Seline examined the Life Map with great focus. "The energy fields are reorganizing, striving for a new equilibrium. Yet this balance... it's more stable than any pattern we've come across before."

Victor pressed closer still. "Let me show you." Slowly, he raised his hands, and pure energy welled from inside him, shaking in absolute synchrony with the Sacred Artifact and the Eternal Ring. Chris' eyes widened in wonder, for he had never seen such a perfect integration of energies. For an instant, the ongoing battle between these two opposing forces seemed to dissolve.

. . .

"This is not an end," Victor said in a low yet firm tone, his belief resonating in every word. "This is a new beginning. On a higher plane, at last, we can understand each other as we should."

2

THE ANCIENT PROPHECY

Miller's footsteps echoed along dark corridors displaying the library. It was the third time he had come up to this strange stone door with ancient runes that refused to yield their meaning to him. Chris followed behind him, a torch clutched in his hand, and frowned.

"Why today of all days?" Chris asked, a little exasperation tingeing his tone.

Distortions within the field," Miller said, his head not turning. "The tide of energy in Abyssal City has been slowly shifting since the day of Victor's arrival. I traced that shift this morning to find where it resonated with the runes on the stone gate.".

. . .

While Seline and Monica waited there, a mixture of excitement and alertness on their faces, there was at the other end of the corridor a stone door with ancient inscriptions facing them.

"Once more," he said, and he unrolled the Book of Life. He nodded for Seline to get ready. As the light of the Holy Amulet streamed into the doorway, its runes flared to life in a blaze of gold.

"Wait!" Chris suddenly exclaimed. "The runes... they're rearranging themselves!"

Indeed, the runes moved, forming a different pattern. The door, with a soft click, started to open and released not dust, as might have been expected, but a wave of soft, pure energy.

"This is..." Monica's Blood Crystal armor vibrated with a soft hum. "Such clean, ancient power!"

Beyond lay a chamber of modest size, if not unimpressive, dominated by the centerpiece of a display that was mesmerizing in a purely energetic sense. Miller pressed forward, his voice shaking with wonder. "This... this is a whole record of prophecies! Everything the old world ever recorded is stored here!"

. . .

"Be careful," Seline warned. Yet, it was already too late. The instant Miller's fingers touched the projection, chaotic energy exploded out of the chamber's energy field.

Shit!" Chris instinctively raised his gun but was then immobilized as the projection grew and their surroundings filled up with its light. Millions of pictures and symbols became a raging vortex around them.

Don't panic!" Seline exclaimed as the Sacred Artifact radiated a soft light. "This isn't an attack - it's. a way of downloading information.

Monica, astute as ever, said, "These pictures aren't random. There's something connecting them.".

In walked Count Roland and Victor, their faces set in a mask of urgency. The very second the Eternal Ring was in the room, it started pulsating furiously to the energy field laid out for it.

"This is not a prophecy," Victor said in a sober tone. "It is almost a dialogue between dimensions."

"Look!" he exclaimed, pointing at the Book of Life. It opened its pages and spread them out without anyone's help. Words on the projection were reflected here: "The prophet is not a seer, but a messenger from higher planes..."

"Wait," Roland said, squinting. "There are still scenes in that projection which are recognizable.

Indeed, within this kaleidoscope of images were fragments of moments they knew: the formation of the Eternal Ring, the rise of the Third Power. But alongside these known scenes were the unknown-revelations of a greater story, binding them altogether.

"Over there—look!" Chris said, pointing to a faint light at the edge of the projection. "That...looks like...

"Now!" In that instant, the images froze and slowly moved closer to the faint light. It brightened, revealing a ghastly sight: the Abyssal City wrapped in a ghostly, crimson hue.

Is that... the future?" Monica said in a whisper, with her hand trembling around her weapon.

"Not necessarily," Victor said, looking around the scene. "The ancients taught that prophecies showed possibilities, not certainties."

. . .

Miller went further into the Book of Life and read out loud: "Prophecies are mirrors reflecting choices, destiny a river shaped by the heart's decisions.

"How interesting," Roland muttered, his face filled with thought. "So, this is actually the room that shows us how the chains of our present choices come into being."

As if to punctuate his words, the projection rippled violently, its myriad points of light shifting to a new pattern. Chris felt his gun vibrate in sympathy, buzzing at selected lights. "The energy is re-forming!" he exclaimed as Seline's sacred artifact flared up ominously. "Something is going to—"

Before she could complete her thought, a new image emerged in the center of the chamber: a vast labyrinth, its pathways alive with flickering lights. At the heart of the maze, a familiar dark energy throbbed with an unsettling presence. "That's..." Victor's voice shook, his tone serious.

"The Shadow Council!" Chris exclaimed, his face as white as a ghost. "But not in its present setup—this is..."

"A possibility in the future," Roland concluded with a firm, serious tone. "Our newly forged alliance with Victor, it would seem, is about to be tested."

. . .

The energy in the room began to dissipate, the projection disappearing, but the weight of its revelations remained. All present knew that was only the beginning. An ancient prophecy had just shown them strands of something far greater: a tempest brewing over the horizon, decisions yet to be made, and consequences yet to be seen.

3

THE MAZE'S RIDDLE

The shocking revelations of the prophecy had just settled in when another crisis unfolded a month later. At a chilly early morning, he came bursting into the chamber, his face an image of urgency.

"My lords," he began with hiccups of breath, "something has been picked up near the northern border!"

Count Roland, amid his conversation with Victor about the intricacies of the prophecy, rose at once. The Eternal Ring floated above him, slowly rotating as its radiance grew brighter. "Where, exactly?"

Near the ruins of the underground maze," Nick said, unrolling a map before him. "Our scouting teams detected strong energy fluctuations in that area-fluctuations strikingly similar to the ones we've encountered in the prophecy.

*   *   *

Victor's face had turned grave. "The remains of the Shadow Council...

"It's more than that." Monica, flanked by a squad of patrolmen, entered briskly. "The maze appears to be restructuring itself. The original maps are now completely useless. Worse, we've lost contact with two scouting teams."

Seline's holy artifact hummed softly as she attuned herself to its energy. "This restructuring pattern. it's so familiar, much like what the prophecy revealed, yet it's happening so much sooner than expected.

"Where's Miller?" Roland's gaze swept the room.

"He's in the archives," said Chris. "He said something about clues as to the true nature of the maze.

In burst the doors with most unlooked-for violence; El entered, gravely stern: "It has reached a full head. The maze extends-not simply rearranges.

As the significance of his words settled upon them, Miller emerged, bearing several ancient scrolls. "I believe I've discovered the answer," he declared, his enthusiasm mingling with apprehension. "This maze isn't merely a ruin. It's a vast energy converter. And at this moment—"

On, Victor said finally, the flicker of unease dancing across his face. By whom is the question.

"More importantly," Roland interjected, pointing to an obvious aberration on the map, "why now?"

Nick was hesitant before he started to speak. "Recently, some patrol teams found strange rune markings along the border. We dismissed them as the work of some rogue mages.

"Let me see those," Miller insisted, and he rolled out a record of the findings. His color had gone while he was looking at them. "Those runes... By the ancients! Those are the control runes of the ancient civilization for manipulation of gigantic energy devices!"

The warning glow shone bright upon her Blood Crystal armor as Monica said, "So, someone has examined these runes and activates the maze?

"No time is to be wasted, " Roland instructed flatly. "We are going to split up: Miller, keep working on those runes; Seline, trace the energy fields; Monica, take some people, and seal up the border; Victor—

"I am going to the maze," Victor said calmly. "Nobody knows the Shadow Council's methods better than me."

"I go with you," El said. "If indeed there be a mind behind the maze, the Third Power may well be needed.

Chris stepped forward. "Let me take a team to guard the maze's entrance."

Before they could conclude the plan, an imperceptible tremble ran through the ground. Everyone felt the energy field quiver with intensity.

"There's no time!" exclaimed Seline, her Sacred Artifact shining in a brilliant light. "The maze linked itself to the surface energy grid!

"Move out!" a very confident Roland said. "And remember to keep in contact. It could be an ambush, so be careful.

The room vacated in a hurry as each faction took to its appointed task. Victor and El were to lead; he charged into a maze where several panicked scouts in retreat met him halfway.

"My lords!" exclaimed one breathless scout. "The maze... it is just fearsome. The space keeps twisting, and... well, we encountered things that shouldn't exist."

"What things?" El asked.

Shadows... dancing shadows, yet not just dark energy. Something ancient. and a lot worse.

Victor turned to him in seriousness, for the dark energy spoken of in the prophecy it was.

Meanwhile, in the archives, Miller frantically scanned through the ancient texts. His hands shook, and his eyes stuck on a terrifying revelation: "These runes aren't for controlling any device. They are part of some summoning ritual. The maze. it was designed as a huge 'gate' leading to—"

His voice trailed off, and then a powerful, powerful shaking violently shook the city with immense power. The heavy forces enveloped the atmosphere, weighing upon all those caught within. Above Abyssal City, strange ripples undulated across the sky as if to announce the arrival of something gigantic. Then the visions of the prophecy began to unfold in real life, one gruesome detail after another.

Victor and El struggled deeper into the very core of the labyrinth, twisting through its ever-changing corridors, their force fields clashing with the turbulent forces of the maze. "Be careful," Victor warned, "this place is more than a trap, it's alive." El nodded, his Third Power glowing faintly around him. "And something—or someone—guides it."

In the very core of the maze, the meandering ways joined into one vast chamber. The core reverberated with a flitting darkness that grew greater with each passing second. Above them, Miller's desperate voice came through the communication crystals: "The maze... it's not only a way in. It is a summoning! Something from beyond our realm of dimensionality!"

His voice projected the gravity of the situation, and that sense of oppression echoed in every direction. The skies above Abyssal City seemed to instantly turn grim as that dark presence began to condense. Prophecy was taking hold, and an opponent, far greater than anything they had ever faced, rose to meet them.

4

THE ANCIENT GATE

Before the maze's entrance, Victor and El faced front in twisted space. A starboard corridor, now, seemed to writhe and twist, as tugged by some strong, invisible force. Extremely soft light glowed from the runes etched into the walls, sending an eerie shine around them.

Can you feel it?" Victor whispered, his voice barely heard. "This energy. isn't the work of the Shadow Council at all.".

El nodded, his eyes fixed upon the twisted corridor ahead. "And it's something the Third Power has never faced before. More like...

"An ancient force," a voice interrupted from behind. Turning swiftly, they caught sight of Miller hurrying toward them, gripping a rolled-up parchment. His breath came in quick gasps, and his hands shook as he presented the weathered scroll. "I've found the key!"

He barely had time to explain before Chris's voice cracked over the communicator. "My lords, something is wrong! The maze is sucking in the space around it, and our line of defense is—" The message cut off abruptly, replaced by static.

"Chris!" El immediately tried to reestablish the link, but only harsh interference answered.

Miller unrolled the parchment in a flash. "I haven't got time for a long explanation. In short, this labyrinth is not to trap anything but to call something. These runes are the seals of some ancient people now-

"Someone is breaking those seals," Victor concluded, his tone dark. "But why now?"

The ground shook with another stronger earthquake than before, and the maze entrance became even more distorted, space folded in, threatening to implode any moment.

"We have to go in," said El, his voice firm, his resolution unmistakable. "But first, we need to find Chris

and his team."

Victor would have replied, but then he suddenly froze, feeling an all-too-familiar energy signature. "Wait... this energy...

A figure materialized out of the distorted space before he could finish the sentence, and it was Chris, but something was wrong with him: his eyes did not focus, and dark, tendril-like streams of energy churned around him, livewire whips.

"Chris?" Miller said quietly, approaching him very carefully.

"Stay back!" Chris suddenly roared in that hoarse voice of his, with an eerie quality. "They're... they're inside... waiting for us..."

Victor took a step closer, his face alight with eagerness. "Whaddya see?

Chris's head was in a vice of pain. "I saw... I saw things that mustn't be. That gate... that damn gate...

. . .

El had tried to use the Third Power to cleanse the dark energy that clung to Chris, but the attempt had been practically for naught.

"Forget me!" Chris screamed, suddenly clear. "The others are still inside! And... and I saw Andrew...

"What?" Victor and El uttered in one voice, faking their surprise. Andrew was a person in the Shadow Council, a missing member who had disappeared a year ago.

Miller's hands ran swiftly over the parchment, his eyes perusing its inscriptions. "The text says, upon the opening of the Ancient Gate, the borderline between time and space becomes blurred. In other words...

"Those who have vanished may not have left at all," Victor surmised. "They could be caught up in some sort of time fold. And as the door opens, all of its being sucked back to this instant of time."

The ground again rumbled, stronger this time. A light beamed from far in the maze, showing the way through its twisted paths.

"The time has come," El said. "We shall proceed but

cautiously. Miller, take Chris with you to Seline and see if you can remove this energy from her body.

"Wait!" Chris exclaimed in a surge of urgency. "Beware the shadows... they can read your memories..."

Victor's face turned grave. "That explains everything. But why now, and why us.

"They need us," El said, the realization out loud. "Each of us carries a fragment of memory they need to open the gate."

"Or," Miller said, his voice filled with realization as he peered down at the parchment, "we are the keys to the gate itself."

A surge of energy swept the air, as distant tremors grew in intensity. Then the communicator produced Roland's voice—fragmentary, urgent: "...several energy anomalies... Seline says the Life Map indicates... some sort of ancient presence is stirring..."

Victor's face turned to El, his eyes speaking volumes: neither would give way, no matter what would happen further. "Keep in touch," Victor said to Miller. "If we haven't reported back within the hour—"

. . .

"Warn Count Roland and sound the deware," El concluded.

Without a moment's hesitation, the two plunged into the distorted space. The door behind them started closing, sealing the entrance to the maze and entrapping them inside. It wasn't like any ordinary door closing but rather a giant, silent mouth that sucked them in whole.

5

ECHOES OF THE ABYSS

In this maze, the interior was much more disorienting than either Victor or El had thought it would be: everywhere, the corridors twisted and warped at unpredictable angles, sometimes straight paths bent at impossible angles, or vanished altogether.

These energy flows." Victor exclaimed, his piercing eyes following the bright patterns that were playing across the walls. "They seem to interact toward one central nexus.

El halted abruptly. "Listen."

A soft murmur stirred in the air, words no more than an incoherent whisper, indistinct to make anything out of them. It was everywhere and nowhere, caroming back through space outside them to the innermost recesses of their being.

. . .

"Be careful," Victor warned. "Those shades Chris mentioned—"

No sooner were the words out than a thick, dark mist condensed at the far end of the hall. Richer than any shadow energy, the mist was ancient, innately steeped in malice. The mist started to build itself into a human-like figure.

"Andy?" El knew the figure at once.

Yet the form contorted in an unnatural way, breaking down into tendrils of shadow that smote towards them. In an instant, Victor was raising an energy shield-but the tenebrous tendrils slid through it, razor-sharp, to cut at their very conscious minds.

"Ahh!" They both tumbled, and an overcoming shooting pain befell them. Images poured into their minds: disjointed, fractured-some their own, while others were unknown, yet all uninvitingly macabre scenes.

"They aren't attacking us," Victor grated out, his mind fighting the onslaught. "They're searching... for something hidden within our memories..."

. . .

He steadied himself with the call of the Third Power and regained focus. "But why our memories?

The communicator crackled to life, and hurried, fragmented snippets of Miller's voice filled the air. "My lords! I've decoded more of the parchment. The gate... it requires specific 'keys,' and those keys are..." Then, abruptly, the signal cut off once more.

The shadows drew back just as quickly, yet the whispers grew louder, the words now coherent. Victor's eyes had narrowed, his brain still racing for comprehension. "Wait. these voices-they're not of this time.

They're echoes of memories," a voice spoke from behind them; they turned to find Andrew here, his appearance fading in and out between solid and translucent as the projection struggled to hold its image. "Welcome to the Abyss of Memories, my old friends.

"You're alive," Victor said, his voice steady, though it bore the weight of unasked questions. "You've been here for the entire year?"

Andrew smiled faintly, his expression remaining inscrutable. "Yes... and no. Time flows differently in this place. I've witnessed so much... far too much. Countless possibilities..."

. . .

"You know what's behind that gate," El said. And softly spoken, the word hit right at the heart of things.

"Of course I do," Andrew said. His form flickered once again. "It's the last riddle from the ancient civilization. But to solve it, one doesn't need strength nor intellect-it needs the truth. The whole truth."

"What truth?" Victor pressed.

But then, Andrew's body began to distort. "You will see soon enough. When all the fragments of memory are put together. when past and future come together in this moment. then the gate opens. And through it." his voice trailed off to a whisper ".changes everything.

"Wait!" Victor called, surging forward, but it was too late: he was gone. The air twisted in vicious curves around them, unrolling into other corridors as the maze realigned itself anew. Behind them, other figures of darkness emerged, the stirring shadows restless, voracious.

"They're coming," El said, his hands clenching into fists of the Third Power. "This time we can't afford to let them enter our memories so easily."

. . .

Victor nodded, his face set in steely determination. "But we've got to find out what they're looking for. That may be the key to opening the gate."

A low rumble ran through the maze, its reverberations shaking cold from the walls. A rumble of rumbling, far away, as if the stirring of some giant beast from sleep, was then heard. The dark figures became frantic, their whispers rising to shrill wails.

"Move!" Victor urged, his voice sharp with urgency. "We must locate that gate before chaos engulfs us all!"

Hand in hand, they ran across the shifting hallways of the maze, pursued without stop by the nameless shadows tearing at their minds. The gate was forward—somewhere ahead—and the secret of it was locked out by veils of truth and time.

It was only when the echoes from the abyss grew louder that the path through the maze slowly began to reveal itself, a mere prologue to a greater discovery.

6

THE MEMORY MAZE

Down twisting corridors now, Victor and El emerged into a large circular hall; its walls glowed with luminous runes and its floor was bestrewn with magical symbols. Around the middle of the room was a huge crystal column, probably with several thousand points of light dancing and swirling inside it in various directions.

These are. fragments of memory? El asked, stepped closer to the crystal pillar, and watched the dancing lights.

Victor carefully checked the trace of the magic array. "This hall seems to be a collecting device; it is like all the memories that the shadows have taken in are collected here.

In that instant, the crystal column vibrated, and an odd memory image unfolded in the air of an ancient civilization lined with robed mages working industriously upon a huge device.

"I see." Victor's eyes narrowed as realization dawned on him. "This maze itself is a huge memory collector."

The communicator crackled again, and Seline's voice issued forth, fragmented: "...Energy resonance... The Life Map is showing distinct signs of extinct patterns..."

Extinct patterns?" El frowned. "You mean... extinct life patterns?

Not extinct, but just suddenly Victor thought in a flash, Time erased those memories. That civilization at that time. was trying to save something.

At this moment, the figure of Andrew appeared once again, but this time he was looking even more frail. "You are slowly catching up. That gate wasn't built to lock something in; it was meant to protect something.".

"Protect what?"

The truth in a weak voice about our world, about the

existence of three powers, from where the Abyssal City was really from.

As if before he could say the end, the darkness streamed into the hall once again, thicker and in greater numbers than before. They fell upon Victor and El; it seemed they had told something very significant from their memories.

"Resist them!" El shouted at the Third Power, in a futile attempt to push back against oncoming darkness. But this time, the shadows merged and coalesced into one vast maelstrom.

Victor sensed an overwhelming force beckoning him. "They're not after our memories... they're attempting to pull us away!"

"The Abyss of Memory," Andrew's voice boomed from everywhere. "You only know when you feel it. Are you prepared, my friends?"

Before they could utter a word, the vortex had completely enveloped them. The world whirled before them, and countless fragments of memories flickered across their eyes: scenes at the creation of Abyssal City, the three powers at their very dawn, and the rise and fall of the ancient civilization.

. . .

The final image hung before them: a cadre of ancient mages were activating some enormous device, and a chilling distortion took shape in the sky. It was the feeling that they were trying something enormous.

"Is that... a spatial-time swap?" Victor stared at the scene with his mouth agape.

"No," El suddenly realized. "That's a rebuilt world. They were trying to change some key rules.

The image fragmented, and with a jolt, the two men were back in the hall; but it was subtly different now, for the crystal pillar seemed brighter, and the magic array on the floor had begun to hum.

"Look!" El exclaimed, pointing across the way. Slowly, one wall of the hall creaked open to reveal a massive doorframe. The frame itself was etched with intricate runes; at the middle of it, three interlocking ring patterns were done in tasteful, interlocking calligraphy.

"The symbol of the three powers..." Victor breathed in, moving nearer to the doorframe in awe. "So, this is the gate?"

. . .

Now, Andrew's voice spoke back, sounding relieved. "The last truth is behind the door. But for you to open it, first, you need to understand what all this we have seen really means."

Victor and El looked up at each other, heavy pressure between them, as if all the points in time of all the world had finally converged here.

"Well then," El breathed heavily, "let's just fit these loose pieces together."

7

THE GATE TO THE TRUTH

Thick air condensed in the hall and weighed upon them. Victor and El were in front of the Ancient Gate, trying to get their minds around what had happened in that crazy hurricane of memories.

"The ancient civilization tried to recreate the order of the world," Victor mused to himself, "and what we're seeing now is probably the experiment in this form with the three powers.

El took up the thread. "Why would they do that? Those visions showed them running, looking like they were responding to a threat of some kind.

In that instant, the crystal pillar burst in a blinding glare, and new fragments of memory unfolded in the air before them, this time revealing a much more ancient landscape: a world dominated by an entirely different order, devoid of the three now-familiar powers, filled instead with one singular, more primeval, unified essence of energy.

"The Prime Power." The soft reverberation of Andrews' voice, "that was its original form. Yet it started to crumble, to unravel, leaving the world teetering on the edge of annihilation. The ancient civilization found themselves with no other choice."

Victor realized, "So they divided the Primal Force into three distinct forms, taking this as a means of maintaining the stability of the world."

"But at what cost?" El said sharply.

Suddenly, the runes on the gate's framework lit up, and three patterns of circles began to move clockwise at a slow pace. The memory shards in that crystal pillar shook terribly, and more visions appeared:

- Members of the ancient civilization that slowly disappear during the ritual

A new civilization was emerging stirred by the influence of the three powers.

- Construction of the Abyssal City and its geographical feature

. . .

"The Abyssal City." Victor said, suddenly something clicked in his head, "It was built at a place where the three powers merge. Is it that.

"It's a node," El went on, speaking as if his thoughts were unraveling, "a site for balance."

A figure appeared in front of the gate: Andrews. "Now you see why this gate was built. It's not only a recording device, but also.

"Insurance," Victor concluded. "In the event that the balance was ever upended-if all three powers were to spiral out of control-this gate would turn on, affording those few of us who know the truth a chance to."

"A chance to recalibrate the balance," El said.

Suddenly, their comms system rang out in a shrill tone. It was Count's voice: "The energy imbalance is growing! Space-time rips have started developing all over town, and the seals laid down by the Shadow Council are beginning to break."

"There's little time left," Andrews said. "The gate is ready, but the final decision is yours. You have to realize-once you open it, there's no going back."

. . .

An unprecedented weight befalls Victor and El because it is not just about them as persons but representatives of their respective factions, and it is all to be decided by them for the fate of the whole world.

"Tell us," Victor said, his eyes fixed intently on Andrews, "what is beyond the gate?"

The form of Andrews began to flicker. "It's a reset switch. Once it goes off, the three powers shall merge into one once more, and the world shall get back into its primal state. But this process.

"All that's being is going to be taken away," El whispered.

It quivered again and cuts in space appeared once more on the wall. The outside world was in turmoil, with the balance of the three forces almost teetering.

"We must make a choice," said Victor. "Either we stand by and watch the present world succumb to the destruction created by the imbalance of power, or...

. . .

"Let's restart tudo, even if that would erase everything we know," El concluded the tough thought.

8

FATE'S CHOICE

The shaking in the hall grew stronger, and the tears in space continued to tear mercilessly. Victor and El were standing before the Ancient Gate, standing at the most crucial choice in their lives.

Suddenly, Victor was announcing his eyes ablaze with resolution: "We still have the third option."

It hit El straight away. "You mean...not a full reset, but to attempt a reconciliation?

"Exactly." Victor strode closer to the edge of the gate, his gaze set in the runes chiseled into it. "The old civilization had divided the Primal Force into three parts, thinking that they have to stabilize the world in an extremely short time. But now.

. . .

"Now we have more time and we know more," El said. "Maybe we can find a balancing point.

Andrews' flickering figure hesitated. "That's incredibly risky. Reconciling the three powers requires perfect control. Even the slightest mistake could."

"Could lead to consequences far more dire than a mere reset," Victor said. "It is nonetheless the only way to preserve our current civilization."

The comms crackled urgent, fragmented warnings: it was the voice of Miller, intermittent, "Energy tides accelerating. detecting multi-dimensional fissures. Shadow Council's seals about to. wait, what is this?

The crystal pillar suddenly blazed into radiance, lighting up the whole hall. The three-circle signs at the gate whirled around, humming. A tide of remembered things welled in, congealed into light tumbling through the air in front of them-the last research notes of the ancient mages.

"Look!" El called, pointing at the symbols. "They did provide for the chance to reconcile. But with limited time to.

Victor promptly translated the notes: "Three anchors, each of one of the three powers are needed. Then, through some special pattern of energy waves, they can be gradually moved into.

"I can be the anchor for the first power," El said.

"I am the second power," nodded Victor.

"And I," Andrews said with certainty, "as one who has already faced the Primal Force, can provide a third anchor.

Yet, no more than when just about to press on, another alarm went off. Seline's anxious voice crackled through the communicator: "Something's wrong! Large-scale spatial collapses detected—the whole city is." The transmission then suddenly broke off.

"There's no more time," Andrews warned him. "Are you certain you wish to attempt that risk? There can be no alternative once we start."

Victor and El exchanged a glance; both knew the firm resolve staring back from each other's eyes.

"Let us go on," said Victor.

The rest of them quickly assumed their positions-standing at various other locations around the frame of the gate. All their different powers let loose, the magic formation on the ground starting to glow, and three pillars of different-colored energies erupted into the sky.

"Focus," Andrews reminded them. "Let the energy vibrate within a single frequency. If it is to be too fast, it will be chaos. If it is too slow, then no resonance."

A sudden current of energy ran through Victor's body; "It's just like the resonance of conducting.

El closed his eyes and went into profound consideration: "I can feel the powers answering to one another."

Space shook to its height as fissures disfigured almost every inch of the hall, but in that instant, the three energy pillars began their synchronization to start spewing out unparalleled tidal waves of energy, surging out to stroke and soothe the rioting distortions in the air.

"It's working!" a startled Andrews exclaimed.

With a groan, the Ancient Gate opened, revealing a space filled with the Primal Force. The three powers began to unite inside the gate to make amends this time, instead of restarting the world, to restore the balance.

. . .

Yet, in that instant, came from outside the rumbling of thunder-as if all of Abyssal City was shaking-and the end finally came.

"Wait!" cried Victor, "this is our only opportunity!

9

A MATTER OF DESTINY

Wild surges of energy tides crashed through collapsing space, interweaving into an intricate, volatile web of power. Right at the heart of it all were Victor, El, and Andrew-standing right at the hub of this huge ritual, with the huge onus on the three to harmonize.

"First stage nearing completion," Andrew said, his voice cutting through the whirling vortex of energy. "Stand by for critical threshold."

Suddenly, the communicator crackled back to life, and Count Roland's voice urgently cut through: "You must hurry! The city's structural foundation is collapsing—Shadow Council's seals are—" The message abruptly ended.

. . .

"It is the critical point!" Victor exclaimed, eyes widened, while the power of energy suddenly surged upwards. "El, turn on the second sequence!"

El nodded, and a stronger burst was released. The three powers began a deliberative cadence of weaving into one another, creating a steady web of energy before the Ancient Gate.

"This is..." Andrew watched the pattern in open-mouthed amazement. "Perfect harmony. The ancients never managed as much lateral synchronization."

Just as they were moving into the third phase, suddenly, the whole area began to distort furiously; a deafening crash boomed across the hall, sending the wall cracks running.

"This isn't good!" Victor exclaimed, sensing the unsettling shift. "The external collapse is accelerating. The spatial structure is disintegrating at a pace quicker than we anticipated!"

"Gotta hurry it up, or else it's game over!" El growled, clenching his teeth.

. . .

"But to increase the speed will take the energy beyond control," Andrew said. "If the rhythm becomes irregular, everything will fall into disarray."

"There is no alternative," said Victor firmly. "We have to take the risk. Program the third phase. Full power!

The energy was put to work, and three of them began to spin the matrix faster and faster. What had been harmonious balance now changed to a wild, turbulent uprising- wild as any storm in its uncontrollability. Even space shook at the strain of such strongly growing energy.

Then, with the crystal pillar quivering once more at that most fragile moment, out came the last vestiges of the fragments of memory-ancient wisdom epitomizing the very substance of the Primal Force.

"I see it!" Victor exclaimed as that spark of light lit in his eyes. "We are not to apply a balance; we are to key into their nature...

Like rivers to the sea, El stuttered as it finally dawned on him.

"Let them sort it out themselves," Andrew finished, quite laconic and cold. The three straightened, relaxed the grip on mastering the energies. As it were, they let themselves be no more than conductors of the currents, so that each force could wander whither it would. A wonder then happened. Those forces which had been so turbulent suddenly wished to balance themselves. The three powers henceforth came and went in a soothing rhythm belonging to themselves and created, from now on, a quite new condition.

"We have done it!" exclaimed Andrew, full of wonder.

The Ancient Gate burst into radiance, a tide of soft, powerful energy spilling out from it. Space collapsing around them reached and began to heal, holding at bay the forces of rampage that would annihilate.

The communicator suddenly crackled to life, alive with voices of jubilation.

The energy tides are stabilizing..." Miller said.

Seline said, "Spatial structures are self-repairing...

Count Roland was dumbfounded. "Incredible. This really happened."

Victor, El, and Andrew dropped to the ground, spent and overcome with emotion; they had saved the world—not with a reset, but by opening up another way.

. . .

"So," El asked, her eyes set on the now-motionless whirlpool of energy, "what now?"

Victor smiled, the seldom-populated features of warmth and hope crossing his face. "We know now how to walk with this new balance. We understand it, we can use it. It is not an end—this is wholly a beginning."

When Andrew's form steadied and was clear, he nodded and said, "At last, I can rest. Yet, previously, I still have much more knowledge to be passed onto you."

Where the light of the Ancient Gate drowned the hall, it became a sign of new life toward endless possibility, as the fate of their world passed out of the threshold into a new, uncertain chapter defined by harmony, understanding, and fragile yet hopeful peace.

10

A NEW CHAPTER

The Abyssal City was finally finding its way back into the silence of life. As the three powers reached a sensitive balance, the subtle yet profound transformation around their world slowly unfolded. Victor and El stood at the highest observation deck in the city, gazing at morning light cascading across the primeval, mystical landscape.

"Can you feel it?" El asked, shutting his eyes. "The flow of power's become so. harmonious."

Victor nodded reflectively: "As if the world found its most natural condition, neither forcibly divided nor all glued together, just living in a state of dynamic balance.

The communicator crackled on, and immediately a voice was heard from it: "All monitoring data is steady. The

Shadow Council's seals have repaired themselves-and they are even stronger than before."

"That is because the seals are no longer a forced restraint," Andrews' voice finally joined in, and his figure seemed to shimmer weakly in the morning light. "Now they act more to guide and regulate.

Seline added, "Interestingly, we've noticed that ordinary people are beginning to exhibit some special abilities. Not purely of the three powers, but rather. a mixed quality."

"That is how it ought to be," said Victor, "for now, power isn't some right of few people, but it has returned to its real status in the world.

The door opened at once and the Count appeared: "The conclave is ready. All parties are there.".

Victor and El looked at each other, and it was time to explain everything to the world, to outline the course of its future.

The big conference hall was full, filled to its capacity with representatives of all sides present in the air thick with anticipation and hostility. A deep silence fell in the room when Victor began to reveal the mystery shrouding the Ancient Gate.

"We are standing at the threshold of a new beginning," Victor said, his eyes scanning the people present. "The differences and disputes of the past shall soon become part of history. Yet, all that does not mean we must abandon our unique traditions and identities."

He added, "The new balance does need diversity, as an ecosystem does in nature. Every group, every tradition, does have value and a place in the world.".

The wisdom of that ancient civilization," boomed Andrews, his voice echoing through the hall. "was never meant to light the way but rather tend us towards our own answers."

The discussions lasted for a whole day. The representatives aired their concerns and suggestions as they worked together to come up with the blueprint for the New Order. At the first streaks of sunset, a landmark concurrence was finally reached.

It would replace the outdated governing systems of the Abyssal Council, a center where all factions would coordinate. The research being done by the three powers was to be shared among all, but in accordance with high ethical values.

Out of the conference hall, El asked, "You really think we can do that? Live in that harmony?

Victor gazed at the horizon-the setting sun. "It is going to be a very long journey, one full of pitfalls and setbacks. But what is vital is our finding the right route.

Andrew's voice came with a ring of satisfaction. "My mission is complete. The rest of the story is yours to write."

His figure dissolved, but this time without the appearance of a forced disappearance-this was a serene adieu. And only before his figure vanished from their eyes did he say the following:
Remember, true strength does not lie in control but in understanding and absorption. It is this that the ancient civilization finally came to realize.

As night began to fall, the lights of the Abyssal City started turning on one by one. A new, fresh energy permeated into the city: the lights shone in a brilliance never seen before, signifying the start of something totally new. In the silent part of the city, a child in wonder watched as a common rock hovered in mid-air at his command. It was not simple telekinesis, nor was it magic in base form; it was something different altogether.

11
___

THE ANCIENT CIVILIZATION

In the Temple of Destiny, as the Book of Life unfurled with languid grace, a vivid portrait of the ancient civilization began to take shape. The tips of Miller's fingers touched the gold, luminous pages softly, his face grave. "These records ... they are so much greater than anything we could ever have imagined."

Seline's Sacred Artifact pulsed softly with the pages. "The life map shows that this information contains an unusually high level of energy purity.

Like at the center of the temple, Count said nothing but watched the Eternal Ring whirl up above him in a slow circle. Victor did not leave him but stood stiff against the drapery of his black robe since he too was part of the process as their research in the ancient civilization had gone far enough.

. . .

"According to these records," he explained, "the ancient civilization was not one but rather included three, including the Civilization of Light, Civilization of Shadows, and most unusually, the Central Civilization.

"Three civilizations?" Chris clutched his weapon tightly almost on instinct. "Does that mean.?"

"Yes," said Victor, "our own personal strife has, in many ways, acted out the strategies of an antique drama.

Instantly, the energy field of the temple started to fluctuate wildly, filling the air with the atmosphere of stress. Miller was hastily flipping through the pages: "There's an even more important finding! It shows that the three ancient civilizations didn't just fight against each other, but on the contrary, they cooperated in building a gigantic network of energies, establishing the Abyssal City as its center!

El's face turned thoughtful. "So, the disturbances within the underground labyrinth.

"Precisely," Victor replied, a shadow of worry dancing in his irises. "The maze isn't just a converter of powers, but the juncture for the three civilizations. The Great Schism back then probably happened here.

. . .

Suddenly, Monica's Blood Crystal Armor sent out a warning: "The energy field is expanding!

Everyone looked up: numerous runic projections covered the dome of the temple now. Merging together, these runes combined in such a strange way that three energy vortices interwove within.

"Look!" Seline pointed to the center. "This flow of such energies corresponds just right with the life map prophecy pattern.

The Count furrowed his brow deep. "Miller, proceed."

"According to the records, there indeed existed perfect amalgamations of technology and magic the three ancient civilizations had come up with. Still, there were more fantastic artifacts: the Eternal Ring, the Sacred Artifacts, and the Blood Crystals-just to name a few. But what's more important is."

Miller's voice caught mid-sentence as the glow emanating from the Book of Life became suddenly brighter; all eyes now turned to it. And then, a previously hidden passage began slowly opening up to them:
"When the energies of the Three Civilizations converge once more, then is the Ancient Gate to be reopened. Beyond the gate lies an end, and a rebirth."

. . .

There was a violent shaking of the earth beneath them suddenly. Chris ran to the window. "My lords, look!"

Far below, in the heart of the underground labyrinth, one pillar of dark red energy was rising high up. Around it, there were outlined dark outlines now-those "mobile shadows" the runaway scouts had spoken about.

"Now is the time to act," he concluded finally. "Victor, thou knowest most about the Civilization of Shadows. Take a group and proceed with the deciphering of these texts. El and Seline, get ready with the ritual with the participation of the Third Power. Everybody else.

Before he could complete his thought, another tremor rattled the temple. This time, the entire Temple of Destiny appeared to sway precariously. Miller's attention was suddenly drawn to the Book of Life, which began flipping its pages unaided, as streams of text poured forth like a torrent:
"Three roads converge, new shadows born.
Today shall bind what ancient oath has sworn.
The fate-weaver's wheel is broken.
A new order shall rise from the void."

The armor on Monica suddenly hummed at the words. "This is no mere prophecy. It reads more like an incantation of activation!

. . .

It was a serious look shared between the Count, Victor, and El-a moment of truth, as it were, when one knew the storm would break loose, changing everything, with the Ancient Gate right in the center of the maelstrom.

12

THE ABYSSAL GATE

Flashes of red light illuminated the entrance to the underground labyrinth to hold at bay the gloomy darkness for that bit longer. An energy shield had been cast at the threshold by Chris's vanguard team, but the waves of "moving shadows" kept on pressing onto them.

"Something's not right," Monica said, her Blood Crystal Armor dutifully scrutinizing the currents of energy. "These shadows. they're looking for something.

Above, the Count stood on higher ground, the Eternal Ring glowing and sending light into the surroundings; meanwhile, Victor stood poring over a copied version of the documents they found in the Temple of Destiny.

"I've found it!" Victor suddenly exclaimed. "These aren't mere shadow creatures; they're 'Pathfinders'—

constructs from the ancient Shadow Civilization, created specifically to reopen the gate."

"What gate?" Chris asked him, his eyes darting nervously into the darkness where treetops loomed like specters.

"The Abyssal Gate," Victor returned, his voice laced with trepidation. "This is the fabled nexus connecting the three civilizations. Yet, apparently from these records, something rather more terrifying is sealed away behind it."

It was then that Seline and El burst in.

"The ritual for the Third Power is prepared," Seline said, "but the energy field remains far too unstable."

El continued, "Miller has been working ever so diligently to decipher the activation spell. He says it's a dual function—a mechanism capable of opening the Abyssal Gate or sealing it forever.

"And what is this to cost?" asked the Count, coldly.

An instantaneous shudder answered his question. A blinding red light burst from the depths of the labyrinth as dozens of "Pathfinders" took solid form, plunging deeper with fixed determination toward the middle of it.

"They've found the trail!" Chris exclaimed. "Should we intercept them?"

"Wait—," Victor said, flipping through the documents in urgency, "it says here that once the Pathfinders have found their target, they initiate something called the 'Reset Protocol.' That will.

Before he could get his sentence out, a deafening explosion boomed from inside the labyrinth. An indescribably huge pulse of energy then coursed out, sending a wave of pressure through the air and momentarily arresting the movements of all present.

Seline's Holy Artifact shook with violence. "The thread of life is completely tangled! It's as if... as if someone or something is rewriting the code of reality itself!

"Move in!" the Count commanded decisively. "Victor, you're with me. El, Seline, prepare the Third Power. Monica, secure the rear. Chris, evacuate the nearby civilians!"

The team was off and running with amazing rapidity. But when they actually entered the labyrinth, they found its interior entirely reworked: gone were the corridors they knew, twisted and curved in unnatural ways, and glowing runes filled the walls.

Victor stopped in his tracks. "Wait, these runes.

"What is it?" said the Count.

"They are the common basic script of the three civilizations," Victor said in amazement. "It goes: 'On the day this gate opens, the Three Powers shall unite. The ancient oath shall be fulfilled'."

While his words were yet echoing in the air, the quaking of the quivering walls surrounded them. Light runes flared into life, outlining the frame of a huge door. The "Pathfinders" walked towards the gate and merged with the frame of it, like so many keys fitting into a lock.

"We have to stop them!" Seline exclaimed, lifting her Sacred Artifact as the Third Power's light enveloped everything around them. But that gate, though hardly visible, remained steadfast and exuded an even stronger rush of energy.

At that moment, Miller's voice crackled through the

communicator. "I've cracked it! That activation spell isn't for opening the gate—it's for making a choice!"

"A choice about what?" demanded the Count.

"Consider what comes forth-or what does not! The gate is double-edged! It was over this, over what lay beyond, that the great schism between the three cultures first took place. And now."

Miller's transmission cut off abruptly, replaced by the gate exploding in a brilliant light. Through the searing radiance now beginning to take shape, a pitch-black fissure. In this overwhelming presence, a force flowed, seemingly with the weight of something more timeless than existence.

Victor pushed forward, urgent. "Wait! I know this! This is no gate, but a selector mechanism; it's waiting for somebody to make a choice."

"What decision?" the Count inquired, the urgency of his tone unmistakable.

"Whether to let the forces of the past re-claim this world..." Victor took another deep breath, ".or rebuild the future on an entirely new premise."

. . .

Before anyone could answer, a series of tendrils of energy, like a wintry vine, began to spill out of the fissure in the gate, unfolding their elaborate dance into an enormous vortex. Somewhere at the center of it, something began to take shape: dim outlines of another world, a mirror of what could have been.

"This was the great question left us by the ancients," Victor muttered on, almost in a stream-of-consciousness.

The Count stared into the churning void, his mind churning over thoughts of foment. Whatever was beyond that gate had the power to change everything from the Abyssal City to the whole world. And now, this impossible decision lay with them. Countless generations weighed upon them, the echoes from some of those ancient civilizations long lost.

Energy pulsed through the gate, impatient. A time had come for the making of choice. Were they to follow the forgotten legacies from the past or forge an unknown future?

And then, standing in the stirrup of their future, they steeled themselves to meet the great choice of a lifetime.

13

CONVERGENCE OF THE THREE POWERS

The vortex-like gate widened further and further until the powerful tug of it was nearly impossible to stand upright against. Beyond it opened a realm-a domain built solely from pure energy-where three currents in it moved in a fascinating dance.

"This is.," Seline breathed, "the origin of the Three Civilizations!

Indeed, the gold light energy, deep indigo shadow energy, and mystery of the Central Energy-being, suspended delicately between the two, swirled ceaselessly within the gate. And what furthermore shocked them was the disquieting realization that these very primordial energies actually began seeping into their world.

. . .

"Something's off!" Monica exclaimed, as her Blood Crystal Armor crackled with energy. "The energy field.it is starting to merge!"

The words were just leaving her mouth, when the first surge of power exploded from the portal. That instant that the three primordial powers clashed with their world, an instant violent response burst forth. The whole labyrinth was shaking in mad fury-the walls inlaid with glowing runes pulsating in time with chaotic light.

"Miller!" the Count exclaimed into his communicator. "Check the Book of Life! Does it say anything about this?

"There is!" Miller shouted, alarm lacing his voice. "But this is not supposed to happen yet! It says in the prophecy that the three powers converging is the very last phase-there is supposed to be some reconciliation process!

Victor seized the Count's arm. "Stop! The Eternal Ring-look at it!

All attention fell on the unyielding figure of the Count, who occupied a place in the heart of bedlam. The Eternal Ring over the Count tingled with the feel of the three streams of energy above, its lustrous shine pulsating in harmony with the powers beyond the gate.

. . .

"Seline!" the Count cried. "To the Third Power!"

Seline and El powered up, locking in the Third Power. Surprisingly, as it started building, there was a turbulence in that area. There was a surge of resistance from the gate itself, breaking their effort into an uncommon and unnatural pattern for the Third Power.

"It's. Central Civilization's technology!" Victor exclaimed with a stunned expression. "They are forcing the convergence!"

Indeed, the mysterious energy from it had already begun to force them-what had been crossing each other-into deep resonance and started to spread, embracing all of the labyrinth.

"No, this isn't the way it is supposed to go." Victor muttered, "Unless.

The Eternal Ring suddenly erupted into an extraordinary brilliance before he could even finish his sentence. At the same time, the Sacred Artifact Seline, Monica's Blood Crystal Armor, even Chris's weapon, started to shudder fiercely.

. . .

"These artifacts." El said suddenly, "they are all relics of the Three Civilizations!"

A crackle of Miller's voice came over the communicator, his tone ecstatic. "I have it! These aren't just weapons-they're 'guidance devices.' Now, it's being activated by the ancient program!

As if to affirm his words, the artifacts released torrents of energy that synchronized with the three powers coming from the gate. The whole energy field started to twist as reality and the dimension beyond the gate began to converge.

"This is the true convergence of the Three Powers." Victor said, his voice with a ring of wonder. "It is not just a simple mixture of energies, but a reconfiguration of the dimensions!"

It was as if, from some maelstrom of dimensions, it came into view that what was left of the Three Civilizations began condensing within the void: the golden City of Light, the deep violet Shadow Temple, and the luminous Central Nexus-each radiant with a light not of this world-crystallized into the crossover realms.

"Look! Over there!" he exclaimed, pointing at the horizon. "The Abyssal City. it's changing!"

. . .

Indeed, the whole Abyssal City was going through a kind of weird transformation. The outlines of its buildings began to merge with the contours of the ancient ruins, forming new, hybrid structures that seemed to bridge the gap between times.

"This is no coincidence," Victor said evenly, though his voice was packed full with determinism. "Abyssal City is situated precisely on the conjoint position of the Three Civilizations.".

At once, an explosion of shock boomed loud within the labyrinth. From the churning vortex of the gate, three beams shot out and struck one of the three artifacts-the Eternal Ring, the Sacred Artifact, and the Blood Crystal Armor-causing them to ring in perfect harmony to form a flawless triangular energy field.

"Miller!" the Count called through the comms device. "What is the situation with the Book of Life?"

"It's gone wild!" Miller exclaimed in wonder. "The pages are turning themselves, and there are the hidden texts showing up. These. these must be the final messages from the Three Civilization!

. . .

It was then that Seline saw her Sacred Artifact before her change: the golden and violet patterns in its energy signaled its extreme evolution.

"The Third Power ., It was always meant for this moment. To unite, not to fight!" he said in a whisper.

Victor nodded. "It is-so, the civilizations foresaw it. They knew the powers, that were divided, would combine when the time was right, when we fully understood these forces."

Before he could finish his thought, a second wave of energy burst forth. This time, the three streams of power did not just intermix-they intertwined in complex patterns, giving way to countless glowing runes. The runes danced gently in the air, slowly gathering into a huge three-dimensional structure.

"This is." Monica said, studying the data through her Blood Crystal Armor. "It's some kind of hyper-dimensional matrix!"

Indeed, the structure gradually came into focus, surfacing as a hugely complex energy grid. Still more astounding, however, was that its nodes matched the essential points of the Abyssal City.

. . .

The Eternal Ring suddenly vibrated with a fierce intensity, sending a message straight into the Count's mind:

"What was once divided shall now be united. The Three Powers converge, heralding the rise of a new order. Only those who transcend opposition can grasp the ultimate truth."

"This is the moment of choice," Victor said gravely. "But it's not us electing the power-it's the power electing us."

In the next moment, suddenly, the energy field changed dramatically: The three forces no longer clashed and merged jumbled but started reorganizing according to some incomprehensible logic. From the Eternal Ring to the Sacred Artifact and then to the Blood Crystal Armour, they simultaneously released their energies, creating a perfect circulation cycle of their powers.

"They're changing!" exclaimed Seline.

Indeed, a miraculous change of some sort was happening to all three; the streaks in the Eternal Ring shimmered darkly, the Sacred Artifact shone brighter, incomparable to any, while the Blood Crystal Armour reflected some strange, dancing play of light and shadow.

Miller's voice came across the comms system again. "I get it! The last prophecy of the Book of Life. this isn't about unifying the power; all along, this is 'full-dimensional reconstruction'! The will of the Three Civilizations is about to be written onto the face of this world!

But before anyone could respond, the third and final swell broke. The wave was stronger, multi-dimensional, and transformative beyond anything they had ever known.

Reality itself began to distort.

14

THE NEW ORDER

As the third wave of energy rippled forward through the labyrinth, a miraculous change began. It wasn't just several forces blending together, it was actually a deep recasting of the structure of space itself. Beyond the Abyssal Gate, finally, was the whole truth of the Three Civilizations.

What lay beyond the gate was not just any ruin or ancient city; before this tapestry, the pure concept was woven. If the Civilization of Light represented order and creation, the Civilization of Shadow manifested chaos and destruction, while Central Civilization, for its part, acted as a balancing and transforming agent for these two opposing forces.

Look!" Monica exclaimed, pointing toward the void. "It's reorganizing!"

. . .

Indeed, the three primordial forces began fully to interact with each other in an utterly new fashion. No longer content simply to oppose or overlay one another, they were yielding a general energy ecology. Creation and destruction, order and chaos-no longer mere opposites, but phases within the same cycle.

Just then, the voice of Miller burst through the comms system, his voice shaking with emotion. "The Book of Life... it's open! The last prophecy is at hand!

With the communicator-amplifier on, everyone heard it aloud: the last prophecy.

"Where three rivers meet,
The world as it once stood will break and fall and give way to a new.
In the confluence of creation and destruction,
Order and Chaos dance as one.
Whosoever wields the Three Powers
Sall found the base of a new world."

The Count, with the Eternal Ring in his hand, stared at it in growing amazement. "Victor, your 'choice'-it's not a question about which side of the gate, is it?

"No," Victor replied, his voice determined. "It concerns how to harness this new power. The Three Civilizations didn't really disappear; they've just been waiting—waiting for someone who could understand and use the combined power they left us."

In a flash, the Eternal Ring, the Sacred Artifact, and the Blood Crystal Armor each shone with dazzling brilliance. The triangle started to spin, its rhythm closely synchronizing with the might of the Abyssal Gate. There was an unbelievably powerful pull issuing forth from the abyssal gate; different from the scene a while ago, it had already transformed from a chaotic force into an orderly and intentional gravitation.

"The Third Power." Seline breathed, "It's guiding this whole process!

Indeed, the Third Power, at first conceptualized as a bridge to reconciliation, finally turned out to reveal its real role-it was the detonator for the powers' final rearrangement within the Three Civilizations, and under its impact, the primordial forces started merging in a way surpassing simple coexistence.

"This is the truth," El said thoughtfully. "The Third Power was never to defend or oppose. It always was to guide this inevitable convergence."

. . .

But in an instant, space began distorting once more, yet this time different from the chaos that had come onto that screen earlier-again with order. They watched in amazement as the very structure of Abyssal City began changing-scattered nodes of energy began conjoining into one huge energy network.

Victor's voice shook in excitement: "This ... this is the true inheritance of the Three Civilizations! The entire Abyssal City was rigged for this day! It's a single, huge energy transmutation device!

With the Blood Crystal Armor wrapping her, Monica oversaw the energy flow. "The network is improving by itself. It's as if. it's like the whole city is awake!"

Now it was Miller's voice, full of astonishment: "The last page of the Book of Life has turned! This is not the end-this is the start! The words say here that the purpose of the three civilizations all along was to create a new world to accommodate all kinds of powers!

With his voice sounding, the energy vortex inside the portal started to shrink, not close, but tighten. The three rays of light wonderfully twisted with each other in an incredible, delicate pattern, finally condensing as a perfect energy core in the middle.

. . .

Undaunted, the Count replied, "This is the final decision; it is not a question of choosing sides, but rather an issue of which way to go with this new strength.

With an instant burst of bright light, the energy core suddenly blew up. The prime forces of the Three Civilizations merged perfectly, forming a new kind of energy. This astonishing energy embraced the creative power of Light, the flexible adaptability of Shadow, and the basic balance of the Central Civilization.

It dawned on every one of them present in this moment that this was the beginning of all, not the end. Thus ends the Era of the Three Civilizations. From the ashes, another age would erupt.

As the core finally stabilized, its energy began to emit outwards, redefining the Abyssal City-its buildings, its streets, and its structures-an ancient design with a hint of modern flair. Pouring down across the city in a cascadial manner, the energy lit it up in brilliance never seen before.

"The city is not only changing," Victor said dreamily, "but it's going to be actually the center of this new world."

El nodded. "The Three Civilizations had anticipated this moment, when they would bequeath their knowledge and power not to enslave, but to ensure that the next generation could rise and create something far superior.

The Eternal Ring, the Sacred Artifact, and the Blood Crystal Armor lit up one last bright radiance before they finally fully changed. From the remains of ancient times, each relic had turned into the embodiment of their predecessors-the combined strength of the Three Civilizations.

Seline clasped her artifact, now gleaming with twisted shades of gold and violet. "The Third Power... not any one particular force, but a manifestation of all three tied together."

He looked down at the Eternal Ring, now shining so much brighter in a silent, equal glow. "This is what they gave us. Not just power, but the greatness of the responsibility for using that power well.

It was Miller's voice that cut the silence. "The Book of Life is disappearing. And its last message is clear as crystal: 'The Three Powers are one. The world is yours to rebuild. But remember-creation and destruction is two sides of the same side.'"

Victor stepped forward with unwavering eyes. "This is our chance. The Three Civilizations have entrusted us with their legacy. It is our duty to establish a new order-not that of dominance, but of balance."

As the light from the gate slowly faded, none of them said a word, their gazes upon the city that had transformed utterly before them. It was from then on that the Abyssal City changed from being a historical relic into a cornerstone for a new era.

A child, in a more secluded part of the city, was growing a small crystal, fascinated by the way it glimmered with an unusual, harmonious light. For the first time, the powers of the world were not fragmented into the possession of factions or civilizations but part of a vaster whole, open to everyone who would seek their understanding.

And so, beneath the new light of the Abyssal City, they stirred as on a new morning-waking, for the first time, in conciliation, not in strife. The best of what had gone before was done and finished now; the future was their own.

15

A NEW ERA

This was an irreversible change which one and all felt when that brilliance finally vanished from the energy core. It had not been a shift in power but a redefinition of the very nature of the world. It was a sight to leave everyone aghast as the light started subsiding.

Now, the Abyssal City was thoroughly different. What was originally a dark and chaotic city now possessed an indescribable beauty. Golden lines of energy pulsed through the city like veins, while deep violet currents were interwoven into them, with the Third Power as the main adjuster that harmonized each and everything in that big system.

"This is incredible," Monica uttered, staring at the readouts coming through her Blood Crystal Armor. "The entire city has become one huge living, organic energy system. It is not a bunch of buildings anymore. It's alive!

. . .

Chris was staring at the Eternal Ring in his hand, his eyes wide in incredulity. What had only been one entity of energy turned out to be a brilliant spectrum now, flickering between the peculiarities of the three powers effortlessly. "Could this... have been what the Three Civilizations were trying to create all along?"

"Indeed," Victor said. "They foresaw this conjunction of powers to happen. Yet, it was only possible by knowing each other and accepting each other, not by conquering or being conquered.

And in that very instant, it was the excited voice of Miller that filled the comms system: "You gotta see this! The Book of Life-its last page, it's recording all of this right now!"

In this projection, the group could almost see new words appearing before their eyes in this book:
"The powers of the past have united into one. A new order has taken shape. From the convergence of the Three Sources, a new world shall be based. Those who can manage this unified power will lead the future with wisdom."

At this time, the Sacred Artifact in Seline's hands started radiating intense brightness, shooting a beam of light into the sky, and in the space, a three-dimensional hologram came into view, detailing the last will of the Three Civilizations.

In the projection, three ancestral figures materialized one after another. Their voices resonated through the corridors of time and space, imparting their final words of wisdom:

"If you are reading this, then you have succeeded in all that we had undertaken," the ambassador from the Civilization of Light explained.

"This is not the end, per se, but an awakening in truth," said the voice of the Shadow Civilization.

"Everything we left will be the ground on which your world will rebuild," concluded the representative of the Central Civilization.

The Count looked upon the remade Abyssal City, a deep sense of solemn realization carved on his face. "This city. no, the core of this new world. is where everything begins."

Victor added, "The Three Civilizations used their wisdom to clear a path for us. But which road to take thereafter—that we must decide for ourselves."

. . .

El spoke thoughtfully, "That's why the Book of Life guided us all along. It wasn't to make us relive the past but to create the future."

A strange pulse emanated from the very center of the city and attracted them to itself. Finally, when they reached the very center of the city square, they were amazed to see that three rays of light rose from the ground, each possessing qualities unique to the Three Civilizations. However, as opposed to the previous times, they did not clash or remain separate; instead, they merged harmoniously, forming a steady energy field at the point of intersection.

"This is...," Monica breathed, "a complete energy matrix! It can..."

"The thing might redesign the energy pattern of the whole world!" she said. "This is no matrix for mere in FIFA of powers, but rather one to rebuild reality itself!"

As her Blood Crystal Armor looked into the field, much minute detail became apparent. "Look at these energy circulation patterns-they are thoroughly free of the restriction of the old rules. In any moment the creative energy may turn into destroying energy, and on the ashes of destruction new creation could arise. It is a complete cycle of energy!

. . .

Victor approached the center, his face grave. "The Three Civilizations had predicted it: they knew one single force cannot maintain a whole civilization. Development genuinely requires balance and the unification of all forces.

Suddenly, Miller's voice burst across the communicator: "The Book of Life is showing new pages! These ... this is some sort of instructions!"

The group watched intently as the book projected intricate symbols and formulas onto the air-elaborate instructions on how to harness the unified power.

The Count took this quite well. "It would appear the Three Civilizations endowed us with not only the power, but all the trimmings of how to use such power responsibly."

At the moment, a miracle happened. The Eternal Ring, the Sacred Artifact, and the Blood Crystal Armor rose and then formed a perfect triangle in the air. And then, the energy emitted by them began to interlace and build up an integral structure.

"They're... evolving!" Seline exclaimed.

Indeed, the artifacts underwent a far-reaching transformation. From simple relics of the past, they developed into an integral part of an organic and unified whole: each artifact was allowed to retain its individual character while it harmoniously complemented the others.

Chris watched in great detail. "It's like... a miniature core for the new world!"

"Exactly," El said. "These are going to be the transition from the old world into the new one. These will give us a new grid that we can gradually spread to blanket the whole world."

Suddenly, the ground started shaking beneath their feet-not in a way that would destroy anything, but pulsating almost to the beat, like the heartbeat of some living animal.

Monica took one swift glance over it. "Fully powered, the energy network of the city is expanding outside, restructuring space!

Victor nodded, the sound of his voice unshakeable. "This is the Three Civilizations' real project-this abyssal city isn't a city; it's a seed, a seed with which to create a new world.

They had watched through sensors as ripples of energy emanated from the Abyssal City, and behind those ripples, pockets of chaos reconstituted as stable space. It was not a violent change; more properly, it was a gentle, almost deliberate rebuilding.

"I see now," said the Count, "The Three Civilizations understood that forced change necessarily breeds ruin. True reformation proceeds only painfully and with time. It is in this city that the starting point for such a reformation will be found."

Seline then said, "Our role is to let this process be stabilized and to take the entire world towards a glowing future.".

As if to confirm her utterance, the last page of the Book of Life unfolded itself completely and showed its deep prophecy:

"The New Era Has Arrived
The old wars to make way for peace
Yet let this be understood
Power is but a means

Wisdom the precept
By my power of the Three as One now
Create a better world."

They stood silent as those words held their heavy weight in gravity. The Abyssal City, at the new world's center, was ablaze with teeming life; it radiated its energy outside to alter reality itself.

This was to be the beginning of a new era, not of the hegemony of one Power, but of the concert of all the Powers. The heritage of the Three Civilizations was now accomplished, and the future was assuredly in the grasp of their hands. And so, with the brilliant light of the newly risen Abyssal City, the first page in this new world order began.

PART II

PEAK OF POWER: THE FINAL GLORY

Under the silvery moonlight, seven figures stood unflinchingly upon the pinnacle of the sanctuary, their powers rising to an unprecedented level. Around El swirled golden Threads of Prophecy, each one a possible future, shining with all possibilities. Seline wrapped herself in the projection of the Life Map, where an infinity of shining runes wove themselves into intricate secret patterns in the air. Her Blood Crystal Armor glowed brightly with silver brilliance, each crystal on its surface already grown to full size.

Yet, however, at the height of their powers, few as they were, the figure of the Count started to dissolve into the ether. Sudden was his sacrifice, yet sure as the movement of the stars. Gently he rose in the air, the Eternal Ring softly rising from his hand, to break into innumerable starlight points sprinkling the night sky. That was the great delineation in the soul of all, and even as if the earth itself had stopped and held its breath for this incredible one moment.

Under them, the seven big energy nodes spread all over the land started shining one after another, turning into an incommensurate net of energy. The darkness of the abyss started changing as streams of light, pure and untainted, surged up from its interior.

It wasn't the end; it was a rebirth.

Each could feel it in that air: this was the world in transition, at its deepest breaking point. And there, in the silvery moonlight, they were real actors, not merely spectators, in this drama of change.

16

THE WAY FORWARD

As the last prophecy fulfilled, the energy in the Abyssal City began to balance itself. The rhythmic pulsation of the energy core slowly came to a rest, but never ceased, similar to the steady heartbeat of an eternally living entity.

"This is just the beginning," Victor said, his gaze fixed on the city now changed. "Yet, the challenges that lie ahead are far from over."

Indeed, although these powers of the Three Civilizations had now united, the most urgent question before them was how to use this new force and lead the world through a smooth transition.

She continued to analyze the data through her Blood Crystal Armor. "The energy expansion still is under control.

The change is currently only within the vicinity of the Abyssal City. That would give plenty of time to understand and follow up."

"That was the intent of the Three Civilizations," El said. "They gave us a system to operate with, but it's up to us to decide how to use it."

At that very moment, it was then that Miller's voice crackled back through the communicator. "You need to see this! The Book of Life. it's still adding new content!"

In it, they saw new text materializing upon its pages- not prophecy this time, but detailed instructions:
"The Way to Rebuild the World:
Step by step, without rush, is the first thing.
Without predominance of any force, a balance should be struck.
Thirdly, the people are the first-they shall not be pressed.
Count read the instructions carefully. "

These aren't just rules. They're a complete philosophy of governance. The Three Civilizations are teaching us how to use this new power responsibly.

Seline's Holy Artifact started to quiver, casting complex-like patterns of energy into the air. "Look at that!

Those are implementation plans. Each region needs alteration with precise calibration of energy."

Chris looked at the diagrams. "It's all one big ecosystem. Any disruption creates a domino effect on all others. It's going to require a great deal of care."

Suddenly, the three beams of light at the heart of the city began to shift. No longer just streams of energy, they coalesced into three semi-transparent control platforms.

Victor approached one of the platforms, his expression filled with intensity. "This is... some kind of control system!"

Indeed, the platforms served as a centralized hub for overseeing the flow and dissemination of the new energy. Through these systems, the speed and direction of energy expansion could be meticulously controlled.

"But," Monica questioned, "how do we articulate these changes to the outside world? Is the world ready for such a huge change?"

El reflected on that for a while. "Maybe this was why the Three Civilizations did things gradually-to give the people time to adapt, to understand, and to accept."

. . .

Suddenly, a light beamed out of the Eternal Ring, and a 3D map appeared, showing the regions around the Abyssal City. It clearly showed how the new energy was affecting the ambient environment right before their very eyes.

"Look!" Chris exclaimed, pointing at the projection. "The energy isn't destroying anything-it's. it's optimizing!"

The surroundings, under this newly influenced energy, had indeed begun to change gradually: the chaotic zones had become well stabilization; everything had changed just so that the changes didn't overpower the people present.

The Count watched with great interest. "Now I see the great motive concerning the Three Civilizations. They did not want us to be world conquerors or world changers-they wanted us to change the pattern of its evolution."

"Precisely," Victor agreed. "This is not a revolution but an evolution. And it's our job to ensure it happens smoothly and in balance."

Right then, Monica came across something interesting with her Blood Crystal Armor: "Look at this! It is like the power of the energy field adjusts to the very nature of what it's passing through."

. . .

They foresaw that this new energy took different features in the various types of landscapes it broke into: in chaotic zones, it found stability and imposed structure; in barren lands, it nurtured vitality and encouraged growth; while in areas of established order, it concentrated on optimization and refinement.

"This is amazing," Seline breathed. "This energy isn't forcing change-just developing each place into being the best it could be."

And then again, Miller's voice was heard: "A new chapter to the Book of Life! Contained herein. are practical applications in the harnessing of the energy!

In these pages, they found complex details about how energy should be used at any given time in specific situations:

"First, in chaotic lands, lead with order, but do not extinguish vitality.

Second, in lifeless regions, nurture growth, but avoid forced infusion.

Third, in areas with existing order, focus on improvement, not upheaval."

Chris started going up and down the entries. "It's kind of like an instruction book-how to use this new skill in many various ways."

. . .

In one swift movement, all three control platforms simultaneously became bright, cascading complex data-flow-a real-time follow-up on the energy's expansion with comprehensive feedback on its effects.

"We need to gather a dedicated crew," the Count declared. "This news needs constant follow-up and decoding."

Victor nodded contemplative. "Not only that," he said, "we shall have to train more hands to harness and make use of this new power. This cannot be dependent on but a few of us."

"And we'll need to establish rules and systems to ensure this power isn't abused," El added.

Right then, the Eternal Ring displayed yet another of its capabilities: projecting a holographic organizational structure in front of them, a fully developed managing system.

"It looks like the Three Civilizations contemplated that already," Monica said. "This system has deliberation, implementation, and supervisory mechanisms—something for every aspect of governance.

. . .

Seline closely examined the framework. "That means power would be well utilized and there wouldn't be too much concentration of authority. It's quite a thought-out design."

Suddenly, in a second, the energy changed, then rearranged itself in the city. This was the proof that even the best system does need a constant readjustment and caring.

"I believe it is time we begin making plans," said the Count. "First things first: we must share these findings with the outside world, but not alarm them.

Victor beamed with approval. "We can start small, showing how much good this energy is capable of, and people will slowly adapt to the changes.

"In the meantime," El said, "we have to start recruiting and training new cadres. It will take time, but there's simply no way around it.

"Talking of training," Monica said, opening a new dataset, "Blood Crystal Armor has already set up an initial program; the training can be adjusted according to specific characteristics and potentials.

. . .

In that instant, the Eternal Ring, the Sacred Artifact, and the Blood Crystal Armour vibrated together as one, reflecting an all-round training system comprising theory, practice, and moral training.

"This is perfect," Seline exclaimed excitedly. "It is not only the training program that teaches the ways of power use, but it instills in the essential ethic principles with responsibility.

Chris was deep in the workings of the system. "It's clear the Three Civilizations thought of everything. They knew those who command must also possess wisdom and integrity."

The last page of the Book of Life shimmered once more, to show a final message:
"Remember:
Power is not the end, but the means.
Change must be gradual—beware haste.
Nurture character above all—choose wisely.
The future is in creation, not preservation."

Thus, the Count gave these thoughts: "Be it this that's their last council to us, not to be dazzled by the powers amongst ourselves, for thence the general idea has its root.

. . .

Victor nodded seriously. "Exactly, whereas the betterment of the world is the far-off goal, rather than just simply maintaining it as it is, or restarting anew.

All of a sudden, a peculiar kind of pulse resounded from that energy matrix at the center of the city, igniting all three control platforms. Before them, a new interface emerged—a boundless, all-around world map dotted with innumerable hotspots.

"This is our roadmap," El said. "Each marker represents a place where we're needed to guide and assist."

Miller relayed through the comms device, "And the map is dynamic-it updates in real time based on changing conditions. That gives us some amazing flexibility.

Monica carefully examined the data before her. "Based on current estimates, it will take decades to complete the world's smooth transition. This is going to be a long journey," she remarked.

"But that's the best way," answered Seline. "This way, each region and everybody will get enough time to adapt and grow accordingly.

. . .

At that instant, the Eternal Ring blazing with one last ray of splendor traced across the air in letters of light:

"A new journey has started. This isn't the end, this is an alternate beginning."

Chris gazed at the words. "Indeed. We've completed the mission entrusted to us by the Three Civilizations, but our true responsibility is only just beginning."

The count gazed into his companions and the alternative aspect of the Abyssal City before him; a faint smile crossed his face, steely in resolve: "Then let us begin. For the sake of this world's future, for the sake of the hope of life.

Victor nodded vigorously. "Yes. This is our task—and our choice."

He looked towards the horizon. "A new era has dawned, and we are going to act as its pioneers and guardians."

A whole new era now started as the very first shades of dawn broke through the veil of energy covering the Abyssal City and spread their light upon this rebirth.

17

THE START OF THE NEW ORDER

While the change of the Abyssal City began to ripple its way outwards, it was far from over yet. Over the course of the next few days, the team set in the task of establishing a new form of governance.

"According to the leading of the Book of Life, we have to create three basic institutions," the Count announced during one of the constitutive meetings. "Those would be a Decision Council, an Executive Branch, and an Oversight Body. These three must balance each other."

As Victor summarized: "The Decision Council will establish overall policies, the Executive Branch will manage the implementation, and the Oversight Body will ensure that things don't get off the rails."

. . .

Monica, enveloped in her Blood Crystal Armor, conjured a detailed organizational structure. "We can establish regional branches within this network, with each being given the necessary men and material.

It was then that these three things-Eternal Ring, Sacred Artifact, and Blood Crystal Armor-began to glow together and cast a detailed model of the governance mechanism in the air right above them. The model not only portrayed the composition structure but also explained the method of functioning.

"This system is truly unique," commented Seline. "It maintains the hierarchy that is needed to administrate, yet allows flexibility and freedom where needed.

Chris took extra caution while monitoring the system. "It's also equipped with multiple safeguards to prevent the abuse of power."

El nodded, with a faraway look on his face. "That's exactly what we want. Moving these changes ahead, we should also make sure that nothing else starts breaking.

Then and there, the Book of Life unfolded to a new set of dictums:
Governance Keys:

Clearly define responsibility, and check it with each other.

Balance central coordination with local adaptability.

Justice and transparency need to be upheld, and the voice of the people heard.

"These principles are excellent," remarked the Count. "We must steer clear of repeating the mistakes of the past, where a new system could regress into yet another form of authoritarianism."

The energy matrix suddenly started to fluctuate in the city, and flows of information materialized on the control platforms. These streams were showing how already so many areas were seeking to inactively fit into the new order.

"It would seem that some places have started to recognize the difference," Victor said. "That's a good omen—that means they've found reason to have hope."

Monica read the requests. "But with caution, we must not be taken over by their eagerness to hurry up the process. Every move has to be done at the right time.

. . .

"Agreed," El said. "We can start with limited pilots in these areas to learn and make our mistakes there.

And in that moment, the Eternal Ring showed a new ability when suddenly the requests coming in needed to be filtered and prioritized by urgency and possibility.

"This is immensely useful," Chris said, "it gives us a scientific edge in the planning of activities."

Seline said, "The ranking system takes all factors into consideration, like regional stability, willingness of the public, and implementation challenges.

What astonished everyone was an unforeseen revelation—some of the requests originated from once adversarial factions.

"This is sweet surprise indeed," said the Count, "and the salutary effects of this change seem to have convinced some of our old opponents of the value of co-operation."

Victor examined the proposals with keen interest. "Fascinating. A number of these groups submitted their requests after experiencing the transformation of the Abyssal City firsthand."

. . .

Monica peered closely at it with the aid of her Blood Crystal Armor. "Most of those factions have survived under a turbulent and unpredictable environment. They desire more stability. We still must consider them cautiously.

In that very moment, three control platforms lit up a set of assessment parameters: factors for the sincerity of cooperation, regional stability, and possible risks.

"Look at this," El said, pointing at the data. "With these steps, there is laid out a basic cooperation framework.

Chris looked at the framework. "It begins with small-scale technical collaboration, goes through resource sharing, and only then goes to full integration. Very well thought out."

Seline picked up on something important: "The framework is mutual. It's not just changes for them, but there are changes, adjustments, and compromising that must be done from our part."

The Book of Life gave further light:
"Which Way to Turn Enemies into Friends: One, meet with an open mind; two, move one step at a time and give time to adapt; three, seek common benefit, grow up, and develop together."

. . .

As they envisioned these, the Eternal Ring tossed up in front of them pictures of what had changed in these places over the last several months. Places around the Abyssal City had already begun the healing, cleaning process.

"This is the best proof," said the Count, "it is a change that speaks louder than words.

Victor nodded. "This change is occurring organically, without a sense of coercion, which further adds authenticity to this development.

Suddenly, Miller's voice crackled through the communicator. "Everyone, I've uncovered something intriguing. Numerous regions that haven't formally allied with us are discreetly mirroring our approaches!"

This was through a projected hologram of this strange occurrence: how certain regions were autonomously reorganizing their governments to be more in line with the success of Abyssal City.

"That's a good omen," Monica said. "That means our message catches on with just about anybody.

"But we also have to remind these regions: 'Don't just

simply mimic us'," El said. "Every place has its particularities. They have to be treated differently."

And it was then that the control platforms sounded a warning that various areas suffered from problems stemming from too-hastily implemented reforms.

"This is the one thing we need to guard against," Chris said. "To charge ahead can create new disorder.

Seline quickly connected to the related information. "We need to make a guidance plan as soon as possible to help those regions avoid the same trouble.

"Agreed," the Count concluded. "We shall forthwith establish special advisory machinery. Every area that is in difficulty shall have its own special assistance."

The next step for Victor was to select suitable candidates. "These advisors not only had to understand the technical aspects but also the essence and spirit of the reforms."

And with that said, the three items rang together one last time, projecting into the air a hologram of an all-inclusive training framework: theory, practice, relevance of cultural understanding, and finally communication skills.

. . .

"This is great," Monica said, working through the framework. "It balances theory with practical knowledge and emphasizes the need to be responsive to local circumstances."

The Book of Life turned to a new page and revealed some intricate principles for guidance:
The Art of Guidance:
First, teach them to fish—do not do everything for them.
Second, understand the local reality—avoid rigid application of rules.
Third, progress step by step—never rush to achieve results.

El contemplated the principles with care. "These are precisely right. Our aim is to assist them in developing their own systems, rather than imposing ours upon them."

Suddenly, the Eternal Ring projected a dynamic map showing global changes in real-time. Orderly regions were slowly but steadily expanding, while chaotic areas were shrinking.

"Look at this for a trend," Chris said, nodding toward the map. "Not great, but it's a step in the right direction."

. . .

As Seline has said, "Most importantly, these changes are organic and stable-not the product of forced interventions.

At that moment, the city's energy matrix shifted once more, and the control platforms illuminated with a fresh development—a framework for a global collaboration network.

"This is incredible!" Monica exclaimed, her enthusiasm palpable. "With this network, regions can directly exchange experiences and learn from one another."

Victor recognized its potential immediately: "That will be a self-reinforcing feedback loop. Each region is able to learn from successes and challenges of the others."

The Count observed the unfolding events, a satisfied smile spreading across his face. "I believe we've discovered the correct path. This isn't a matter of coercion; it's a process of natural evolution."

"Exactly," El said. "It's a matter of making it possible for every region and community to find the way that will work most naturally for it. That basically is the new order."

. . .

With night falling, the three rays emanating from the Abyssal City remained in the sky, lighting it up. The three rays, once images of horror, were now the lighthouses of hope and advancement.

The new order was beginning to take shape—not through conquest, but through understanding; not by force, but through guidance. Although the process would unfold slowly, each step was both deliberate and firm.

A pointer into the future had been laid, and it was only the beginning.

18

THE RISE OF NEW TECHNOLOGY

As the new order was being established bit by bit, the Abyssal City gradually took shape, at the forefront of a technological renaissance. It naturally wove in the technological legacies left by the three civilizations and integrated them into the prevailing systems, thence causing miracles.

"Look at this," Chris said, triumphantly showing a breakthrough finding in the lab. "Combining quantum computing with Life Energy leads to a completely different model of computation altogether.

Victor leaned in closer, his eyes bugging at the streams of data. "This is incredible. Computation speed has increased many hundredfold, while energy consumption has gone down to an absolute minimum."

. . .

Monica, in Blood Crystal Armor, pressed further into the analysis: "In addition, such a new computational model would seem to simulate the trains of thought of living things; this may lead to a new generation leap for artificial intelligence.

Every one of them shone dimly with the Eternal Ring, Sacred Artifact, and Blood Crystal Armor; a small formula embroidery, diagram after diagram was cast into the air, showing all possibilities in the fusing of new technology.

"This is great," Seline said. "These formulae show us the deep interrelation of energy, matter, and information. It totally overthrows everything that we have so far thought."

El meticulously studied the projections. "And what's more, these technologies are entirely sustainable. They cause no harm to the environment. This is exactly the direction we've been striving toward."

And suddenly, the pages of the Book of Life began to flip fast to yet another set of legislation for the development of:

"The Way of Technology:

Imitate nature first—never go against the way of nature;

Benefit all human beings second—never harm others and society;

Develop with time third—never cling to yesterday's means."

. . .

As the Count reflected, "It just reminds us that technological development has to be purpose-driven; it is not just a question of developing for the sake of developing without considering what impact it will have.

At that moment, the laboratory's energy matrix began to fluctuate, causing all the equipment to display new data at once. This information unveiled a remarkable breakthrough: the energy field was capable not only of transmitting energy but also of conveying information.

"This... this is revolutionary!" Chris exclaimed. "If we can master this technology, it will totally change the face of communication."

Victor soon realized the enormous importance of such a discovery: "That means we can create an international Pisper-instant communication network, virtually insensitive to physical restrictions."

Monica quickly analyzed the emerging data. "Even more astonishing is the fact that this energy field communication would seem to transcend even the bonds of space-time. In theory, information transfer could approach the speed of light.

. . .

With that, the Eternal Ring brightened up and projected in front of them, in great detail, a model of an Energy Field Communication Network: how a non-self-sustaining but self-improving network could be achieved through the creation of several energy nodes.

"Perfect," El commented. "Effective but with very minimal, if any, additional feeding into the power source."

Seline said, "And this means of communication will not interfere with any other electromagnetic systems, it can be compatible".

In an instant, all three control platforms lit up simultaneously, revealing one major discovery: the energy field was apparently capable of purifying and renewing the environment.

"Look at that," Chris said, turning back to a holographic projection. "In areas completely enveloped by the energy field, the pollution is lessening while the ecosystems are starting to rejuvenate."

Immediately, Victor knew how significant this finding was: "This means we can solve both communication and ecological problems at once. It's a double discovery!"

. . .

THE BOOK OF LIFE REVEALED MORE INSIGHT:

"The Way of Integration:

First, complement strengths and offset weaknesses—let systems enhance one another.

Second, innovate boldly—pioneer new possibilities.

Third, test cautiously—progress step by step."

WHILE EXAMINING THESE REVELATIONS, A WARNING SIGNAL came from Monica's Blood Crystal Armor, hinting that several sets of experiments had shown instability within that energy field.

MONICA SAID, "THIS SHOULD BE A POINT THAT PUTS ONE AT caution. Any new technology introduced needs rigorous tests and its validation.

EL NODDED IN AGREEMENT. "PRECISELY. WE NEED TO DEVISE A broad-spectrum safety testing model whereby not one technology is released before proper scanning.

BY THEN, FLUCTUATIONS IN THE ENERGY MATRIX OF THE LAB were indicating a host of new possibilities. Energy field technology gave way to supposed applications in health care, agriculture, and construction.

"THIS TECHNOLOGY APPEARS TO HAVE MUCH MORE POTENTIAL than we had ever imagined," he said. "Of course we have to be very cautious-one step at a time."

. . .

The Count contemplated the revelations, his voice imbued with thoughtfulness. "We must find a balance between the pace of development and safety. Advancing too swiftly may result in unforeseen consequences."

In a flash, the three artifacts shook again and mapped out in mid-air a minute technology development roadmap, with key milestones highlighted at each phase of development, further emphasizing possible risks to be mitigated.

"This roadmap couldn't come at a better time," Victor said, looking at it closely. "It doesn't only light up but also warns about impending perils.

Monica further analyzed the roadmap: "Interestingly, it is of a spiral nature in development. Each breakthrough realizes previous developments, and at each step, it considers societal impact."

It was at this point that the three control platforms started unfolding an exciting phenomenon-energy efficiency throughout the city had jumped by about 300% thanks to the integration of the new technologies.

"This is an unexpected bonus," El said, "Apparent

synergistic effects of these technologies are way larger than anticipated."

Seline gestured toward the data. "The best part," she remarked, "is that this increase in efficiency has been accomplished without any detrimental effects on the environment."

The Book of Life then unfolded another enlightening set of collections:
"The Way of Balance:
First, efficiency and safety are equally stressed.
Second, innovation and stability coexist.
Third, it develops while preserving.
Chris studied these words, deep in thought. "
Exactly. No technological advancement should come at the expense of the environment. We've already paid the price for such mistakes in the past.

Then the Eternal Ring unfolded a tapestry of what the visions could be-clean energy, smart cities, and balanced ecosystems-none of which now seemed an impossible dream.

"This is the future we must aspire to," the Count said. "Let us see to it that technology truly serves man, not heralds his destruction.

. . .

Victor elaborated, "The key is in a proper assessment mechanism where all new technology must go through proper safety and environmental impact assessment."

When the energy field started getting into tune, a humming noise filled the lab as if suddenly, in the harmony, another discovery unraveled: it showed that the energy field was indeed able to maintain continuous energy cycles.

"This. this is a revolution in energy science!" Monica exclaimed. "If this theory holds, we've truly solved the energy crisis."

El did the calculation in his head straight away: "With this theory, we would need only a tiny initial energy to keep it all going. That changes everything when it comes to thinking about energy consumption.".

Seline examined it centimeter by centimeter. "The best thing is," she said, "this system is totally clean, producing no pollution at all. This truly represents the very heart of sustainability."

With the coming of night, the laboratory was brilliantly lighted. The scientists resumed their labors, and now, more than ever, the awful powers were wielded with awful frontiers. This time, however, research into novelties was not casual but intelligent and purposive, so that every step moved in full harmony with the general good.

This was a time when new technology was emerging and the world faced an unimaginable change.

19

THE PROPHECY OF OLD

Deep within the records of the Abyssal City lay a finding that really astounded everyone. Sorting through many ancient documents brought into view by Victor was one mysterious parchment scroll.

"Fantastic," said Victor, cautioning as he unwrapped the parchment. "This scroll indeed seemed to predict all that we're going through now."

Monica peered with her Blood Crystal Armor through the ancient scroll. "Judging from the material and the energy pattern, it is at least several thousand years old."

The Count leaned in to see the carvings. "The text... it is the Ancient Tongue of the Three Civilizations. Yet, apparently, it is more than can be discerned with a first glance on the surface level.

. . .

In an instant, these three items vibrated and shone onto the scroll: the Eternal Ring, Sacred Artifact, and Blood Crystal Armor. In that light, some of the hidden texts showed themselves piece by piece.

"I'll try and translate it," Chris explained, as he started interpreting those ancient words:
   When three lights stand and shine,
   When the ancient wisdom again returns to the world,
   When in harmony chaos and order stand,
   A new era shall rise.
   Three guardians walking together,
   Transcending time and space boundaries,
   Combining new and old wisdom,
   Guiding the trend in the world.

El pondered what it could be. "These verses... they describe everything that is happening now. The 'three rays of light' have to be the three energy pillars of the city, and the 'three guardians'... may they imply the three artifacts?

Seline proceeded to read the following lines:
   "When the Gate of Knowledge shall reopen,
   When the Energy Web covers the globe,
   When the Tree of Life grows anew,
   Hope shall pierce the darkness."

. . .

It was then that the Book of Life suddenly turned its own pages, showing things pertinent to the prophecy-those pages which told in graphic detail the process of the rebirth of a world.

"Look here," said Victor, pointing at another part of the scroll. "The prophecy speaks for this critical time:
  When threefold powers come into conjunction,
  When borderline of past and present dissolve,
  Then unimagined might could appear,
  Giving passage unto the higher worlds.

Monica's Blood Crystal Armor shone brightly. "There are huge energy fluctuations. This prophecy doesn't just record words but conveys embedded energy information."

Then in an instant, the Eternal Ring suddenly flared up into the air, bursting with a multitude of holographic images: three kinds of energy intertwined in a complex energy matrix.

"This should be the 'threefold powers' mentioned in the prophecy," Chris analyzed. "Through some kind of process, these three forces can achieve a qualitative leap."

El scanned the projections. "What's interesting here is that the pattern of this energy matrix is just like the new energy field we've been working with lately."

. . .

Seline continued to interpret the prophecy:
> "The river of Time is whirled into eddies,
> The dams of Space break,
> Ancient sages reappear,
> Bringing the final guidance to the world."

Suddenly, all three control platforms flickered on simultaneously, flashing warning lights of strange data fluctuations, as if some great spatial temporal anomaly was to occur.

"A moment," said the Count, "this 'time vortex' of the prophecy-might it not relate to the time distortions of late?

Monica began her analysis immediately: "That does sound probable. According to the latest intelligence, the space-time continuum around Abyssal City has begun to show some minor changes.

The Book of Life flips a new page:
> "Gate to Truth
> M.S.S.A.:
> First transcend the limit of time and space.
> Break the limit of perception, second.
> Thirdly, allow the incidence of a new possibility."

. . .

Further revelations by the subjects deeper into the matter: three artifacts lit in brilliance cast an awesome vision in the air. There was some web-like, interwoven complex of timelines.

"That's terrific," said Victor. "It appears to reflect how many timelines all interrelate. See these nodes-they're major points in history.

Monica gazed out at the projections through her Blood Crystal Armor. "But the most astonishing fact, these timelines are not static. It keeps on changing as if... as if it is searching for the best path.

Then suddenly, the scroll revealed its final prophecy:
> When the wheel of fate is turning anew,
> When the light of wisdom is guiding the ones astray,
> When the feeling of life is awakening anew,
> The greatest truth shall appear.
> Not an end, a new beginning.
> Not a goal, a new exit.
> Through mist of times,
> Up to the high spheres.

At this point, the energy field of the archive suddenly surged, and three control platforms sent back alarming information-the changing of the spatial-temporal structure had never been seen before.

. . .

"It would seem the prophecy was correct," El said. "For after all, we do stand at a crossroads.

Chris continued, "This tipping point does not only concern ourselves, but also the course of the future for the entire world, probably."

Maybe that is the reason why the Will of the Three Civilizations left it here to anticipate this day." The Count said nothing more for some time.

Turning to them now, Seline watched the unending shifts in information. "The question is… how do we respond to the forthcoming changes?

Once more, a page had turned in the Book of Life to reveal its final advisory:
"The Path of Preparation:
First, an open mind.
Second, admit the possibilities that could not be conceived.
Third, face change with courage."

When night began to fall, the archives slowly slackened their dialogical undulations of energy. This, though, was the calm before the tempest–even then, everyone knew it. Greater changes were afoot, and one needed to be ready.

. . .

It was now confronting them with its fulfillment, bit by bit, and this was just a beginning. As nobody knew what times were coming next, the one thing which was for certain was that they stood before the door of a completely different epoch.

20

WHIRLPOOL OF TIME

The energy matrix in Abyssal City suddenly started to violently fluctuate. At the same time, these three huge energy pillars turned into dazzlingly bright beams; one huge mass of energy condensed in the sky above the city.

"Something's wrong," Chris said quick, his hands already flying across the control panel. "The power surges in the energy field are too great."

In an instant, Monica's Blood Crystal Armor flickered with warning signals all over. "It's detecting large-scale spatial-temporal distortions; it seems that this is about the 'time vortex' mentioned in the prophecy."

Immediately, Victor brought out the map of the energy

distribution of the city: "Look at this energy flow, the power of the three energy nodes is gathering together."

It was at this moment that these three things, the Eternal Ring, Holy Artifact, and Blood Crystal Armour all lit up once more. The Eternal Ring presented an integral map of the surrounding space-time structure and showed some changes which have never appeared before.

"This energy pattern," El said, studying the data intently, "appears to be opening some type of portal."

Seline added, "The energy flow is strange, too; it's collapsing in, whereas it should be expanding out.

Abruptly, the Book of Life commenced turning its pages swiftly, disclosing an urgent warning:
"When threefold powers are in tune
When the Gate of Time and Space is near opening,
The Guardians must decide
Whether to stop or lead the metamorphosis."

Count Contemplated the ever-widening vortex: "We have little time to make a decision. This vortex grows much faster."

. . .

The protecting barrier of the city started to flicker, showing some signs of instability induced by energy fluctuations in the city's systems.

"We have to act right away," Monica said, as her Blood Crystal Armour was gauging the situation at an incredible speed. "Otherwise, if it keeps spiraling out of control, it is going to put the entire city in jeopardy."

Chris worked hard on the control panel. "We could try to shift the flow of energy to balance it out."

However, before they did that, the three control platforms saw something shocking: at the middle of the energy vortex was a structure resembling a wormhole.

"This is something else," Victor said, staring into the holographic projection. "According to the data, this structure is linked with numerous spatial-temporal dimensions."

El explained further, "Besides, it is not just a relation; it seems to seek some points in time and space.

The Eternal Ring emitted a beam of light that pierced the vortex's center. Under its illumination, the wormhole's structure became clearer.

. . .

The Book of Life presented in details:

The Gateway of Dimensions: First, a door into the past. Second, a bridge to the present. Third, a door to the future.

Seline examined the changes carefully. "This isn't just some sort of random spatial-temporal rift; it's a deliberate call.

Then suddenly, all the three energy pillars are humming in powerful tone while the vortex itself started spinning faster.

"Energy readings are spiking fast," Monica warned. "If this keeps up, the whole energy system for the city could collapse."

The Count did not waste any time. "We must stabilize the vortex. Chris, switch on the emergency energy redistribution system. Victor, raise the secondary energy matrix."

But the affair wasn't quite that straightforward: the faster it spun, the stranger the visions that appeared in the vortex-a mixture of remnants of the past with bits of the future, like dynamic pieces of light in a kaleidoscope.

"These images," Victor cried, transported with wonder,

"these are no fantasms, but the actual relics of time and space!

Monica's Blood Crystal Armor sensed that something was off. "Something is coming out of the Vortex-a being from another dimension is headed toward our timeline!"

Then, all three Items lit up brightly and created a sort of shield of energy. It was behind that shield that they were finally able to see the figures emerging from the vortex.

Three figures moved forward in steps older than time itself, as if one stood between life and space.

"We have been waiting for this day," the first figure said, his voice thunderous, ancient-sounding as if it were carried across centuries. "We are the Guardians of the Three Civilisations -and your ancestors."

The Book of Life began operating independently and recorded events relevant to these Guardians:
"When the world is in turmoil, and at every crossroads of civilisation, the ancients will come out to shed light on the way forward."

Chris was shocked. "They... they're the ones who left all these artifacts and prophecies thousands of years ago!

. . .

The second Guardian nodded. "Yes. We knew it would be so. While for now time and space no longer exist, new dimensions open their doors.

The third Guardian continued, "Yet, all that was just a start. Much greater trials and possibilities remain ahead."

Suddenly, the vortex started to tremble violently and the outlines of the three Guardians began to blur.

"Time is short here," the first Guardian began, "and remember, the things you have in your hands are not just tools-they are keys to ascend to the highest realm.

"The second Guardian continued, When the threefold powers shall truly unite, then shall a new age be born.

The third Guardian said good-bye with, "Be wise, be strong-the cross-road of fate is nigh."

Said that, his body and those of the other Guardians disappeared into the vortex, which now began to shrink and rotate at a much slower speed until it finally just collapsed into a light shine and disappeared into the night.

. . .

The town went back to normal, but in the know was every last citizen that this encounter had changed everything. The three artifacts pulsed with energy anew and shone brighter than ever.

The Count observed the city, which had now attained stability. "It seems the real challenge is just beginning."

Victor nodded, his eyes glittering with deep thought. "Yes, we have to understand their powers, but also what lies beyond mere artifacts.

Monica watched it all with her Blood Crystal Armor on. "This will change time and space beyond recognition no more, for sure."

As night fell, the Abyssal City went back to its usual silence. Yet, everybody knew that nothing would be the same again.

A new chapter was about to begin, whereby they would be both the witness and the pioneer.

21

THE LAST ALLIANCE

Golden afternoon sun bathed the Abyssal City. Gusty soft light diffused through thin clouds, coloring it with its rich tone as it stood in continuous reconstruction. The spire of the Shadow Council's new headquarters, the dome of the Silver Star Temple, and the shining surfaces of the Temple of Destiny all seemed to be varnished by this fading light into an uneventful yet subliminally tense panorama.

El, standing in the great hall of the Temple of Fates, looked intently at a three-dimensional map made by the Whirlwind himself. All the representatives of the big factions stood in a line, sitting around the round table, their faces twisted by gravity and hope-the conference that would determine the future pattern of the world.

"The world is undergoing unprecedented change," El began, shattering the heavy silence that enveloped them.

"The Count's sacrifice has granted us this opportunity, yet maintaining balance will demand all of our wisdom and courage."

Seline unrolled the Life Map silently; the complicated network of energy started to unfold, extending into the air. "The current energetic living system has just been balanced, yet its vulnerability still exists. If no new order is set up soon, chaos will break out once again anytime.

Salena leaned forward, the new Speaker of the Shadow Council; her voice was husky with import. "The Shadow Council is ready to impart our knowledge. But let me warn all of you—some knowledge comes with great danger. We need very strong mechanisms to control its use."

High Priestess Elena of the Silver Star Temple clasped her hands before her chest. "The Temple is ready to open the Prophecy Library. However," her keen glance swept around the room, "the prophetic power may well be more dangerous than even the sharpest blade. We must proceed with caution."

At that moment, the ring released a soft light and spread a protective field through the hall. The Blood Crystal Armor on Monica's body quickly analyzed the phenomenon: "Energy field forms a resonance pattern. Looked like some kind of contract-like force of nature!

. . .

The dark form of Victor waltzed to the corner of the room, his skills delving deep into the nature of the energy. "Interesting... the energy signatures of the representatives are interlocking themselves automatically. It is not being forced-this is in line with shared ideals."

Miller flicked the leaves of the Book of Life until he landed on a shining golden page. "It's here! The prophecy labeled it the 'Natural Alliance': the moment different powers really understand each other, they will naturally choose the most excellent way to unite.

Chris, who had remained quiet until that moment, abruptly rose to his feet. "Even as a humble soldier, I recognize the truth—this is not the time to bicker over factional interests. If we cannot genuinely unite, then all the sacrifices we've made will have been in vain."

His words sent a ripple down the table. El looked around the room very carefully; his eyes were deep and reflective. "Chris does have a point. We don't need an alliance that is bound by rules but cooperation based on mutual agreement."

Seline's Life Map began to shift as new energies started to reveal themselves. "Look at this," she said, "the energy signature of each group is slowly changing, consciously seeking its points of resonance.

Tapping the table lightly, Salina explained, "What the Shadow Council would offer is multi-tiered knowledge sharing: the bedrock knowledge would be available to all, while the advanced form, which could be dangerous, would be provided, in due course, through apprenticeship.

"That's a great idea," Elena assented. "It could be emulated at the Silver Star Temple's Prophecy Library. But then we have to come up with some rigid qualification protocols."

Monica's armors crunched the figures posthaste. "Given current energy trends, this tiered sharing model offers higher than an 87% success rate. There is, however, one crucial factor missing."

"Public sentiment," Victor interpolated, his dark good opinion stretching over the city. "The general populace is generally in favor of this publicity; however, there remains a residue of concern-most especially among those who have been burned in the past.

Miller has noted this epiphany in the Book of Life. "It reminds us that a new union cannot just be about power integration. We have to be sensitive as well to the sentiments and anxieties of ordinary people."

. . .

The deliberations continued well into the night. As the surrounding dark of night fell, a structure of the new alliance began to take shape-one in which the unique characteristics of each organization were retained, yet effective machinery for cooperation was established.

El wrapped up his meeting with these few words: "This coalition won't be based on regulations but on mutual understanding; not on force, but on liability. Let's altogether observe the very beginning of this century.".

And with that, the inner energy field of the Eternal Ring pulsed softly, washing the room in a wave of warmth; every person within it felt a reassuring presence, the residual consciousness of the Count, speaking silently his approval.

Monica's armor then showed the final result of her analysis: "The energy field has now stabilized into a structured whole. This is going to be the base for the new alliance."

The voice of Victor rose from the shadows, full of conviction. "The whole city rises with it. It is not an alliance of factions; it is the rise of a whole civilization.".

. . .

With the final agreement signed, the first light of dawn began to crest over the horizon. There was no need for elaborate ceremonies to mark this alliance, as the most significant bond had already been etched in the hearts of everyone present.

El looked at his new allies and hailed, "This is not the end but the beginning. Later on, even more difficult challenges will arise, but so long as we cling to this consensus we have reached today, nothing can shake this alliance."

Seline folded the Life Map with care and whispered, "Yes, let us prove it through action that the Count didn't die for nothing, this world is worth fighting for.".

Beneath the expansive night sky, the lights of the Abyssal City sparkled like distant stars, embodying the weight of this momentous evening. A genuine Final Alliance had been forged—not through force, but through a deep and heartfelt consensus.

22

THE CLEANING PROCESS

The first rays of the morning sun cast a warm glow upon the dome of the Temple of Fate below, where vivid shades of every color tumbled through the stained glass. Refracted colors danced elegantly across the floor, playing upon ancient runes carved into the stone-ages of being there, softly shimmering now in gentle harmony with the morning light.

"It is now unraveling," Seline exclaimed against the view of the Light Map, whose light points started compacting. "This, however, is but the first step. The process of complete purification will be far more complicated than we had ever thought it would be."

El nodded and then took the Eternal Ring in his hands, humming softly. "Although the energy within the Abyss has already become stable, there is still a lot of chaotic element within it. If that's not fully cleansed, it will become a latent menace."

Her eyes gleaming with acuteness, Monica uttered in a high-pitched tone; her Blood Crystal Armor amplified her analyses. "At this energy-conversion rate, it would take a minimum of three months to purify this whole Abyss region. But..." A deadweight seemed to fall, and then her tone was grave: "We may not have that much time."

"Why not?" Chris frowned, furrowing his eyebrows. Though he was a warrior and may not fully understand such intricacies of energy analysis, he surely could feel the heaviness of her worry.

Victor stepped into the light; his tone was even, grave. "Because elements of the Shadow Council are mobilizing. My shadow network has intercepted movements-they're gathering their forces for one last stand."

Miller opened the leaves of the Book of Life till he had come upon a line shining brightly with meaning. "There's something here-a record of some sort about an ancient purification ritual. It says, 'As embers is the strength of chaos; when the Seven Stars are aligned, so shall the True Power of Purification awaken.

. . .

Elena scrunched up her brow, deep in thought. "The Seven Stars... something about that concerned an ancient prophecy in the Temple." Reaching into her robes, she pulled out a parchment scroll. "I recall, it was stated quite clearly in the prophecy: 'Thus, the day of purification must come in ritual simultaneously at seven nodal points.

Life, Wisdom, Power, Balance, Creation, Guardianship, and Hope," a hoarse voice echoed from Salina in the darkness. "These seven nodes must perfectly align with these cardinal forces.

El's Prophetic Power surged strongly, and his face turned solemn. "That's not all. Each node requires a specific guide. If a person is inadequately chosen, then the ritual will not only fail but can also bring terrible consequences.

In an instant, the whole temple was shaking. The Luminous Runes on the floor began to form a huge seven-pointed star diagram, filling the whole hall with energy.

"The energy is guiding us," the wonder-struck Seline exclaimed. "Really it is-it's showing us where it is!

The instant this happened, Monica's armor initiated immediate recording and analysis of the patterns. "The first node should fall at the Tree of Life, where Life Energy is strongest."

. . .

"The latter one is at the old Shadow Council headquarters," Victor said calmly. "That place retains the most ancient vestiges of wisdom."

"The third," El gestured toward the horizon, "is placed at the ruins of the Tower of Power."

One after another, all the seven places were announced, and when the last place was confirmed, the seven-star diagram on the ground glowed brightly, sending a ray of light.

"But," Chris jumped in, grasping toward perhaps the most important question, "can we actually get the right people to run these nodes?

El said to Seline: "The Life Node is yours for the taking. You are the most powerful Light Bearer, and nobody else could control Life Energy like you.

Seline nodded with determination. "I'll take responsibility for it. But what about the other nodes?"

"The Node of Wisdom," Salina whispered. "I'll take it. Being the former member of the Shadow Council, I understand its ancient knowledge more than anybody else."

"Power Node," El volunteered, "I will be able to handle that thanks to my Prophetic Power about the volatile energy over there.

Victor stepped forward. "I shall take the Balance Node. The power of shadow has always been one of balance."

"The Creation Node belongs to the young," Elena said. "It's a symbol of hope and possibility.

"I shall take responsibility over the Guardianship Node, supported by my Blood Crystal Armor," Monica replied confidently. "In one sense, technology embodies the guardian concept."

"And finally the Hope Node," he said, closing the Book of Life; "to this the priests of the Silver Star Temple are to be given charge. Prophecy and hope inextricably intertwined.

And when the sevenMeadeums received confirmation, the Eternal Ring cast seven rays, each to fall at a place appointed for the purpose.

. . .

"We do not have that much time," El said, his voice filled with tension. "I can feel it-the Shadow Council stirred its forces. The ritual needs to be finished before they strike."

Monica cleaned the numbers again in a flash. "At this rate, at least three days would pass. The thing is."

"The problem is the Shadow Council won't give us that much time," Victor cut in. "According to my network's intelligence, they could launch their final assault as early as the day after tomorrow."

"Then we will go all the faster," Chris said with serious assurance. "I will dispatch the warriors to firm up our defenses at the nodes. We will work night and day to give you the time you need."

He surveyed the room, his eyes locking into each of his companions. "Chris is right. We're on our own from here on out. Remember, once the ritual starts, a stop will not be possible. Whatever happens, node workers stay at their position till the end."

They all nodded gravely and then went their separate ways to start working. Time was running out, but unyielding determination fluttered in every heart. It was a race against time, for one single wrong move would have meant disaster for all.

As night started to fall, the seven nodes began to condense, their energies running between them, molding the growing form of the purification net. But this was just the beginning, as the greater task was still ahead.

"By this time tomorrow," El said, his eyes fixed on the stars above, "we will know if this path of purification can really work."

Seline stood beside him. "Whatever happens, at least we'll know we gave everything we had. That's enough."

In the distance, unseen forces began to stir. The horizon promised a greater storm. But in that moment, one thought remained in the mind of every guardian-this world was worth saving.

One path was the Path of Purification, to which retreat was impossible but advance irresistible.

23

THE SHADOWS STRIKE

In the depths of the grand, sullen night sky, the Abyssal City was shrouded in grim silence. These seven nodes burst with shafts of light that crossed star-like across the sky with soft, fluttering brilliance, which pieced the darkness now angled around.

Chris was up on the wall, his fingers absently tracing the hilt of his sword as he peered into the shadowy horizon.

"They're here," Victor said out of the darkness, his words etched with worry. "At least three armies-more than we'd have thought.

Monica's Blood Crystal Armor gave a real-time reading. "Massive energy fluctuations detected, estimating numbers between fifteen to twenty thousand. Worse." Her voice caught and fell low. "They have successfully performed an ancient corruption ritual it seems.

A deep alarm klaxon boomed across the City, shearing through the silence. El materialized in front of the Temple of Destiny, his body haloed by the Eternal Ring, which floated above him, shining steadily and watchfully.

"Mobilize all defense forces," he ordered in a crisp, cold voice. "Remember, our top priority is to defend the seven nodes. The purifying ritual cannot be interrupted once it begins.

Seline spread the Life Map before her, revealing a troubling visualization. "The enemy's corruption energy is starting to wear down our energy shields. If this persists..."

Her words were cut short by the shrill, doleful blast of a war horn, echoing across the plain. The next instant, hundreds of shadowy forms appeared at the horizon, surging forward to engulf the city like an unending tide of darkness.

"Form defensive positions!" he yelled, his sword drawn. Hundreds of warriors took a position at the walls, the bowmen reaching for their bows.

. . .

The first wave of the assault struck with ferocity. The vanguard of the shadow army unleashed ancient shadow spells capable of corroding the city's protective energy shields.

"Something's wrong," Victor exclaimed suddenly, his sharp eyes scanning the ground. "These hits. much too accurate. They know our defense system.

Elena, High Priestess of the Silver Star Temple, burst into the bedlam. "A traitor lurks among us! The Prophecy Library has informed me that our strategic plan of defense has been divulged.

"It's too late to be concerned with that now," El calmly replied. "Turn on the backup defenses immediately. Salina, escort the Shadow Guard to protect the Wisdom Node. Monica, amplify the energy feed to the Guardianship Node."

A deafening explosion cut through his words. On the western side, the city's protective shield splintered, affording a wide breach for hundreds of surging shadow warriors.

"I'll handle this!" Chris rallied a team of elite soldiers and charged forward. Amid the clash of steel and shadow, the battle descended into fierce close-quarters combat.

. . .

Meanwhile, Seline watched as fluctuations in the energy field that encased the Life Node started to happen. "Something's interfering with the focusing of the ritual. If we don't stabilize the energy field soon...

"Miller!" El called out through the communicator. "Look in the Book of Life! Does it mention anything about countering this corruption?"

"I'm looking!" Miller's voice cracked over, laced with a tinge of urgency. "Wait. I have it! The book reads: 'When the power of corruption strikes, only through the resonance of pure hearts can it be purified.'"

Monica's armor crunched through it in an instant. "This tells us we must have all seven nodes, all at resonance, for a complete defensive circuit.

That is when the second wave attacked; this time, it wasn't just physical, a strong blow packed with energy. It was here that the Shadow Council brought out their trump card: the Power of Chaos.

"This is terrible!" Victor exclaimed. "They're not trying to destroy the nodes, but to corrupt them! And if even one node is corrupted, then the ritual of cleansing won't work!"

. . .

El made an immediate decision. "Everybody listen! It's time to implement the "stalemate scheme". Let's change into the Stellar Guardian Formations, as we have rehearsed!

With one word from him, the seven node guardians fell into position. Seline's Life Energy was attuned to Elena's prophetic powers, while Salina's shadow means merged seamlessly with Victor's perceptive capabilities. Monica's technological expertise lent precision and stability to the entire defense network.

"Hold the line!" Chris yelled from the front, his sword flashing in the chaos. "We gotta hang on for just one more hour! When the morning comes, the rite of purification can start!

Yet the attack by the enemies did not cease. The Shadow Council, resolute to conclude this battle this night once and for all, summoned dark powers imbuing the battlefield with a hostile and depressing aura.

"This cannot go on," Victor said seriously. "It's beginning to gnaw its way into the very bones of the city. Unless we do something.

At that moment, the Eternal Ring burst with brilliant light. Within the bright halo, a ghostly form appeared-this was the last bit of the Count's consciousness.

. . .

"Initiate the emergency protocol," the ghostly figure ordered, firm and commanding. "We will tap the power of the Eternal Ring and utilize its power to preponed the date of the ritual of cleansing. And the cost is..."

"The price," El said finally, heavily, "is that the Eternal Ring will lose much of its power. And your soul will cease to exist entirely."

The ghostly figure of the Count bowed his head. "This is the only chance. Still, it must be unanimous."

A moment of silence reigned on the battle field. That said, it sounded heavily in the air the burden of this decision-to lose the guidance of the Count forever was a heavy price, but there was no alternative.

"I do," Seline said, her voice cutting through the quiet. "For the future of this world."

"Agreed," said Salina with no deliberation.

They followed one by one the desire of the guardians, until the final agreement was sealed, at which time the

Eternal Ring shone like never before, pouring its light on the entire city.

"Prepare to perform the ritual cleansing!" El shouted with commanding authority. "Everybody, get into position!"

With this, the ghostly form of Count began to dissolve into nothingness. His words still echoed in their hearts: "Remember, true strength lies in unity. Never... never forget that."

His image disappeared, and within the Abyssal City, the skies began to develop an incredible storm of energy. All through the night of the shadow attack, the night of the intestine-jolting clash of light and darkness would be chronicled in history.

While the battle raged at its wildest, to the east a pallid light of morning proclaimed hope. The Way of Purgation had started; a new world was being melted within the crucible of this crazed struggle.

24

THE BATTLE OF GUARDIANS

Before the break of dawn, Abyssal City was engulfed in its most intense battle. Seven energy nodes were burning defiantly against the approaching night, their beacons punching through the darkness like the last stars before the morning sun rises. Light from the Eternal Ring cast protection over the whole city, but the attacks from the Shadow Council continued to press in like a tsunami.

"The energy shield can only hold for another fifteen minutes!" Monica's voice came through the communicator, laced with urgency. Her Blood Crystal Armor showed critical data: huge pressure had been built up at the Guardianship Node.

Chris was in the very front, fighting with all his might; his whizzing sword cut through sharply. "They're concentrating their attack on the west defense! Monica, pour in energy support!

"We cannot," a voice came from the darkness, steady, steely, belonging to Victor. "Deregulation from the nodes would collapse the entire defense net. We must retain the current flow.

Suddenly, without any warning, some shadowy assassins breached the outer defenses and rushed towards the Life Node. She immediately turned to the Life Map and produced a shining barrier of golden energy to manifest. Unfortunately, those assassins were equipped with weapons imbued with some strange power that could pierce through the barrier to an extent.

"Look out!" El shouted, using his Prophetic Power to open a subsidiary line of defense. "Chaotic energy in their weapons!"

A tremendous explosion boomed from the Wisdom Node, and then Salina's voice crackled through the communicator, "There's a huge attack on the eastern front! They are utilizing an ancient array for teleporting!

Elena, High Priestess of the Silver Star Temple, was quick to act: "Seers of the Temple, to your posts! Raise the Starlight Barrier!

. . .

Brilliant light of pure silver burst out across the eastern sky, creating for one instant a barrier of energy. But everyone knew this was only a temporary reprieve-the actual challenge was yet to come.

"Miller!" El called into the communicator. "What is the preparation status for the purification ritual?

"Five minutes," Miller replied. His voice was thick with exhaustion. "The Book of Life said the energy of all seven nodes needs to perfectly align to activate the ritual. But...

Before he could complete his thought, a colossal surge of energy erupted from the heart of the city. A devastating wave of pressure coursed through the air, compelling everyone to halt for an instant.

"It's the Chaos Source!" exclaimed Victor, his voice now laced with a sense of urgency. "The Shadow Council is trying to wake it up!"

This was an alarming conclusion, until Monica's systems quickly processed the data. "If the Chaos Source is fully awakened, it won't just disrupt the purifying ritual; it would cast the whole city into catastrophic chaos!

. . .

It was getting out of hand really fast. The main forces of the Shadow Council launched a general attack, driving the defenses of the city to their limit. If that was not enough, chaotic energy emanating from the Chaos Source desynchronized the nodes.

"We need a new plan," Seline said firmly, though chaos licked at every word she spoke around her. Keeping the stream of energy in the Life Node, her brain seemed filled only with one need-to know the solution of how to contain this Chaos Source.

At this, the Eternal Ring heaved with an incredible turmoil; its light was nearly blinding in its intensity. The Count's ghostly perception burst anew, his face properly somber.

"One final solution," his voice rumbled with weight. "The Eternal Ring has the power to seal the Chaos Source for a time. But this would require one to guide it. And this guide...

"...will have to sacrifice their life," El concluded, his eyes steady and resolute. "I'll do it."

"No," Chris said with force, stepping forward with resolution. "Let me handle it. All of you have an important role to play in the purification ritual. This is something I can do.

"Chris!" Seline exclaimed, with a chilling of her voice.

"There is no time for discussion," Chris said briefly, after which he turned right toward the centre of the city. "Victor, guard the back. El, the moment I seal the Chaos Source, you can begin the ritual immediately."

Nothing could bring him back. His eyes told of this determination. Just then, this very ordinary warrior outshone his mundane humanity.

"Remember," the ghostly figure of the Count intoned as it started to disappear, "the timing is of the essence. The Eternal Ring's power must contain the Chaos Source before it fully awakens to life. Precision is key."

Chris nodded, his fingers clenching over the Eternal Ring. He disappeared into the turmoil, running toward the very eye of the storm.

"Listen, everybody!" El shouted above the fighting din. "The instant Chris begins the sealing, we must start the purification ritual. Whatever happens, the ritual must not be stopped!"

. . .

It was a continuing battle, but heavy was laid the feeling that fell upon the city. Every defender knew how much the forthcoming moments weighed upon them: the future of the world.

The first whispers of dawn sliced through the heavy cloak of darkness in the east. The battle of the guardians was at its most critical point.

Undulating masses of energy stroked the Chaos Source right in the heart of the city, pulsing with a malign life of its own. A weighty moment, but he didn't flinch.

"Let's do this," he whispered, raising the Eternal Ring high atop his head. In response, the artifact blazed with light as it flowered into a protective shield, encircling him.

The source of Chaos erupted with such a fury that waves of energy lashed against the barrier. Chris ground his teeth as he siphoned all his will into keeping the ring's power up.

The guardians positioned themselves at the nodes, their feet set. Seline's golden light became one with Elena's silver prophecy as they laced a balancing embrace around the Life Node; Salina's shadow techniques supported

Victor's balance at the Wisdom Node, while Monica kept precise calculations at the Guardianship Node to maintain steady energy flows.

"Synchronize the nodes now!" El ordered, his prophecy powerfully entwining the threads of energy together with perfection.

The Book of Life suddenly shone bright and its pages began to spin in a flash. "The nodes are synching!" Miller screamed. "We are really close!

As the ring at the center surged with energy, Chris felt a final, resounding voice of the Count inside his mind: "Thank you, Chris. It is your courage that will save us all."

Chris gave a weak smile, fingers clenching on the ring. "Do it now!"

Fully opening, the Eternal Ring cast a display of blinding brightness upon everything, encasing the Chaos Source. It confined the malicious energy in an instant, its dark tendrils recoiling into the void.

"Now!" El shouted, "Let the purging ritual begin!

. . .

All at once, the seven nodes burst in a resounding harmony, their beams of light combined into one huge energy vortex enveloping the city. The cacophony of energy cleansed through the united power of the Guardians and thus started to break the corruption apart.

As the first light of dawn washed over the city, the fight was gradually ending. The forces of the Shadow Council fell back, their last desperate attempt foiled. Yet, the price paid was steep.

Chris was nowhere to be seen. Sprawling in the dirt lay the Eternal Ring, his light not snuffed out but rather tuned down, testimony to that one warrior who gave himself for the world's sake.

El stood silent, triumph and sorrow welling in his eyes. "He did it," he whispered. "Chris saved us all."

Seline fell to her knees beside the ring, weeping openly. "He was... more than a warrior. He was a guardian, in every sense of the word."

Above them, the sky stretched clear and bright, the light of dawn heralding a new beginning. The Path of Purification was finally over, but the memories of tonight- the Battle of the Guardians-would be etched in their minds forever. A new chapter was born-one forged in a crucible of sacrifice, courage, and unity. Though the scars would still linger on, the sheen of their future now shone more brilliant than it ever had.

25

THE FULFILLMENT OF PROPHECY

In the last hours before dawn, Chris stood right at the center of the Source of Chaos. The Eternal Ring in his hand began to hum with a faint vibration, as if it was attuned to the fate that was about to come. Inside the thick, churning blackness, chaotic energy surged out of control, struggling to break through the last seal.

"Chris is in place!" Victor's voice boomed out over town via the Shadow Network. "All nodes, standby!"

Suddenly, some unexpected fluctuations were evinced in Seline's Life Map. "Wait, the Life Node shows some kind of weird energy pattern. This frequency. it seems to be resonating with something."

"The prophecy," El exclaimed suddenly, his eyes flashing

serious. "The oldest prophecy is unfolding before our very eyes. Miller, consult the Book of Life right this minute!

In an instant, Miller's voice was back, full of wonder: "The whole book is illuminated! The prophetic texts are rearranging themselves. Hold on, I've got it!"

"When the light and darkness entwine, the brave shall submit their spirits. If the Seven Stars are in place, the vow of old is redeemed. The end is not death; it's the start of rebirth."

The energy of the Source of Chaos is reaching critical levels! Chris, now!" Monica's Blood Crystal Armor suddenly warned her.

Lifting the Eternal Ring high above his head, Chris initiated the seal at the center of the city. In that instant, golden light intertwined with the violent darkness in a grievous, beautiful display across the sky.

"Turn on the Purification Ritual!" The voice of El crackled over the communicator. "All nodes, full capacity!

Seven rays of light shot upwards all at once, meeting high above. Seline called upon the Life Node, El protected the Power Node, Salina was in charge of the Wisdom Node, and Victor and Elena were both working together to maintain the Balance Node. Monica watched over the Defense Node while the priests of the Silver Star Temple supported the Hope Node.

It was then that the prophecy unfolded, unfolding in a manner as told. Where the seven beams of light met, one gigantic energy vortex appeared and started sucking in the turbulent energy around it.

"This is..." Monica exclaimed, her voice filled with shock. "The energy conversion rate has reached an unprecedented level!"

Yet, the resistance from the Source of Chaos was getting stronger. Chris felt his life force slipping away with increasing speed, yet he desperately clung to the Eternal Ring, determined to complete his last mission.

"Wait!" El called. "Just one minute more, and the purifying will be complete!"

It was then when everything got new twist. The last shred of Count's mind in the Eternal Ring met the will of Chris. A shining gold light flared off the ring.

. . .

"This is..." Seline mused as she peered through her Life Map. "Life energy! The Count's final gift!"

The voice of Miller shook with emotion. "The writing in the Book of Life is rearranging itself! A new prophecy is unfolding!

"Not sacrifice, but rebirth. Not an end, but the birth of something new. The moment a pure heart connects with eternity, a miracle shall emerge.

Then, a light of unbelievable brightness suddenly burst out of Chris' body. The power of the Eternal Ring completely merged with Chris and took the form of a perfect energy field. This energy did not only seal the Source of Chaos but cleansed everything in its surroundings.

"Look!" exclaimed Victor. "The Shadow Legion... they're having their weapons and armor dissolve!"

Indeed, with the purifying power radiating away, corrupted shadow energies quickly vanished. A beginning of disintegration appeared in the attacking formation of the Shadow Council, and their hitherto mighty chaotic technologies faltered under the attacks of pure energy.

. . .

Elena had been astonished-something overcame her from the Prophecy Library. "This isn't just a victory, this is a rebirth! Chris, he.

Before she had said her words, there was a shining beam of brilliance at Chris's position, fusing seamlessly into the other seven rays. Eight rays of lights overspent with one another before engulphing the whole Abyssal City in a mild field of energy.

"Life signs!" Monica exclaimed suddenly. "I can still feel Chris's life signs! They're weak, but they're there!"

Seline instantly tapped into the power of the Life Map. "I see it now clearly! That was the real prophecy! It wasn't referring to death, but rebirth! The Eternal Ring didn't take his life-it transformed him into the new Guardian!

Indeed, with the first sunbeams shining through the clouds, the battle was over. The remaining members of the Shadow Council had either been cleansed or had turned themselves in. They found Chris, still upright and right in the middle of the city, but he was different, wonderfully so.

"The prophecy has been fulfilled," El said softly, "though certainly not as expected. It is a purifying that has cleansed not only the city, but the hearts of its people as well."

. . .

Miller's face turned solemn as he wrote in the Book of Life these historic words: "When free will meets the power of eternity, a miracle is created. This is not the end, but the start.

When morning finally arrived and the sun was high up, Abyssal City bathed in the morning light. And so the eight rays went their way, turning from what had been a simple omen of protection into profound testimony of hope.

26

INTO THE ABYSS' TRANSFORMATION

This change was unbeknownst to anyone as the first rays of the sun began to caress the land in the Abyssal City. The ground softly vibrated, not in the rhythm of chaos and destruction, but to one of life.

"Look there!" Seline exclaimed, her finger pointing out toward the hidden depths of the city. Her Life Map unfolded a great revelation: "The essence of the Abyss... it is undergoing a great change!

But the prophetic power of El showed an even deeper change. "It's not superficial. Right down to very involved energy structures, there's a reorganization going on. It's a metamorphosis."

Monica's Blood Crystal Armour continually developed new data. "The energy conversion rate is still growing and has surpassed 95% meanwhile. More shockingly, this transformation is taking place naturally, without any interference from the outside."

Chris was reborn, standing at the center of the city, shimmering between matter and pure energy. The Eternal Ring floated in the air before his chest, benignly glowing soft and white.

"I can feel it," he said, his voice all but otherworldly. "The Abyss is no longer just a source for chaos and destruction; it's becoming a wellspring of creation."

Victor stepped forward into the light, his face wearing a seriousness unusual for him. "Yet, this transformation has come with unexpected results. The Shadow Network... it grows, and its very purpose shifts.

Suddenly, cracks opened up across the whole face of the city, but from these fissures poured, instead of chaotic energy, a vibrant new power teeming with life.

"New Revelation from the Book of Life!" The communicator suddenly crackled with Miller's voice. "The true nature of the Abyss has awakened. It was at first a holy place where an ancient people bred new life, yet later it was corrupted and distorted."

. . .

Elena, at the forefront of the Temple of the Silver Star priests, began laying down protective sigils. "We must focus this energy, channeling it along the right pathways."

"No," El interjected, his gaze transfixed upon the scene before him. "Look."

And suddenly, before everyone's very eyes, the forming energy did not require controls over its direction. It moved instinctively into the most perfect ways and means. Ground cracks started to heal, leaving behind them a huge web of fine energy vessels, looking like a great Life Network.

"It is the will of nature," cried Seline, astonished. "Abyss is returning to its antient form."

Further processing of data revealed to Monica increasingly detailed complexities: "These new veins of energy are developing a complete circulatory system. They're not just purifying the environment-they're creating completely new life forms!

Where the flows of energy crossed, peculiar forms of life began to spring forth. They were not just entities of pure energy, nor were they typical life-they were perfect mergers of the two.

. . .

"This is the true transformation of the Abyss," Chris said as he finally tuned himself to the changes. "It's not about ridding the darkness, just finding that perfect balance between light and shadow."

Throughout the city, massive changes were in action: crumbling buildings were on the mend, desolate landscapes began to bloom anew, and the atmosphere became infused with renewed life.

Victor saw all in his shadow perception. "The most amazing thing is that this change has not washed away the original features of the Abyss; the shadow energy is still there, just that it is much purer and more regular."

Seline's Life Map began reacting with a sudden intensity. "Look! Life energy is mixing with these new forces. They're not fighting each other anymore; they're working together and strengthening each other."

Miller pressed on, revealing more from the Book of Life. "This," he explained, "was the original blueprint of the ancient civilization. The Abyss was supposed to act like a perfect energy conversion field where all the forces changed into creative springs.

And suddenly, a deeper realization washed over Chris. "Ma'rika. There's more... The transformation of the Abyss won't stop with the city. It'll just keep on welling up-not an invasion, but a fertilization."

Monica did a rough calculation in her mind: "At this rate of expansion, it will engulf the whole known world. But it may take years, maybe decades ".

"That is the best way," El said. "It gives every place ample time to adjust and adopt it.

Then, the Eternal Ring flared up in a dazzling spectrum of colors, its brilliance casting into the firmament an all-encompassing map of the world-to-be. The sketch of that map revealed the eventual result of the Abyss's transformation into a realm where light and shadow existed in exquisite balance.

Seline's eyes were fixed on the projection, a glitter in her eyes of tears she wouldn't allow to fall. "This was the dream the Count always dreamed. He wasn't trying to conquer the Abyss-only wake it up."

It went on to last for three whole days. Within that time, the Abyssal City underwent its full transformation from what it once was. No longer did the "source of sin"; it had now transformed into a hotbed of new life.

. . .

"This is only the beginning," said Chris now, fully accustomed to his changed self. "The actual work is to guide this transition in a manner that it works for the benefit of the entire world."

El nodded in agreement. "Not only do we need to protect this change, but learn about it and utilize it-a formidable, unwieldy affair, yet an opportunity unparalleled.

In the final stages of this transformation, the Abyssal City would then reveal itself in all its glory: a most vital city of hope that shone bright enough to have light and darkness melt into one another with ease, suckling into being a brand new life force.

This summed up the very essence of the change of the Abyss: not to delete but to wake up, not to change but to restore. All learned a big lesson on the journey there: true strength does not lie in conquest but rather in understanding and embracing.

27

TAPESTRY OF LIGHT AND SHADOW

It shone with an brilliance that was never seen at dusk, neither blinding nor dim, but just a perfect blend of light and shadow together. It was from the top of the highest possible observation tower that Chris saw this flow of energy, for the first time, through his newly gained perception.

"Beautiful," he breathed, and the Eternal Ring purred softly along with his thoughts. "Like a tapestry, wrought of light and darkness.

Then the Life Map of Seline appeared in the air, fully capturing the sentient convolutions of energy. "Each thread of energy so seamlessly sewn, like the rhythm of life itself, almost.

. . .

It was then that El's prophetic power sensed something amiss. His expression turned grave. "Something's happening. There's a massive energy fluctuation in the field."

"I'm getting the same readings," Monica reported as her Blood Crystal Armor processed the data. "But this fluctuation... it's strange. It doesn't feel like a threat—it feels like a summons."

The figure of Victor emerged from the shadow. "I feel it, too. The energies of the city are restructuring on their own, according to Shadow Network contacts."

Then, an amazing sight appeared: the firmament showed a view not comparable with anything else; uncountable strands of lights and shades interwove far above into one huge vortex of energy. However, this vortex showed a balance that none had seen from any other phenomenon.

"The Book of Life is answering!" Miller's voice came over the communicator. "This is the Great Weaving. It was said in the prophecy that once light and shadow are really in balance, the world will go into a new phase.

Elena instructed the priests of the Silver Star Temple in a prophetic formation. "The conflux is shifting. The energies, where light and darkness merge into one, are no longer just mingling but actually blending into one on a deeper level.

Chris felt the overwhelming surge of tremendous power. "It's here!"

As he spoke, seven beams of light exploded from the heart of the vortex this time, each centered on a major node of the city. This time, though, the beams shone both in pristine light and deep shadow, intertwined in perfect harmony.

"This is... — Seline was staring aghast at the Life Map. "The life energy is trying to shift! It no longer is pure light; it carries the depth of darkness too."

Monica's statistics told the unbelievable truth: "Energy efficiency is up more than 500%! It is as if this united state has taken energy consumption to the next level."

Victor was to muse, "Not only that, the very nature of shadow power changed; instead of being destructive, it became creative."

In that moment, Chris felt the status change of the Eternal Ring: what had been a golden halo turned into a ring with a characteristic glow, carrying inside as if all the colors of the spectrum.

"I see now," he said, "this is not just the marriage of power, this is a leap of comprehension; light needs darkness for its value to be told, and darkness needs the light to define its entity.

These were the subtle changes that began to manifest across the city: textures of buildings that shone in the sun, absorbing shades; veins of energy running across streets in a hardly tangible net of light and shade in perfect balance. Even the air had its unique signature of energy that could envelope people in comfort not previously experienced.

"Look over there!" Elena pointed toward the city's outskirts. Strange phenomena began to appear. Once barren lands now sprouted new plants—plants capable of thriving in bright light and flourishing in darkness.

Miller kept clear the sense of the revelations given through the Book of Life: "This," he said, "is the Sign of Rebirth prophesied. When light and dark are really balanced, new life will appear."

Monica's systems showed an even greater quantity of changes. "It's not just physical changes; the energy structure of the whole city is remodeling itself at its very foundations.

Every energy node contains the properties of light and darkness.

"And it's a stable one," Victor thoughtfully pointed out. "The Shadow Network called that condition of stability self-supportive. It needs no interference from outside to be maintained.

Chris closed his eyes, letting the changes happen around him, washing over him. "It's as if... the world has finally found its truest state. It isn't just black or white anymore; it's a combination of the endless shades in between."

Suddenly, the life map of Seline showed the big picture: "The change will not stop at Abyssal City; it will go on to flood the entire world. However, it will be soft and will cause no disturbance."

"That's the best-case scenario," El said. "It gives every place the ability to change then adopt this in their own time.

When night began, the Abyssal City was the most magnificent of all. Innumerable lights fluttered in the darkness, like stars falling to the earth. These points of luminescence didn't dazzle the eyes or weigh depressingly on the senses but created a soft play of light and shade.

. . .

"This is true balance," said Chris, "not the eradication of differences, but their counterposition in space. Not uniformity, but embracing the differences."

When the last shreds of twilight slipped over the horizon, Abyssal City turned into a different world, no longer the field of bitter struggle between light and shadow, but a haven of congregation for the two in the most perfect of harmony.

When light crossed with darkness, a new beginning began. During such a time, everything that was opposite would turn to be a complement, and dissonance would give birth to harmony. It was not yet the final, but a beginning of a far greater saga.

PART III

THE FINAL SHOWDOWN: A LAST GAMBLE WITH FATE

In the dark before the dawn, the last ritual circle of the Count shimmered on the ground. Seven figures stood at the cardinal points of the formation; their silhouettes reached across in the pale moonlight. The armies of the Shadow Council surged from a distance, like an unstoppable tide, a myriad of hostile eyes glinting ominously in the blackness.

The loud crack of thunder broke into the battlefield. In threads of gold, the prophetic power of El wove an intricate over-net, mapping the chaos of the battlefield. The life energy of Seline diffused onto the war-torn field, resurrecting all the wounded and bringing them back into the fray, while Monica's devices projected real-world battlefield information into the air to guide each strike with proper precision. He slid through the shadows like a ghost, the augury of death, laying waste to enemy after enemy with precision.

. . .

At this moment, in the rise of violence, Miller plunged himself right into the heart of the formation. Like a stone thrown into the still waters of a lake, the shock sent ripples of energy emanating from its center outwards without end. The Eternal Ring blew up in an explosion in mid-air and rained shards of starlight onto the battlefield-one for each particle of the last hope of the world.

A fierce wrestle of light and darkness was on in the heavens, with flashes of sparks bursting into brilliance like fireworks, bathing the battle-field with their light. The impact tore night into an auric fabric sewn with black, almost as if heaven itself was a witness to this last fight.

28

THE LAST OPPORTUNITY

At midnight, an odd surge of energy tore the stillness in Abyssal City apart. It was Chris who felt the anomaly first, as the Eternal Ring vibrated hard on his chest.

"Something had broken through the barrier of dimensions," he said solemnly. "It is ancient... and incredibly powerful."

With one sweep, El's prophetic power unfolded-instantly-but this time, the vision of the future seemed strangely blurred. "The prophecy is being disrupted. Whatever this is, the power in it is strong enough to send ripples through the times themselves."

Seline went forward hastily, clutching the Life Map in her hands, its surface breading erratically. "Do you feel it?

The life energy quivers like never before. It is as if.the world itself were shaking."

"I've found the source," Victor stepped into the light, his face ashen. "It's the remnants of the Source of Chaos. They weren't fully purified. They've come together and are attempting to reform."

In an instant, a flurry of warning signals burst forth from Monica's Blood Crystal Armor. "It's worse than we thought," she said. "These leftovers of chaotic energy have actually developed a kind of consciousness. They're working actively to revert the purification process!"

Suddenly, Miller's voice burst in on the communicator, hinting at panic. "The Book of Life shows this as the start of the Final Trial. If we do not nullify this threat before the break of dawn, then everything that we have done will get undone!

Elena and the acolytes of the Temple of the Silver Star, that very moment, launched their protective circles- which proved to be futile. "This is chaotic energy. they found some way to neutralize our powers. A different approach is needed!"

Chris closed his eyes, feeling the situation with the help of the Eternal Ring. "There is still a chance." Then he opened his eyes, stern and unyielding. "We can use the newly-created energy field due to the interplay of light and shadow. In any case, all your cooperation is needed.

"Really what is expected from us?" Seline asked.

"We have to channel the interwoven energy at all seven nodes all at once," Chris explained, drawing an elaborate diagram of energies interlinking with each other in the air using the Eternal Ring. "There's just one problem..."

"Time," El said, cutting to the meat of the issue. "Building an energy circuit of this nature is going to require at least three hours. And in two, what remains of the Source of Chaos is going to fully regenerate itself."

It was Victor who presented a slightly bold suggestion: "What if... we transmit the energy using the Shadow Network? That would save so much in setup time."

"The risk is too great," Monica protested without any hint of hesitation. "The Shadow Network is so susceptible to chaos energy corruption, and if it goes bad, it will be a complete disaster."

While the group had been in hot dispute, Chris

suddenly received a message via the Eternal Ring with the Count's last revelation:

"When light and darkness merge, and disorder reigns, believe in one another, and the test will be endured."

"It all makes sense now," said Chris. "We have been trying to avoid danger, whereas it was simpler than that. Victor is right—the Shadow Network is the only way out."

He stood a moment, thinking, before he nodded. "This is no time for hesitation, but we need to be prepared."

Thus, they quickly concocted a plan, wherein Chris was to serve as the base in holding the energy field via the Eternal Ring, Seline guiding the flow of Life Energy, El and his prophecy foretelling imminent dangers, Victor controlling the Shadow Network, and Monica's Blood Crystal Armor in charge of specific calculations in terms of energy output per node.

"Just one more thing," Elena warned. "Once this gets under way, it cannot be stopped. One break in that chain, and everything's at risk."

"Then see there isn't any failure," said Chris decisively, "all have to contribute everything they can. It is our last opportunity."

. . .

And then, the operation kicked off. At Chris's command, the seven nodes booted simultaneously. The Shadow Network split like a huge spiderweb, linking up the nodes together. Light and shade sprinted across the net, twisting the rigid energy matrix within.

Feeling an emerging danger, the remains of the Source of Chaos heave mighty waves of interference that might break the circuit. The tension is extreme, and even Chris starts to show signs of overexertion.

"Stop!" El yelled. "One-third of the energy circuit is complete!

Without warning, the third node began to destabilize. "Chaos energy's trying to penetrate the Shadow Network!" Victor exclaimed the instant he caught the problem. "I need more power to stabilize it!"

"Take mine!" Seline cried without even thinking, sending her vital force into Victor.

Monica's Blood Crystal Armor began to fracture under the immense strain. "Energy output has reached its limit. The system won't endure for much longer!"

. . .

As if matters couldn't get any worse, the unthinkable happened. Those areas cleansed so far began to hum and emit innate energy vibrating in tandem with the seal.

"This is...," exclaimed Miller, "the world itself is aiding us!"

Chris felt it-the Eternal Ring shone, brighter than it ever had before. "Now! Everyone, give it your all!"

At that instant, they all had transcended their limit. The dance of light and darkness formed and rose to become a perfect seal; nothing remained of what once was the source of Chaos.

It disappeared at the first light of dawn in the city. But it was understood from everyone present that what had taken place was, rather than a victory, a representation of the realization.

Only when light and darkness work together with mutual reliance, when trust prevails over fear, will this last chance turn into eternal hope.

29

EVE OF THE DECISIVE BATTLE

The night just struck midnight, wrapping the Abyssal City; the air inside the Temple of Fate quivered. The defeat of the Source of Chaos would mean to them that the actual fight was going to take place, at most, in just a few moments.

Chris stood right in the middle of the temple, the Eternal Ring serenely floating before his chest, shining into space with soft, unwavering light. He could feel the pulsars of energy crossing the city through it. "What's left of the Shadow Council is gathering. They're getting ready for the final counterattack."

The prophetic strength of El unraveled, though these visions were still hazy and fragmentary. He furrowed his brow. "The timeline is unusually chaotic. Something strong interferes with the clarity of the future.

. . .

It's not just prophecy, Seline said, the edge in her voice weaving a thread of concern. The Life Map she held ruffled as if uncontrollably. The life energy shows weird anomalies. As if. something were consuming it.".

The normally collected Victor emerged into the light, shock palpable on his features. "It's worse than we'd thought. The Shadow Network picked it up-they're trying to perform some kind of ancient, forbidden ritual."

Warning lights flickered across Monica's Blood Crystal Armour as she ran the data. "Multiple high-energy sources detected. Energy signatures would indicate there are at least five shadow lords."

Then, right in the middle of that, Miller's voice crackled over the communicator, threaded with urgency. "I found something in the Book of Life. This is the 'Annihilation Ritual', some sort of ancient spell that can reverse the purification process. If they succeed...

"They will have no opportunity," Chris said firmly and confidently. "But we have to make some good plan."

Elena sullenly came with some seers from the Silver Star Temple. "A new vision from the Prophecy Library is revealed. The final battle will happen at tomorrow's dawn. We have to conclude all the preparations before it.

. . .

Immediately, everybody went into the temple and pressed around the great sand table at the center. Using the capability of the Eternal Ring, Chris projected a three-dimensional field model in front of them. "The enemy's major forces will strike from these three directions," he said. On the sand table, radiant points suddenly quivered, showing the most probable ways of their attack.

"We cannot defend the three fronts with our forces," Victor explained. "We will have to devise some stratagem to divert their attack."

"Or," Seline said, "we could use that twisted energy field of light and darkness to create a different sort of shield along the outskirts of the city."

Monica's armor ran a quick simulation: "That's doable! But it is going to use lots of power, and setting that up will take at least four hours.".

"Time is our biggest enemy," El said in a firm and grave but unshaking tone. "And the time for the prophecy's attack was supposed to be at dawn, meaning that we should make good use of every second.

. . .

Chris took a moment to ponder before arriving at his decision. "We'll divide into three teams. The first team will establish the defensive barrier. The second team will ready the counterattack forces. The third team..." He paused, his gaze unwavering. "The third team will accompany me to accomplish a crucial task."

"What assignment?" Seline asked.

"The Eternal Ring has told me that an ancient device is sealed beneath this temple; if we can awaken it in time, then it would turn the tide of battle. But the process of its activation is fraught with a great deal of danger."

The whole gang was silent, knowing full well that all of them were really taking a gamble with their lives.

"I will go with you," Victor said finally, breaking the silence. "My shadow perception can help us avoid the traps below."

"I'm coming too," Seline added firmly. "Life energy can stabilize the artifact's power."

El nodded. "The rest of us will handle the surface preparations. Monica, you'll coordinate the defenses. Elena, keep the seers on high alert. Miller..."

. . .

"I will have to continue translating the Book of Life," Miller said. "Something valuable is bound to be hidden between the lines thereof."

And with a scheme finally determined, to work they went. All Abyssal City, hooded in night, became an organic thing, whose every part travailed incessantly toward those impending hostilities.

And Chris led Seline and Victor down through underground chambers beneath the temple, down and down until the heavy, ancient oppression weighed in upon them, and the light of the Eternal Ring was all that lit their way.

"Careful," Victor said, halting. "Ancient protection spells up ahead."

She opened her Life Map cautiously; Seline suddenly spoke up, "It's not just protection. Those wards seem conscious about something. They are .testing us."

Chris closed his eyes as the message spread across the Eternal Ring. "This is not a test but recognition; when the true balance of light and darkness really comes, it will be possible to cross these seals.

. . .

After finally making it through the layered trials, they finally reached the innermost chamber. At the room's center lay a crystal coffin, and on the surface, it contained innumerable runes glowing. Wherever there was air, it was so still-as if time had just stopped.

"This is it," Chris said, pushing forward. "There is, however, a price for operating it.

"What kind of price?" Seline asked with a softness no louder than a whisper.

"Someone must sacrifice their life force to infuse the artifact with its initial energy," Chris replied, his voice steady. "And I'm prepared to make that choice."

"No!" exclaimed Seline and Victor, in a breath.

Yet, before anything more could be said or done, the air inside the chamber began to distort. A being of pure energy appeared—a faintly glowing projection of the last moments of consciousness of the Count.

"No sacrifice is needed," the projection in a low-soothing voice said. "I have prepared all this some time in advance."

It swept over them as a tide. Even in the last paroxysm of death the Count had seen it. It was he who had assured that they should not have to meet the supreme penalty.

It was to be the last preparation for the coming combat, the last peaceful moment before the storm. The great test of life was in store at dawn.

But at least they knew they did not face it in solitary.

30

THE CHOICE OF FATE

Within those several seconds before dawn, a brightly shining aura enveloped the Abyssal City. Chris stood firm atop the rampart, his eyes fixed on the faraway Shadow Army closing in. And upon his chest, the Eternal Ring was humming ominously.

"They are here," Victor's voice whispered from the darkness, urgent. "Stronger than we had thought. The Shadow Council gathered not only all their remaining forces but also called an ancient amplification ritual.

Monica's Blood Crystal Armor gleamed with a stream of unceasing, red alerts: "Energy readings are way above the warning threshold! Their combat strength surged by nearly tenfold."

. . .

Eternal Time

"It's worse than that," Seline replied. Her Life Map resembled a grim tableau. "They're distorting the life energy around them. It goes on at this rate...unless we do something pretty soon, it'll make everything we've done pointless, as far as purification goes."

El stood at the pinnacle, whirled around by a vortex of prophetic energy. "The timelines are in complete disarray; each of the possible futures shrouded in a veil of uncertainty."

Suddenly, a piece of the Count's soul, which was preserved in the Ring of Eternity, burst out: "The time has come. Now, activate the ancient artifact; it is the key to turn the tide in this battle."

He nodded towards his companions. "To your posts! No matter what happens, hold the line to the last possible second. This is no mere fight-this is a moment of destiny."

Instantly, the defenses roared into being. Seven energy nodes flared in that instant burst to make one gigantic shimmering barrier of light and shadow. Still, the huge energy barrier before the tide of the Shadow Army looked so fragile.

"There's the first wave!" Victor exclaimed.

. . .

Thousands of shadow energy projectiles shot across the sky like driving rain, cramming themselves onto the barrier. It shook violently under the constant bombardment, though held-for now.

"Deploy counterattack matrix!" Monica exclaimed. Countless turrets vomited beams of interwoven light and darkness energy that met the enemies' attack in the middle and blew up with deafening roars.

Yet, all that would be just the start. Here was the real beginning of the attack of the Shadow Council. Five shadow lords moved forward and rained down prohibited magic spells, while a massive vortex of chaos materialized over their ranks.

"No!" Elena exclaimed, "It's them trying to tear open a dimensional rift!"

Miller's voice was laced with panic, crackling over the communicator, "The Book of Life confirms it-they're finishing the Annihilation Ritual. If they manage to actually pull that off, then everything within a hundred miles radius will get sucked into the abyss!

Chris's face went steely. "Seline, Victor, come. It's time to bring the artifact online."

. . .

The three hastened toward the underground chamber, guided by the lingering will of the Count. The glow of the Eternal Ring sliced through the encroaching darkness, illuminating their path. The moment they reached the crystal coffin once more, the earth overhead began to shake violently, and the battle overhead was growing in intensity.

"Remember," the Count boomed in the chamber, "the thing requires a perfect balance of light and darkness to engage. And now, you three are just the personification thereof.

Chris nodded. "Let's begin."

The ritual began immediately. The power of the Eternal Ring combined well with the life force of Seline and the dark energy of Victor, forming a very steady energy field enveloping the room with its dazzling light.

The crystal coffin creaked open, and there it was—a Crystal Heart glowing with seven shades of spectral light.

Suddenly, the ground right beneath their feet began to shake violently. Monica's voice came across the communicator in urgent tones. "The barrier's failing! The shadow lords are accomplishing their ritual!"

. . .

"Now!" exclaimed Chris. The three pairs of glittering eyes, bright as the sun, focused the pent-up force upon the Crystal Heart. Thick streams of light burst from the relic, blowing downwards through the rock and earth while it continued upwards into the firmament.

Above, the battle raged; most of the guarding screens were broken, and the forefront of the Shadow had already swept forward past the outer defences.

Then came the impossible. The beam from the Crystal Heart suddenly fragmented into a thousand tendrils and turned inwards, entwining together into one huge web of energy stretched across the battlefield. Where it touched, the empowered energy of the Shadow Army started to disappear in utter amazement.

"This is... the Web of Balance!" El exclaimed. "The legendary artifact said to harmonize all forces of opposition!"

Realizing their peril, the five Shadow Lords threw their now meager powers into the Chaos Vortex, pitting it against the newly coalesced Web of Balance. Theoretically, the moment of reckoning had at last arrived when the two would meet in an explosion of energy, both beautiful and terrifying to behold.

. . .

Everything was in suspense, with light and darkness wrestling each other above, apparently furiously, casting their light into view over the spectacle in great and terrible display upon this field.

"Wait!" Chris screamed. "Just a few more seconds!"

Finally, with the first light of morning seeping above the horizon, the Web of Balance unleashed its final surge. The vortex of chaos exploded, sending the forbidden ritual to nothing. As happens with everything that goes through the circle, the backlash engulfed the shadow lords and their army, swallowing them into the very void they tried to invoke.

The light faded to leave an unnaturally heavy, stifling silence over the battlefield. All that remained of the main force of the Shadow Council were minute, quivering ripples that danced in the air.

"It's over," Seline whispered, her tone drenched with relief. "This time, it's really over."

Chris stared into the Eternal Ring, from which the final echoes of the Count's self died out. "Nein, das ist kein Ende. Das ist ein Neuanfang.".

. . .

When the sun finally rose completely over the Abyssal City, all the ruins and survivors were all bathed with this warmth. It was at that moment that light and shadow finally harmonized with each other, exquisitely promising a new era.

This was the last call of destiny, a finding by the ways through which the two would be allowed to live together but not between camps, each one got a reply and simultaneously a look into a better tomorrow, here.

And as the first wind of dawn swept over the battlefield, carrying with it the promise of renewal, it finally hit all: True victory was not in demolishing the other side but in embracing the difference.

A new chapter was only just beginning.

This would be that pivotal moment, etched in memory as a great turning point in history; the tale was far from over, however-it would extend and change in quite unforeseen ways. Nothing is permanent in this world, merely growth and modification.

This is its indispensable and ineluctable lot.

31

THE BATTLE BEGINS

The moment the Source of Chaos was sealed, a great explosion rocked the skies above the Abyssal City. The temple was still covered in dust, until the cacophony of trumpeting horns rent the air from afar. From afar, the main army of the Shadow Council was forming up: a grim, unending tide of soldiers stretching across miles of landscape, their ranks shining with a mysterious ghostly light.

El slowly opened his eyes, and instantly, the light of the Eternal Ring flickered in his pupils as the prophetic power surged ahead in him. His voice was quivering; tones were all contorted as visions before his eyes danced. "There are three critical breaches in the line of defense. The Shadow Knights to the east are preparing the Obliteration Array. The Mechanical Legion lies in wait to the south. But the greatest danger is..."

. . .

"The west," a low voice of Victor appeared out of the darkness, cold and solemn, "there stand three shadow behemoths, each filled with forbidden chaotic energy; they aim for the heart of the temple.

The life map spun in front of Seline, golden threads weaving a picture of omen upon omen upon the battlefield. "This isn't just a military incursion," she said. "Look at the energy nodes they're turning on-they're building some kind of ancient war formation."

Monica's Blood Crystal armor was warning her crazily. "Estimated enemy units at 157,632. About 30% of those are elite. And worst yet, they have brought five Eternal Night Forges with them. These machines will grant constant energy to its army."

"This is worse than I thought it was," Chris said, clutching the Eternal Ring tightly. "But we have no choice. This city is the key to the Abyss's transformation. If it falls, everything we've worked for will be undone."

A faint rumble of vibration shook the floor, as of the tremors from a great, far tread. Then the dark colossi appeared, their feet falling like meteors, buckling the landscape.

. . .

"Split up!" El ordered, "Seline, get the Life Guard positioned and set up, eastern front. Monica, get the Tech Corps, southern exposure. Victor..."

"I know," Victor whispered as his figure silhouetted darkly, slowly turning into the night. "The Shadow Task Force will molest their flanks. We won't defeat them, but we will buy all the time we can.

Even as the words left his lips, the first wave of the Shadow Army launched into the fray. Several thousand shadow warriors lifted into the skies, their forms now empowered by the Eternal Night Forges, their ranks awash with a tide of dark energy. Then a storm of black arrows blotted the sky, falling like a deadly storm.

"First line of defense, ready!" Chris yelled. Several hundred Light Guardians raised their energy shields in radiating formation. The arrows continued to rain without exception, shattering against the shields with an explosive riot of black and gold.

On the eastern front, Seline moved with purpose along the line of defense, her life energy forming a tracery of golden vines ensnaring any enemy who broke through their ranks. Yet, despite her efforts, there were too many, and the line was being forced backward.

. . .

In the south, Monica's Tech Corps clashed with the Mechanical Legion in a shower of firepower. Few in number, the Blood Crystal Warriors were fearsome in their power, enhanced with the newest and most advanced augmentations. Energy cannons fired non-stop, one after another, in a lethal tapestry of ruin that barred the enemy machines from pushing forward in waves.

But the full brunt of the assault fell upon the western front. Three shadow behemoths towered like walking fortresses, their armors impervious to any conventional assault. Victor's Shadow Task Force maneuvered around them in search of weak points, but the energy barriers were far too robust to break through.

Inside the temple, Miller and Salina were working hard to keep the core formation up. From it streamed swirls of energy, strengthening the outside defenses. Yet, the looks on their faces were those of growing concern.

"The energy output is reaching its limit," Miller remarked, wiping the sweat from his brow. "At this rate, I'm uncertain whether the formation will hold."

Salina's face suddenly darkened. "The southern defense is breached!"

. . .

A huge shell of energy fell from above down to the weak point in the south barrier, and that explosion seemed to shake the temple itself, its very foundations.

"Send reinforcements at once!" El ordered, but his words were soon enveloped by an even bigger threat-the shadow behemoths reached the first line of defense, their energy cannons glowing an ominous blue.

"Attention, all!" Chris's voice boomed over the communicator. "The dark behemoths are going to fire! Everything in their path will be vaporized!"

Then the Eternal Ring blazed bright, casting a shield of pure gold before the temple. Behemoths fired beams of annihilating energy; they slammed against the barrier in an explosion that shook the very air, seeming to contort and ripple under such incredible force.

"It is the Count's last defense," El hissed, showing his teeth. "But it is able to stand only against one blow. We must destroy those monsters right now!"

Seline looked at the situation using her Life Map. "There's a weak energy flow near the joints of their armor. Could be a weakness. Thing is, it's hard to get close enough to exploit it..."

. . .

"I have a plan," Victor said, his voice fatigued, well modulated but still firm. "But it is going to require perfect coordination. Seline, can you use your life energy to jam their sensors? Monica, can the Tech Corps disrupt their firing?"

"We'll try," Monica replied, running calculations. "Success rate is only 37%, but it's better than nothing."

And then, as the fighting continued, came that glimmer of hope: surely against all odds-the steadfast resolve of those who fought back, knowing full well that each decision had the power to tip the balance in this war.

The last residues of the dusk cast the battlefield into a red-gold hue, the surreal sort of prettiness that belied the carnage. The early stages of the battle had begun-but the hard part was yet to come.

32

THE DESCENT OF SHADOWS

In a flash, black clouds shrouded the Abyssal City, and a gigantic tornado swirled ominously in the sky. These clouds were nothing but one great surge of energy emanated from the Shadow Council. The figure of the Eternal Night Sovereign stood at the very center of the tornado, his body flickering, sometimes brighter, sometimes out of sight, as his staff reached toward the sky and let loose a cascade of black lightning streaking across the heavens.

"Your resistance is futile," he screamed, his voice booming across the battlefield, distorted yet commanding. "The Source of Chaos has stirred. Soon, this world shall fall into the eternal embrace of the night!

His words were still in the air when the vortex above whirled with increased speed, filling the atmosphere with a force so heavy that every one underneath felt stifled.

. . .

Suddenly, his clairvoyant powers flared up the strongest, and in a quavering voice, he shouted, "Look at the sky! That vortex... he's trying to open some kind of space-time portal!"

The alarmingly wriggling intensity on Seline's Life Map sent a foreboding warning. "This is bad! These portend the signs of Eternal Night Gate! Some say it summons the ancient creatures of shadows, an eldritch forbidden ritual!"

Frantic alarms buzzed across Monica's console. "Energy levels are exceeding all known bounds! If he completes the ritual, that whole city is going to get sucked into the Shadow Plane!"

Victor stepped out of the shadows, his voice full of ominous undertones: "It's worse than that-through the Shadow Network, I can feel a large quantity of unknown lifeforms beyond that gate. Whatever is locked away there... it's an ancient shadow army-styles we've never seen.

With a deafening crack, the air split in two in the middle, revealing a gigantic tear. Bursting from within this tear were numberless dark forms, soldiers that were no such thing: wholly composed of shadow energies and fuming with a noisome miasma of fear.

. . .

"This. this is the trump card of the Shadow Council," Chris said surely, clutching the Eternal Ring in his hand. "It isn't just destruction they want; they want this whole world to change into a domain of shadows!

Miller's voice crackled urgently through the communicator. "I've found it! These creatures... they're the Eternal Night Sentinels. Legends say they're formed from the fallen wills of ancient warriors. They feel no fatigue, fear no death, and their only purpose is to expand the dominion of shadow."

Salina gasped in surprise. "It's not just them! Look at the Eternal Night Sovereign... his form is changing!"

Indeed, the body of the King-in-Waiting began to swell and contort as his humanoid form twisted into a grotesque parody. Then six pairs of wings unfolded from his back, with every feather shining with some dire light.

"He's given himself over utterly," Elena said, her face pale. "For the powers of an ancient shadow king, he's lost the last shreds of his humanity."

Excluding Eternal Night Sentinels that advanced toward the city, the battlefield was turned upside down. Weapons cut through energy shields without any resistance, and all ordinary attacks were utterly useless against them.

. . .

Cover the retreat!" Chris yelled, "All non-combat personnel, fall back to the temple! We must protect the core at all costs!"

Seline's Life Guard fought with unparalleled bravery, golden energy barriers forming and reforming as the embattled mass strove to push back the oncoming horde. Yet the sheer multitudes of enemies proved too much, and slowly the defensive line started to buckle.

The most powerful of her Blood Crystal Warriors could barely stand against such otherworldly foes, their high-tech war machines falling one after another, each corroded by that infallible shadow energy.

"This isn't looking good," Victor said, his voice strained. "The Shadow Network is being assimilated. If this keeps up, we'll lose all ability to predict their movements."

This brought on a desperation that begat an unlikely twist: the long-dormant Source of Chaos stirred to life once more, and in an altogether different vein.

"Wait." Seline's eyes suddenly widened. "This is not chaos' energy; it's. creation energy! The change of the Abyss is finally over!"

. . .

El's prophetic senses quickly affirmed her realization. "Yes! Our efforts were not in vain. The Source of Creation is actively resisting the encroachment of the shadow!"

Light and darkness contended to a frenzy. The Sovran of Eternal Night ordered the last, desperate, all-out attack of his shadow army. Great tendrils of shadow cascaded down from the vortex in an attempt to eradicate every last shred of defenses the city had. But the Source of Creation answered with a burst of gold light, spawning vines beyond count, which crossed the tendrils in a tug-of-war heavenward.

"Hold the temple!" he yelled above the din of noise. "We can hold here if we only stick it out until the Source of Creation awakens, then we win!"

The battle was relentless, with every moment balanced on the brink of disaster; every decision and every action did seem to carry the world's fate. And so began the final confrontation of shadow and light.

"For this world's future!" El said, grasping the weapon stronger. "We'll fight until the last moment today!

As night wrapped the world, the battlefield brightened in a way it never had before, and light and darkness began a bright, hazardous dance. At this moment of destiny, everybody knew the most critical test was yet to come.

33

A LIGHT SUDDENLY APPEARED

Lighting stretched across the sky as the gold light of the Origin Essence fought back fiercely against the dark energy pouring out of the Entrance of Eternal Night. Sparks of energy rained down like falling stars, igniting into explosive contact before boring deep craters into the ground. The manic laughter of the Eternal Night Lord was echoing through the turmoil of clouds.

"Did you think the source of creation would stand a chance against the power of the eternal night?" he roared. His six pairs of shadowy wings dramatically unfolded behind him; each feather shone with malevolent light. "Today, I will show you what darkness is!"

Before his words had time to dissipate, he dove downward, his immense shadowy figure slicing through the protective barrier in an instant. A suffocating wave of darkness enveloped the temple square, smothering the air and plunging it into despair.

"Look out!" Chris yelled, bringing the Eternal Ring up and casting a barrier of golden light to block the attack. But the force of the collision rippled in all directions, and almost immediately, the surface of the Eternal Ring showed signs of cracking.

Seline's Life Map flared in a fierce, blinding brilliance. "Something's off! The attacks of the Sovereign aren't just for destruction but part of some ritual. It's etching intricate patterns onto the ground with that shadow energy!"

The information in front of her was worked fast by Monica's system. "Confirmed! These patterns are creating the Eternal Night Seal. If it completes, this whole area will be pulled into the realm of eternal night!

Victor dodged through the falling shadows quickly and resolutely. "We have to stop him before he accomplishes the ritual, but given his powers, this is an almost impossible approach.

All of a sudden, Miller's voice came from the temple. "Wait! I found something in the Book of Life! There's a countermeasure against the Seal of Eternal Night-the energy of the Source of Creation needs to be focused into seven key nodes all at once to trigger the forming of the Dawnbreak!

El sprang into action. "Time to surround! Chris, you keep the middle. I'll take the eastern node. Seline, Victor, Monica- each take one. Elena and Salina.

"Leave it to us!" the two priestesses said in unison, as they hurriedly led all the forces of the Silver Star Temple to make preparations for this ritual.

The Eternal Night Sovereign seemed to have sensed their plan. The vortex in the sky roared loudly as it spun faster, releasing an even more tremendous cascade of Eternal Night Sentinels that fell upon the field of battle like a waterfall of darkness.

"Hold them off!" Chris ordered, focusing the power of the Eternal Ring into the ground. Blazing trails of creation energy exploded upward against which the shadow army was forcibly met.

One moment, the battle had been joined; the next, it would not cease. Seline's Life Guards fought on the eastern front: shebs of gold bursting from her energy, wrapping around oncoming enemies, tearing limbs off and growing those limbs back again in endless repetition. In the south, Monica's Blood Crystal Warriors were hacked down in droves, but not one yielded an inch. Meanwhile, Victor led his Shadow Task Force in a desperate operation: creating an entrenched path through enemy lines and destroying the energy points of the Eternal Night Seal.

"Eastern node stabilized!"

"Southern node activated!"

"Western defenses critical—requesting immediate support!"

"Northern node energy output at 75%!"

Reports filled the comms as the battle raged on. Finally, a pained roar filled the battleground as Elena and Salina combined their powers in some sort of secret technique and destroyed one of the wings of the Sovereign.

"Bugs!" he bellowed, shaking with rage. "You really think this will send me running?

His body began distorting, swelling up to a far larger and more grotesque monstrosity. The shredded wings reintegrated, now made of nothing but shadow energies, finally pulsating with alarming energy.

"This is terrible!" Miller's voice choked. "He's sacrificing his essence! His power will increase, but..."

. . .

"But it also makes him more vulnerable to the Source of Creation!" El suddenly realized, his voice shrill. "Here's our chance! Let's go, all with everything!

In the blink of an instant, the seven nodes erupted into brilliant golden light, and with it, the energy of the Source of Creation swept across the battlefield, casting his radiance into each nook and cranny of shaded darkness. The outlines of the Dawnbreak Formation began to take shape on the ground, an ingenious pattern shining brightly against the dark lines of the Eternal Night Seal.

The Eternal Night Sovereign launched into a furious roar as he plunged to the heart, smashing the formation. But Chris was prepared; his eyes blazed with resolution.

"Here it ends!" he shouted, siphoning all the residual energy of the Eternal Ring into one brilliant spear of light. With precision and force combined, he struck the spear right into the chest of the Sovereign, piercing into his energy core.

A deafening explosion reverberated across the battlefield. The Sovereign's colossal figure started to crumble, his shadowy form shattering into countless fragments. Yet, even as he disintegrated, a contorted smile stretched across his face.

. . .

"Fools," he spat with his last breath. "You really think this would be the end of it? The power of the eternal night... will never subside!

As his body disintegrated, a huge wave of energy burst forth, threatening to engulf the temple and everyone who occupied it. However, at the same time the wave surged, the Source of Creation unleashed its most powerful might. Countless golden tendrils wrapped around the ravenous energy, rendering it totally harmless.

In that instant, when light and darkness wove their dance, an even purer, brighter light exploded. It wasn't a light for the destruction of darkness, but to light up the way ahead. The Eternal Night Sentinels disappeared into stardust, their outlines once again rising toward the starry heavens.

With the first light, the first broken rays across the horizon revealed that the Eternal Night Sovreign was long gone. Though scarred and bruised, the Abyssal City pulsed back to life with a rhythmic refreshing energy. A bright gold light cascaded from the Creation Source onto the grounds, soothing the wounds of war.

"It's over." Seline whispered, the sheen of tears in her eyes. "We did it, really."

. . .

Chris's eyes gazed down in the palm of his hand to where the Eternal Ring lay, broken. A mix of relief and sadness on his face, he muttered, "No, this isn't the end. In many ways, this is just the beginning."

Where the clouds had parted and dissipated, the sun shone upon the city in warm golden light. This was a victory of light, but deep inside, everyone knew the real work was to be done. Rebuilding their home and maintaining peace-appropriately required more valour and wisdom than the battle that had just been fought.

But one thing was for certain: darkness would never consume the light, so long as a speckle of hope remained in their hearts.

A new dawn had broken in, promising better times to come. For the first time in what seemed to them like an eternity, they could look to the horizon and envision a world full of endless possibilities rather than despair.

The story wasn't over; it was only just hatching.

34

THE QUAKE OF THE ABYSS

When morning sunlight was able to seep through the remaining smoke of the battlefield, a strange, pulsating flow of energy was emanating from the heart of the Abyss. The earth violently shook-in no form of destruction, in great rhythmic cadence, reminding one of how a heartbeat of something colossal stirred from its slumber.

Chris was the first to notice the anomaly-the gaps in the Eternal Ring suddenly lit up with meek light. "Some sort of awakening." he whispered.

"No, this isn't just a wake-up!" Seline's Life Map suddenly raged with manic readings. "It's rather that the very essence of all the energy in the Abyss is fundamentally changing!

. . .

El closed his eyes, and his clairvoyant strength plunged right into the very heart of the turmoil. "I see it... the Abyss is finishing its ultimate transformation. However, the process... it is much stronger than we could have imagined."

Monica's Blood Crystal Armour blared to life with alarms: "Multiple energy waves detected! The depth, frequency and intensity are all escalating at a rapid rate. At the present course, the whole city is liable to be torn apart!

Instantly, the earth blew itself apart with gaping chasms. However, from these, different from before, instead of chaotic energy, a seven-colored light flowed radiantly from the fissures.

"Miller!" El exclaimed over the urgent communicator. "Does the Book of Life say anything about this?"

"Yes!" Miller exclaimed in shock. "This is the sign of the Great Purification. When the Abyss finishes its transformation, it faces this very huge reformation in energy. But the problem is..."

Another quake coursed through the air, this one even stronger than before, before he could finish his thought. The very foundations of the temple shook as if the deep earth suddenly sought to writhe into a new shape.

. . .

Victor stepped into the light, his face etched with an unusual tension. "The shadow pathways are collapsing! The network is restructuring itself, yet the new configuration... it's utterly beyond anything I've encountered before."

"Evacuate the civilians!" Chris ordered with full confidence. "Monica, mobilize all available transport vessels. Seline, reinforce the major passageways with bio-force. Victor, if necessary, use the shadow passages for emergency teleports."

And suddenly, from nowhere, Elena and a throng of priests from the Temple of the Silver Star swoop into the room. "The prophecy said two hours," she gasps, "after which. the Abyss will have reached its last phase of transformation."

"Two hours?" Salina's face clouded. "That's barely enough time. The actual evacuation of the city's population will take at least four hours by itself."

The group had been arguing over the urgency of the affair when Chris felt a sudden surge of energy emanate from the Eternal Ring. Darkening his face, he said, "There's one more way. If we can push this new energy into seven key nodes all at once, it may well stabilize the change and keep the town from breaking apart."

. . .

"That is much too dangerous," Seline said quickly. "In the event of something going wrong, the channels could backlash and destroy those channeling the power."

"There's no choice," El said resolutely. "Either embrace the risk or let the town get torn apart."

Chris nodded. "We split up. I take the central node. El, you are east. Seline, south. Victor, west. Monica, north. Elena and Salina, you guys take the southeast and southwest nodes.

"How about the northwest node?" Monica asked.

"I'll take care of it," Miller said through the communicator, his tone firm. "The power of the Book of Life ought to be sufficient to sustain it."

With the time running out, the group hurried towards assuming their positions; reaching the nodes became quite an impossible task. The ground cracked open, and the wild currents of energy lashed out in unpredictable fits.

"Look out!" Victor shouted, narrowly avoiding a puff of glittering energy. "Those currents of energy aren't random. They're moving with a purpose, as if they're searching for something."

And the seven-colored streams of light did fill them with their living, exuding grace, as if in search of an outlet for an amazing amount of energy.

"In position!" Chris's voice came over the comms. "Once we start channeling, there is no turning back. Regardless of what happens, steady till the very end!"

He gave the word, and the seven willed the energy into its sockets. It was an operation that required superhuman precision; even the slightest mistake promised lethal feedback.

First minutes were a torture-acute discomfort for each of them under the massive weight of energy which pressed with the force of a giant, timeless organism, watching them through flashes of light.

"Wait!" El called out. "I can feel it... the energy's starting to balance out. It's finding its own equilibrium!"

Seline's Life Map corroborated his words: "The energy flow is aligning itself. It's. it's seeking harmony!"

. . .

Eternal Time

But just as hope had begun to well, tragedy descended. From the northwest node, the strained voice of Miller broke through the communicator in a crackle: "Something's wrong. the energy is too strong. the Book of Life is going to break!"

"Miller!" everybody shouted, but of course none dared to leave his own node lest stability of the whole be destroyed.

At this desperate moment, golden light cascaded from heaven and bathed the northwest node in its embrace. It was the shining energy of the Eternal Ring.

"Go!" Chris gritted his teeth and gave even more energy to the central node. "The Eternal Ring can sustain a part of it for a while. Miller, focus on controlling the Book of Life!"

Afterward, the seven-colored light strings started their interlacement; it was as if they did that because they were too disdainful, turning into a dazzlingly fine net extending over the whole city and forming a perfect energy circuit.

The earth's vibration slowly died, while the surging tides of its power stabilized into a regular beat. A fragile balance was found in the Abyss.

. . .

For now.

While the immediate threat was gone, it had been just a beginning, and the change was anything but complete. The city would rest-but just until another attempt would follow.

The guardians fell on the ground where they were standing, exhausted but with high hopes. They had given them a thousand precious moments in the city-and, perhaps, a slim chance for survival.

The Abyss pulsed in rhythmic trepidation-no more chaotic but measured, purposed. It was as if the very land had started to breathe, its heart beating in promise of renewal.

35

THE GUARDIAN'S SACRIFICE

When the last rumbles of the Abyss were dying away, Miller stayed on his feet at the node north-west, his hands clasped on the Book of Life, its soft golden glow fluttering, dying down with every second that was passing. He could feel its energy being spent, slipping from his grasp like sand pouring through an hourglass.

"Miller!" Seline's urgent voice echoed with panic, filtering through the communicator. "Your life energy readings are going down! Fall back from your position, now!"

Miller just smiled serenely, an acceptance now in his eyes. "It's too late. If I stop now, all our efforts will be for nothing."

. . .

"Let me go in your stead!" El's voice cut in urgently, and the soft susurrus of motion implied that he was already preparing to quit his own node.

"Stop!" it thundered from Miller, with a depth of authority quite suddenly there. "Nobody is to leave their station! El, your visions are crucial. Seline, life itself depends on you. Victor, the Shadow Network needs you to keep it in check."

Chris, deeply attuned to the Eternal Ring, suddenly broke the silence, his voice laden with gravity. "Miller... you knew this moment was coming, didn't you?"

A momentary silence fell across the comms.

"Yes," Miller finally admitted; his tone smooth, almost calm. "Since the very first moment I opened the Book of Life, I saw what my end would be. That is the job of a Keeper of Knowledge-to give the ultimate sacrifice when the time comes, pass on the torch of knowledge for another to continue the journey.

Monica's Blood Crystal Armour pulsed anew with urgency. "Anomaly detected! The Book of Life is resonating with the energies of the Abyss!

. . .

Indeed, the Book of Life began to shine brightly and radiate an extraordinary light. The pages began to turn on their own; waves of pure golden energy began to flow out of each one, rolling outward like ripples on a pool.

"What's happening?" Elena exclaimed. "The Book of Life... it's absorbing the energy of the Abyss!

"No," Salina whispered, her voice shaking with the weight of her revelation. "Miller... he's channeling his life energy into the Abyss through the Book of Life, giving it stability."

Victor's voice turned urgent. "The Shadow Network's energy tides are spiking. If they are not controlled...

"That's why someone must remain to guide it," Miller said, his voice growing weaker but no less resolute. "I'm sorry, my friends. This will probably be the last time I'll speak to you."

"Miller!" Seline exclaimed, her voice cracking into a sob. "There must be another way!"

"There isn't," Miller said with a soft voice. "But let me remind you: this is not the end. As one guardian falls, another shall rise in their place. It is an endless cycle. the will of the guardians."

Scarcely had anyone begun to respond when, in an instant, a column of resplendent golden light burst forth from the node northwest, shooting into the air. The Book of Life unfolded completely now, and its pages themselves dissolved to pure energy, mingling with the essence of Miller. Suddenly, the entire city was bathed in radiance.

The turmoil in the Abyss stirred, the currents of violent energy slowing to a stop until they lay still, their shaking stilled, their storming pulses hushed and steadied into a calm rhythm.

"He did it," Chris whispered, his voice shaking with emotion. "Miller gave his life to make the change complete."

When the gold light had spent itself, the northwest node was silent, except for the light particles that drifted through the air like feathers on a wind. Gone also were Miller and the Book of Life, their substance dispersed into the very fabric of this place.

El closed his eyes and let his clairvoyant ability stretch out to find Miller's last moments. "I can see him now. Miller hasn't actually disappeared. His soul has turned into a myriad of sparks, lost in a sea of information.

. . .

Seline's Life Map showed a wondrous vision. "The life energy network is readjusting! Miller's sacrifice didn't just stabilize the Abyss; it woke up something much deeper.".

Monica's systems were chiming in to confirm it: "The energy conversion rate is higher than ever before. This could persist for centuries..."

Victor continued, more in step with the Shadow Network than he was, "It's not just the energy that changed. The flow of information has changed, too. The closed repositories of knowledge stir. It's as if Miller's sacrifice broke something loose... as if he opened the door."

Elena and Salina shared a fleeting glance, tears shimmering in their eyes. Both recognized the significance of the moment they had just experienced. This was the authentic journey of a guardian—not merely to shield, but to offer, to secure the future through acts of selfless sacrifice.

Chris looked down at the fractured Eternal Ring that lay in his hand, his fist clenched over it. "Miller, your decision will not be forgotten. We will protect this world, and the hope for which you sacrificed so much.

. . .

As the last rays of the sun laid their gleam upon the battlefield, so was the transformation of Abyss complete. A new order started to emergicate, yet it came at the price of that forever in the hearts of those who endured. Peace, which they fought for, was tenuous, and sacrifices endured to attain it would bear heavily on their shoulders.

And so, it was when Miller died, a beginning, not an end, had taken place. For so he had always taught them: when one guardian falls, another rises, takes up the torch. The cycle that was endless, life's and hope's holiest inheritance.

A miracle happened as night began to pour into the space at the northwest node: from the charred earth, a miniature Tree of Life was sprouting. Golden were the leaves, as if their each part carried the last blessing of Miller.

It was the Guardian's Sacrifice: life to hope, and hope to light the way. In those few seconds, they grasped what eternity really means.

36

THE BATTLE OF DESTINY

On the first light after the change in the Abyss, a great golden tear ripped across the sky. The Eternal Ring convulsed with renewed vigor, screaming a new message, a deep, more primeval warning of disaster.

"The barrier of space-time is breaking!" El cried out; his prophetic power ran wild, and then his voice shook with emotion as he saw the unfolding vision: "It is... the River of Fate running backwards!"

Seline's Life Map flared uncontrollably. "It's not just fate. The fundamental laws of the world are collapsing! It's as if something ancient is breaking free from its chains...

The Eternal Ring clutched firmly in hand, Chris wore a solemn expression. "This is the last test. The final defender of the ancient civilization has been activated. Everything will be restored to what it originally was."

The tear in the sky opened further and more gold chains fell out of it. Every one of them was permeated with some blood-curdling, heavy power that distorts air space as if it warps reality itself.

"The Chains of Fate," Monica's system analyzed rapidly. "Time-space energy is reversing! These chains aim to erase everything we've accomplished!"

With every word, Victor stepped into the light, and his voice spoke with gravity. "It's not erasure; it's my belief that all they want is just to bind anew the world into its eternal cycle of chaos and order.

Elena entered, holding the last remnants of the prophecy, as pale as a ghost: "The Prophecy Library has collapsed! The ancient texts are self-destructing! We probably don't have even an hour!"

Salina's eyes blazed with determination. "We mustn't let that happen! If we lose our battle, all that Miller sacrificed-all we've fought for-would go in vain!"

. . .

Chris closed his eyes, a murmur joining the hum of the Eternal Ring. His voice was on an even keel when he spoke, yet carried a weight of purpose. "There is one final hope. If we can overwrite the old laws with new ones before the River of Fate runs backward.

"But what's the price?" Seline asked, her intuition sharp enough to feel his hesitation.

Chris took a deep breath and steadied himself. "The price is. all of our energy has to be transferred to the Eternal Ring. Which means...

"It means we'll lose everything," El finished somberly. "Our abilities, our connection to the forces that define us... maybe even more than that."

"No time to tarry!" exclaimed Victor, panting for breath. "The fetters have touched the earth!"

Indeed, there were golden chains coiled upon Earth, and uncurling hard-won transformation of the Abyss. Chaos welled out, and again light and shadow struggled in desperate combat.

"Move!" Chris ordered, his voice tearing through the bedlam surrounding them. "El, your prophetic power can disrupt the River of Fate. Seline, your life energy should stabilize reality. Victor, use the Shadow Network to slow down the chains. Monica...

They all knew their job well enough. Silent and strong, they moved to form a circle around the Eternal Ring; it was in the center of their circle, serenely waiting. Chris started the incantation of the words of old-the legacy given by the Count to Chris during the last lesson.

A column of brilliant energy exploded upward in the air and fought fiercely with the Chains of Fate. Prophetic power unfolded huge golden wings, shining brightly. Life energy blossomed with verdant ivies. The shades danced in intricacy, weaving into complex nets that were meant for entangling chains. Monica's technological matrix set up an unyielding fortress of light.

"Wait a minute!" Chris screamed then, his voice taut with urgency. "I can feel it... the Eternal Ring siphons off our force, turning it into new laws!

But the Chains of Fate lashed back in their fury. They writhed and tangled into a great web, seeking to snare the whole world anew and drag it down into eternal bondage. Asunder sundered the earth, the very texture of reality rived in splintering fragments like those of some broken glass.

. . .

"We're at our limit!" Monica cried. Cracks spread across her Blood Crystal Armor. "Energy output is exceeding critical levels!"

At that moment, a warm and familiar voice echoed in their minds. "Don't forget, you're not alone."

It was Miller, yet not just Miller; it was the will of the Count, the spirits of all the guardians who had fought and died for this land combined. Their presences glittered like starlight, focusing into this field of battle via the Eternal Ring.

"Fate has never been a fixed river," the voice boomed, firm and powerful. "It is a tapestry made of a great multitude of choices. Now, let us interlace a different fate together."

Chris sensed the powerful surge of energy emanating from the Eternal Ring, intensified by the collective wills of those who had come before him. "This is it! Everyone, give it everything you've got!"

They began to unleash their full power, in perfect harmony with each other. The Eternal Ring suddenly flared up in an intolerably bright light as its rays tore through the Chains of Fate. Shattering one by one, the chains disintegrated into golden particles, drifting lazily back into the River of Fate.

. . .

By the time the fight was at an end, their powers were gone. The light began to mellow, the battlefield silent once more. Each buckled to their knees, trying to fill that part of themselves where the powers used to be: El's prophetic visions were gone, Seline's Life Map dulled, the Shadow Network went down, Monica's matrix powered down, and even Chris's Eternal Ring had blackened where its once brilliant surface was dulled and lifeless.

Chris watched the quiet relic, a soft, knowing smile dancing on his lips. "This... this was the true struggle of fate. It wasn't a struggle of power against power, of beliefs standing firm against inevitability. We didn't just fight to win-we fought to change the very rules."

Overhead, the sky lightened, the golden rent sealing as the Chains of Fate vanished. The shift in the Abyss did not shift with it, its new peace preserved. They had lost their incredible abilities, but they were at peace.

For the first time, they grasped a profound truth: true strength lies not in clinging to power but in possessing the courage to relinquish it. Genuine guardianship is found not in domination, but in having faith in the future entrusted to those who will follow.

. . .

Hence, the Battle of Fate means that the moment the guardians gave their powers up on their own, the world received the right to create its fate.

When morning sunlight fell, a new era was in birth: an age unshackled by tethers of fate, filled with hope and unbound.

Those sacrifices that day assured the world-a world not anchored in its past-would be their province, those whose daring dared dream of greater things to come.

37

CONVERGENCE OF LIGHT AND SHADOW

Morning sunlight gently shrouded every inch of the Abyssal City. It had long since surpassed the dazzling brilliance of purity and the oppression of dark shadows. Now, it shone with a soft, harmonious glow that seemed to embrace everything.

Standing on top of the temple, she looked down at the now-transformed city, though this time it could be felt in an utterly new and deep way because the power of her Life Map was now gone.

"How curious," she whispered, the barest ghost of a smile playing on her lips. "Un-empowered, I see so much more.

Chris stood beside her, cradling the now-dormant Eternal Ring. Although its light had completely faded, it emanated a soothing warmth. "Perhaps it's because we're no longer bound by the constraints of power. It feels like... we've finally discovered how to view the world through our own eyes."

Suddenly, a soft humming of energy began to seep from the core of the Abyss: not a warning of impending danger, but a rhythmic, joyful vibration.

"Look!" El, bereft of his prophetic vision, was sensitively aware. He pointed in a far-off direction. "The Abyss... it's balancing itself!"

And of course, streams of crossed and interwoven light and darkness began to arise from beneath; and they flew easy, of their own accord, and intermingled into an organically complete and self-supporting system.

Victor watched with ardent intensity, his face reflecting: "Perhaps this is what true balance is-not something imposed from without, but rather allow all things to find their proper place."

Although Monica's Blood Crystal Armour had abandoned many of its advanced functions, its basic surveillance systems still functioned. "Energy fields throughout the city are stabilizing. The whole environment is undergoing a change, and it is in great harmony."

. . .

And then the even more astonishing transformation took place now: the ruins of the city began rebuilding themselves. Shattered buildings reassembled, the cracked earth sealed itself, and withered plants erupted riotously into colorful life. Amazingly, it required no intervention whatsoever.

Elena marveled at the sight before her. "These changes... they're following natural laws. It's as if the world has gained the ability to heal itself," she observed.

Salina added, her voice full of wonder, "And it's not only within the physical realm. Haven't you noticed? The emotions of people... the hatred, the prejudices-they're melting away, as if purified by the energy surrounding us."

Chris delicately brushed his fingers over the Eternal Ring, feeling its waning vibrations. "This is the ultimate truth. True harmony requires not the burden of overwhelming power to endure; it simply needs all things to revert to their natural state."

Suddenly, soft droplets of luminous light began to fall from the sky: what was left of the energy from the Battle of Fate had become too weak even to restart the world and had transformed into nourishment for all living things.

. . .

"Look!" Seline exclaimed, her finger pointed and her voice full of wonder. "New life is being born!"

Where the sweet rain reached the surface, grotesque new forms of life began to spring forth. Nor were they beings of pure energy, neither organisms either: they were a beautiful symbiosis of both. Since the very moment of their engendering, they instinctively knew how to live in balance with the light and with the shadow.

Victor watched with silent amazement as this scene unfolded before him. "What is great," he mused, "is that these new lifeforms do not disturb the ecosystem. They have integrated and are simply coexisting with everything that is around them."

In a flash, to be brilliant, the Eternal Ring brightened once again. An outline began to take form, a mere coalescence of energies from all the wills of the guardians.

"Children," he said, his voice soft but unwavering. "You have finally understood. True guardianship doesn't come from great power but from wise choices. From this day forward, this world won't need any more extraordinary forces to maintain its balance. Every creature has learned to live with nature.".

. . .

As it flickered on and disappeared from their sight, it called down one last blessing: "Go forth now and make your own fate-a place without excesses, free from an imposed balance.

When the last golden rays disappeared, the Eternal Ring fell deep into silence. "It has done its job. Like us, it's time for another journey," Chris replied, looking at it with a poised and calm expression.

Seline looked out upon the sea of writhing new life forms stretching to the horizon. "This is a rebirth, and not only of the world, but each of us."

El nodded, deep in thought. "Losing our powers wasn't an end; it was a beginning. Perhaps the greatest gift we've received is the ability to see the extraordinary with an ordinary heart."

Monica lifted her helmet from her armor and inhaled deeply, savoring the freshness of the air. "You know," she remarked with a smile, "I believe that technology now holds even greater potential. By setting aside our obsession with power, we can concentrate on how it can genuinely enhance life."

Victor had turned to the sun bursting across the

clouds: "Light and darkness finally learn to love each other. This is a beginning worth being part of."

The glint of hope sparkled in Elena's and Salina's eyes as they exchanged a fleeting look. "The prophecy was right," Salina whispered softly. "The most beautiful future isn't one the strong have ruled; it is one touched by each life.

As night began to fall, the Abyssal City was at its most dazzling. In the absence of superpowers' glorious brightness, the stars shone with an intense brilliance. Under the starry sky, every person was sent to his or her position.

It enclosed within itself the spirit of light and shadow intertwined, where opposition changed into complementarity, where strength surrendered before wisdom, and the world opened up its deepest harmony.

A new era had crept in, silently yet unmistakably.

38

THE FINISHING BLOW

In the dead of night, a strange surge of power burst out from the depths of the Abyss and fractured the hard-won tranquility of the Abyssal City. Even without powers, Chris was the first to recognize that a looming danger lay upon their doorstep. Even the faint remnants of the Eternal Ring pulsed softly to warn of a threat greater than anything they'd ever faced.

"Something stirs," he said grimly, "Something... older than the Chains of Fate."

Seline's face contorted as it dawned on her. "It is the fail-safe of the ancient civilization! They had to sew some kind of last safeguard into the very fabric of the world."

Once more, the skies ripped asunder above them; this time, however, it was not in the form of golden Chains of

Fate. Instead, it was a surge of pure chaotic energy, twisting into an array of uncountable writhing tendrils that reached greedily toward the earth with the goal of sending the whole world into rampant disarray.

"The World Reset Protocol!" El breathed, his eyes wide with recognition at the essence of the energy. "It's got to be that the ancient civilization foresaw the world spiraling out of its control-something like this would be the last resort, to reset everything to primordial chaos!"

The armor of Monica let out the last warning and fell completely silent. "This is not just a normal surge of energy. It is trying to destroy all signs of evolution, to push everything back to its primeval, chaotic element!

Victor watched the flow of energy and turned around, saying in urgent tones: "It's headed for the core of the Abyss. If that succeeds, then all our achieved transformation will be negated.

There was literally no hope left whatsoever. They didn't have super powers, nor did they have weapons of defense. Amidst all despair, Elena's voice pierced through the gloom crystal clear. "Wait! Miller once said that real strength doesn't come out of one's power; it comes out from everything's relation to everything!

. . .

"Exactly!" Salina's eyes sparkled. "We have lost our abilities, but the world has woken up. Every form of life on it-every plant, every person, every newly born energy life-they have all evolved. They've all gained awareness!"

Chris's resolution set as he comprehended exactly what they were saying. "Round them all up! Not just the guardians, but all life-the people, the animals, even the plants that have just started to stir again. We need the will of the whole world!

In no time, word spread, and within a very short period, several thousand had congregated in the temple square. Warriors and villagers alike pressed forward; even redeemed members of the Shadow Council joined their ranks. They reached out and clasped hands with one another-a great circle of unity.

The newly born energy entities answering the call merged in a kaleidoscopic explosion of color and light as they contacted the humans in their peculiar way, building a resonance across the species divide out of light and shadow.

Look!" Seline exclaimed, shaking with wonder in her voice. "Even the Abyss is answering!"

And forthwith, the Abyss started radiating a soft, rhythmic beat, like the heartbeat of some gigantic organism.

Every living thing felt that pulse in its heart, and all breaths and heartbeats involuntarily adjusted to it.

The turbulent tendrils, by then, had dug deep into the earth, clutching at its very foundation. It was this time, however, which for once found its match in an entirely different league altogether.

"Now!" Chris raised the dark Eternal Ring high above his head. "Let the old civilization know, too: This world is different, and we have the power to decide our destiny ourselves!

The mass moved as one, without smiting bursts of energy or spells. One single grain of strength from each person wove together their hope, courage, and determinations into the unstoppable. The unleashed will of each and every life force burst forth, now condensing into an unimaginable torrent of energy.

The wild tendrils began to slump and squirm, their opposition well beyond their strength. But the ancient failsafe was not so easily defeated. It unleashed one final burst- a wave of destruction that would annihilate everything in its way.

"Hold the line!" El shouted across the square. "I can feel it... something greater is awakening!"

. . .

And then, the miracle happened. The Eternal Ring, inextinguishable yet in fact quite long deprived of its power, now flared up in a light that nobody had ever seen. It was now sustained not by feed but by the will of uncounted thousands of lives. The glow wasn't a sear of raw power but a steady rhythm-a pulsing of life.

The great confrontation of chaos against order unfolded. Great waves of gold, essences of all life, clashed with a great deal of violence against the twisting tendrils of chaos. Rumbling thunder, the heavens lit up in combat, shaking the world right to its roots.

"This... this is strength! The mere scale of it!" Chris exclaimed in wonder. "Not the power of individuals, but the unity of all life!"

That struggle culminated in a deafening explosion. Chaotic tendrils shattered, disintegrating into myriads of specks of starlight which sprinkled the heavens. Not by brute strength, but by will-the will of a world grown beyond its needs for such safeguards-the ultimate failsafe of the ancient civilization had been surmounted.

As the mayhem finally began to subside, a hush fell over the Abyssal City. Everybody was slumped down, wearied and spent, as bodies and spirits were completely depleted. But even in that exhaustion, deep-seated joy started quivering along the faces of people. They did it. They didn't just win a war, but transcended.

"It's over," Seline whispered, her eyes blind with unheeding tears. "This time, it's finally over."

Chris looked into the Eternal Ring, whose surface had plunged into darkness once more. A smile beamed across his face, but one of serenity rather than sadness. "No, this is just the beginning. From now on, everything in this world depends upon us-all types of life.

When the first light of dawn finally pierced through the receding clouds, it marked the end of an era, a time when the ancient civilization had reached its close and when a new chapter, written with the toil of innumerable lives, had begun to be written.

That summarized it all in a nutshell with the last strike: where every heartbeat as one, even the greatest force would shatter and where all wills combined, nothing can hamper the life process.

The first light of the new day lit up every face, shining bright with promises of the warmth of rebirth. Thus, the world plunged into an age released from its shackles unto the steering of the combined might of all that was inhabiting it.

39

PRICE OF VICTORY

With the first light of dawn, as if the last starlight had vanished from behind the clouds, the Abyssal City donned an uncommon stillness. This silence was not that of death, but one dripping with heavy exhaustion and pain. Under a sky where light and shadow danced together, all began to count the cost of the hard-won victory.

Chris stood atop the temple, staring at the Eternal Ring cradled in his hand: once radiant, patterned with intricate lights, now it lay totally dull, its surface bearing irreparable cracks.

"It's core is utterly shattered," Seline whispered, tracing delicately over the fine fractures. "It is not only broken on a physical level, but it has lost all that it once had at its heart.

. . .

El looked around them, and his eyes finally fell on the scars that surrounded them in the wake of the fight. "The city's energy web is at an edge, near its breaking point. Most of the balancing points that we fought for and tried to tune to were destroyed.

A few faint beeps later, Monica's Blood Crystal Armor fell silent forever. "All technological systems are failing. To repair even the basics will take... years."

Victor emerged from behind then, his actions sans the subtlety with which he was accustomed to cloaking himself. "The Shadow Network is completely severed. All the shadow creatures that once stood at our side have all reverted to nothingness."

"It's not just the systems," Elena said grimly. "The prophetic crystals of the Silver Star Temple-all have been shattered to pieces. Centuries of collected prophecies have ground down to dust.

Salina watched as the land before her slowly healed. "The deepest cut has been to the spirit of the people. They have lost their special gifts and need now to learn to live within this world once more."

It was then that a very weak pulse of energy shot out

from the chasm of the Abyss-this time not as an omen, but as a faint call for help.

"It's the Source of Creation!" Chris exclaimed as he knew this energy right away. "It was gravely injured in the last battle.

The group hastened toward the core of the Abyss. What lay at the core took their breath away: the once-brilliant Source of Creation had now dimmed, its light flickering no more. It resembled a dying flame that struggled to stay alight.

"Is it... dying?" Seline's voice hushed.

"No," El said after a considered perusal. "It's just tired. Like us, it has given all it had."

Victor knelt beside the Source, his fingers brushing its more-subtle-than-subtle energy. "It's going dormant. It will be ages before it's fully recovered."

"But until then," Monica interrupted, "we have to find a way to keep the city running. Without the special powers that kept it going, many of the systems are already beginning to break down."

. . .

Elena and Salina looked at each other, knowing full well the reality that lay before them. Now deprived of any prophetic foresight, with an absence of energy to keep their civilization going, they had to restart everything.

Long afterwards, Chris spoke, not having budged an inch. "Perhaps. this is what we need."

They said to him, "What is it?" And they turned to him.

"Consider it," Chris said, his voice even. "We have grown so used to the gifts that we've totally forgotten how it feels to live properly. And now, well, we get a second chance to learn how we must survive in this world as it is, rather than using powers that we don't even understand.

"You mean." Seline's voice shook; her mind raced.

Chris just nodded wistfully. "Yes. To lose these powers isn't a punishment; rather, it's an opportunity-an opportunity to relink to the world in its pure form."

At this moment, the Eternal Ring shone with the last, subtle flutter. A hologram of light scrolled before the air, revealing all the transformations happening in the city.

. . .

The powerless didn't fall into despair. Rather, they united and rebuilt homes with their hands: carried the materials themselves since they had no energy devices; used medicinal herbs due to their lack of healing magic; and rather than being guided by prophecies, they relied on one another-the bonds between people in battle against the common unknown.

"Do you see?" Chris said, his voice tinged with quiet awe. "This is the true victory. We may have lost dependency, but we gained an opportunity for growth.

Seline observed the citizens as they coordinated their efforts, her eyes shimmering with unshed tears. "You're right. This isn't a price—it's a gift."

"And," El considered, "even though the Source of Creation is quiescent, its resonance still ripples. This world has been much changed. It's up to us now to learn about it.

Monica looked at her dead armor. "Perhaps the time has come to delve into more mundane technologies-not the flashy energy weapons, but the tools that actually change the world."

A faint smile curled up Victor's lips. "For the first time sans Shadow Network, I see things crystal clear. Sometimes constraints are the best teacher.

. . .

When night once again fell, Abyssal City shone under the starlight. Without the sparkle of special powers, the light of the stars was, instead, even brighter.

Chris gave one last glance at the Eternal Ring and then placed it on the altar of the temple with care. "Let it stay here," he told them. "It was a witness to an era, and that era is over.

The price for such a victory came with the promise of rebirth. The denizens of the Abyssal City were deprived of their extraordinary powers; one of the few opportunities to recapture the essence of life.

The old world's stumbling blocks-stumbling blocks which crippled even more than they enlightened-were gone; every person would create a story-but not through gifts, rather through determination, wit, and hope.

This, perhaps, was the most intoxicating future of them all.

PART IV

LIGHT OF REBIRTH: NEW LIFE FROM THE RUINS

The rays of dawn were spreading softly amongst the ruins, as the energy of the Starseed spread like dew on earth during morning hours. Miracles happened amongst the broken wall and pieces of remains that the pieces of stones could easily join, the fallen rose and the dried plants flowered. Thus this worn-out city that was marked with wounds of innumerable tests underwent reincarnation.

The Abyss was no longer a dark plane; instead, the energy of the Source of Creation cascaded from within it like a golden waterfall. Above, the power of the Seven-Star Guardians condensed into a large energy barrier, shielding this land in revival. Past enemies laid down their arms as one, united in common work to restore their homeland. The Library of Knowledge opened itself to all, and thus, flickering sparks of wisdom came alive amidst mutual comprehension.

. . .

Upon this soil of renovation, the wheel of destiny hummed, alive on air. In truth, the chains of Time were broken, and undreamed-of possibilities opened before the individual. Here was more than the re-building of a city: it was the re-birth of an entire civilization.

40

A NEW DAWN

The mountain peaks were kissed by the morning sun as the silhouette of the Abyssal City appeared soft through the rosy glow of dawn. Sans the dazzling bursts of energy that once characterized it, it has begun to reverberate with the most basic cadence of life: the warmth of everyday living. For one thing, early risers had started work for the day, the commonly rhythmic clanging of hammering serenading the city in testimony to its ongoing reconstruction.

Chris sat on an unfinished part of the city wall, his heart heaving strangely in view of the mere vision before him. Without the power of the Eternal Ring, he somehow felt closer to the raw leading rhythm of life itself.

"So beautiful," Seline whispered, inching closer to him. "More touching than the shine of energy could ever be."

. . .

Gone from her grasp, the Life Atlas, and everywhere around her was still alive, to minute detail: a wildflower grown through a crack in the wall, a flight of birds flying in a circle in greeting of morning, farther off the sounds of children's voices in laughter from the residential district.

El joined them in a moment on the wall, his eyes shining with a resolve unprecedented. "Without prophecy's power, I'm even more excited about the future-for now, every day is a mystery full of endless possibilities.

"You're right," Victor replied, a rare smile gracing his lips. "When we cease to depend on extraordinary powers, we uncover all the small things that are truly worth cherishing."

Monica stepped forward this time in plain working attire, such a far cry from her Blood Crystal armor. "With technology back to basic, I find so many techniques so very basic that we overlooked before. No flash and dash there, but they can seriously improve lives.

A sudden cheer rose from below. All eyes turned to Elena and Salina as they supervised several children in planting saplings in the middle of the central square-these tender shoots eventually growing tall enough to shade and give new vitality to the city.

. . .

"Look," Chris said, nodding toward the serious figures working in the dirt, "this is real hope. It is not based on crushing force but rather on the most simple, honest work-making something beautiful one step at a time."

Seline explained that the saplings were from the Abyssal Core region. "Where the Source of Creation has silenced itself and the essence still remains, these flora have been imbued with the abilities of purification and healing.

"It's not just the plants," El said. "Haven't you noticed? People are so much softer now, too. All the old conflicts, prejudices-they're dissolving out as we pull together in our rebuilding."

Victor nodded in agreement. "Yes, the moment everybody has to rely on each other, all those apparent differences mean little.

Monica, busy chronicling the rebuilding, interrupted, "What's amazing is the way people have started finding ways for themselves. Without energy devices, they find more useful implements. Without healing spells, they resort to herbal studies. Without prophecy, they learn to deliberate and decide.

At that moment, an unexpected discovery surged forth, igniting a wave of excitement. In the Abyssal Core region, a plant unlike any they had ever encountered had broken through the soil. Its roots radiated a soft glow, while intricate patterns that resembled energy veins wove through its leaves and branches.

"This is..." Seline breathed, crouching down to stare at the odd plant in fascination. "It's developing on its own! It has found a totally different method of receiving energies."

El pondered, turning contemplative. "Maybe this is the true path of evolution-upon not relying on outside power but letting life explore and flourish for itself.

Chris hunched down and caressed the leaves of the plant lightly. "Remember what Miller once said? 'The true miracle doesn't lie in the strength of power, but in the wisdom of life'.

As the sun higher, bigger numbers of people appeared in the square beneath the city wall. Nobody any longer separated them. By themselves, they divided the work: some cleaned rubble, other carried provisions, others tended the wounded, and others instructed the children.

"This is what we're protecting," Chris said, standing and surveying the crowd. "Not some grand display of power, but these ordinary, precious moments of everyday life."

. . .

Seline smiled warmly. "Indeed. Indeed, when we let go of pursuing the extraordinary, we return back to life's essence with a deep, deep beauty.

El motioned with a wave of his arm toward the rising sun visible in the distance. "A new day begins. We may not know what the future holds, but as long as we walk forward together, we'll create our own legend.

Victor watched as gay life whirled around him, dumb-eyed. "Perhaps this is the best ending we could have had. Not triumph of the strong, but peace in flower.".

Monica shut her notebook, her eyes shining with an unsaid resolve: "Let us record all here, not for any great praise, but to comprehend this unimportant journey of self-renewal.".

When the golden light of morning enveloped the Abyssal City, a new era, tender as a warm embracing, entered quietly. Here in this land without superheroes, every life told its story up straight and with emotion.

One hundred days later, the first new houses were completed.

. . .

One year later, the basic infrastructure of this city was restored.

Ten years later, a brand-new civilization began to take shape.

One hundred years later, people still told the tale of the battle that changed everything.

Yet, of course, it was the real poignant moment, that ordinary morning full of hope.

When the last words finally touched the pages of history, the story of the Bottomless City was nowhere near its end. By that time, it had grown into thousands of stories of ordinary people. And that, if anything, was the real eternity of the legend.

This is a new dawn, where for an instant the dazzling tinsel disappears and only the purest gold that never tarnishes shines forth.

The ending of this story is the beginning of so many more.

41

REBUILDING THE RUIN

Now, officially, it was the start of Abyssal City's reconstruction. It no longer replaced simple physical damage; instead, this time it would pursue complete change. The energy the Starseed spread throughout the ancient city poured into every corner, renewing the aged structure.

El stood in front of the broken part of the city wall, closed his eyes, and let the power of prophecy unfold into space; countless timelines crossed in his head, bringing up a different possibility with every turn.

Interesting," he said in a low tone, "each brick, each stone in this wall has recorded the steadfast trace of history. From its first raising, through repeated circles of demolition and re-erection, and now.

. . .

Seline stepped towards him, fanning the Life Atlas out before her. "Anything odd come up?"

"Yes," El said, pointing at a crack on the wall. "Look closely at that. It isn't merely wear and tear; it's the times. Every renovation has strengthened it.

Seline studied the wall intently, her Life Atlas in hand, and a sense of delight washed over her as she discovered its secrets. "You're right! The energy of the Starseed resonates with these historical scars. It's not erasing the past but rather absorbing its lessons."

Monica's powered exosuit hummed quietly, crunching the complex calculations running in its systems. "Energy structures are undergoing qualitative change. The ruins aren't simple, lifeless construction materials anymore; they are turning into conductors of energy.

Victor stepped out of the darkness, his eyes shining with interest. "Not just this wall, but the whole underground shadow network beneath Abyssal City has been going through such a change; the secrets buried in the dark little by little come into view.

At that moment, Elena appeared, accompanied by a group of priests from the Silver Star Temple, her hands cradling a softly glowing crystal. "Everyone, you must see this. Among the ruins, we found it."

This crystal was no different than any other recording device, yet at the touch of this Starseed's power, it started, on its own, to disclose well-guarded memories, the Abyssal City in all its ancient glory, capturing times forever past.

Salina peered at the projections. "Is this. the original Abyssal City? It looks utterly unlike the one we've ever heard of.".

El felt that the crystal vibrated with much prophetic power inside. "Wait, this isn't just a record but an architectural blueprint that some ancient civilization has left behind!"

Seline's Life Atlas showed some important information. "You are right! How these houses are arranged. It is a huge energy conversion matrix!"

Monica quickly worked through the data. "This schema indicates that the whole city is one big energy grid, with each of the buildings serving as nodes.

Victor confirmed it with his shadow perception. "No

wonder the underground shadow pathways were along lines in such great order. It's essential to the system."

The finding brought the whole reconstruction effort into a completely new dimension: more than the repair work, the reconstruction of the city according to the insights of the ancients was in order to rejuvenate its grid of energies.

Elena forthwith started to organize the temple priests to make detailed construction plans. "We must mark every energetic node. This will be a monumental task.

Salina made a crucial suggestion. "We can't replicate the ancient design exactly. The new energy system will require modern adaptations."

El nodded in agreement, his expression thoughtful. "Exactly. We need to preserve the core wisdom while integrating new elements to make the city future-proof."

As they argued about ways, a miracle happened. The pieces of the Starseed, scattered all over the city, started to pull together, and vortex-like structures became visible.

Seline's face showed surprise. "These vortex

structures. they completely coincide with the key nodes in the ancient blueprint!

Monica's system had explained it: "The energy is finding, by itself, its most preferred ways. Those places are the most effective points of energy conversion.".

Maybe this was how reconstruction should go: just letting the energy take their reigns and lead; just having to follow in its steps.

And with this in place, the rebuilding was done systematically. Even the building materials were influenced by the Starseed to have extra, special properties. There was nothing lifeless anymore, whereas everything pulsed with life.

Elena pointed to the certain behavior of these materials. "They can change their shape for different purposes, as if they are conscious."

Salina added, "They still remember their past forms, and that makes the restoration work a lot easier.

Yet El prophesied more. "It is not only physical reconstruction, but a complete change in the energetic structure of this city."

. . .

Then Seline opened the Life Atlas to a breathtaking view. "Behold, life force stirs in ruins; that with every mark of death bursts with life.

Monica's analytic system lit up in a series of warnings: "Energy conversion efficiency growing exponentially, the velocity of self-repair far beyond the initial predictions.".

Victor felt deeply resonated with the shadow network and noticed, "What is more amazing is that the process does not reject the energies of the shadow; instead, it integrates it.

While the reconstruction was in process, miracles started to appear-amazing phenomena: what earlier had been called no-go areas became hotbeds of energetic activity; injured structures of defense, which earlier looked threatening, now guarded everything as energy barriers.

Among the flowing texts, Elena found an ancient prophecy. "That brings to my mind a very old prophecy: 'When the city is reborn, the forbidden zones turn into sources of blessing.' It was over.

Salina instinctively sensed what he meant: "All these changes somehow point to a common destination — from violence to conciliation, from oppression to symbiosis.

. . .

At that moment, a groundbreaking discovery captivated everyone's attention. In the very heart of the city, where the Eternal Ring had once stood, a new energy core was beginning to take shape.

El perceived the phenomenon through his prophetic abilities. "This is not just a plain concentration of energy. It's as if a new nexus has appeared, connecting past, present, and future together.

Seline's Life Atlas went further to reveal, "It forms a completely different energy cycle herein that stabilizes the operation of the Eternal Ring and increases its elasticity significantly.

Monica's system ran a deep analysis and said, "The data suggests that this new core is capable of developing itself independently. It will adapt to the city's needs over time.

Victor could feel the ripples emanating through the shadow network: "No longer is it one lonely control center, but rather an exchange platform.

This greatly accelerated the rebuilding process. The new core of energy now could conduct the work of rebuilding-a sort of thinking command system.

. . .

Elena's eyes shone with amazement. "It's fabulous. The city is alive, and it heals itself.".

Salina said, "We are more a guide and collaborator than builder.

And as the work went on, wonders multiplied. Wounds that once seemed irreparable began to scab, reversed under the gentle tag of the new energy system. Battlegrounds of former wars became flower-filled gardens; discarded weapons reversed into channels of life-giving energy.

El watched the whole scene in front of him with an unconscious smile. "This is what Miller wanted to see: not an utter erasure of the old, but a new beginning out of the scar.

Seline's Life Atlas unfolded as a breathtaking panorama: "Every ruin tells a story, and every act of rebuilding creates new possibilities," she reflected.

Monica's system was showing promising timelines. "At this rate, restoration of basic infrastructure will be 80% early.".

. . .

Victor watched as the city now changed profoundly in front of his eyes. "This is no longer Abyssal City; it transformed into a whole different thing in which light and darkness coexisted.

As night fell, this renewal city was showfully brightened up. The Starseed shone up against darkness, bringing on a shining star river. This is to say, "In memory of the past, to light a way forward.".

This was a capturing of the very essence of rebuilding: not deleting the past but forging the future, embracing it- not hiding scars, but letting them swell into the seeds of new life. And in this journey of rebuilding was a person renewed, with stories of rebirth in every nook and cranny.

42

REBIRTH OF THE ABYSS

While the city was in fervent rebuilding, a more fundamental change had been underway secretly at the core of the Abyss. The earth that inspired terror a moment ago now shined with an incomparable vigor. The nature of the abyss itself, as a result of energy from the Starseed being constantly channeled in, was about to undergo its ultimate transformation.

El and Seline stood at the edge of the Abyss, looking down into the roiling tides of energy surging beneath them. Whereas formerly it had been wildly turbulent, those currents now seemed to be flowing in a peaceful and harmonious rhythm.

"Look over there," El said, pointing to an energy vortex. "The Landscape of the Abyss is morphing into itself. Like. it finally found its shape."

. . .

Seline unwrapped Life Atlas for a view of the change. "That's amazing; this change isn't being compelled. The energy is trying to reach its high plane of existence.".

Monica's system was working overtime to collate an incredible amount of information. "Energy conversion does indeed follow a pattern. It would appear that the Abyss is reconstructing itself from some sort of ancient plan.

Victor came forward with his face showing an unusual surprise: "The shadow network is outputting some weird signals. Those ancient energies, long-sealed, began on their own to wake up and purify.

Elena and Salina hurried to the location, Elena clutching a measuring crystal in her hand from the Temple of the Silver Star that shone brighter than it ever had.

"This reaction...," Elena said, flipping through the ancient texts she carried, "is mentioned in the temple's records. This is a sign left when the 'Source of Creation' has begun to awaken."

Salina added, "Have you noticed? The various energies within the Abyss no longer repel each other. Light and darkness, creation and destruction — they are finding their balance.

. . .

Then, in an instant, there was a strange resonance welling up from the very utter deeps of the Abyss, caught between melody and pulse as though the chasm were speaking uttering some ancient hymn.

Almost instantly, the anomaly was picked up by Seline's Life Atlas. "This is. the rhythm of life! The Abyss gives birth to whole new forms of life!"

Monica's system worked tirelessly, processing the data with fervor. "Confirmed! A multitude of unknown energy structures is taking shape. They are neither conventional material lifeforms nor entirely composed of energy."

Victor had already gotten used to such changes. "What's really striking is that those new creatures will have duality in their character-a mixture of light and darkness. They are the real children of balance."

More acutely prophetic, El stared into the phenomenon. "It is more than just energy transformation; this is one great leap from the course of the very evolution of life. The Abyss becomes the crib for a new form of life.

As the group marveled, an even more breathtaking scene unfolded. Across the Abyss, countless Starseeds began to bloom simultaneously, their radiant flowers illuminating the darkness. Each "Flower of Light" contained potent and pure creative energy.

Elena's voice trembled with expectation. "These are those 'Abyssal Flowers' the prophecy spoke of! They were said to bloom only when the world finally reached out in true harmony."

Salina gazed at the glowing flowers with much attention. "Each flower is like a small cosmos, full of endless possibilities.

Then, suddenly, an intense energy surge came out from the centre of the Abyss. Tension gripped them instantly, but they soon realized that it was not a danger signal. A complex energy structure was forming into shape, and the structure's form left everyone staring in awe.

"This is... "El's eyes narrowed, "a new 'Eternal Ring'? No, way too intricate for that. It is just a multi-dimensional energy matrix!"

Seline's Life Atlas had more complexities: "It's not just one ring; it's an enormous web-like structure of millions of energy circuits. Each one represents a different possibility.

. . .

Monica then explained that "this structure is adaptive and evolutionary; it can adapt and optimize itself when necessary.".

The most amazing thing about it, he said, tapping into the shadow network, "is that it links the material world and the dimensions of energy at the same time. A real bridge.".

But as the new energy matrix has solidified, the whole Abyss began to dramatically change: hostile energy vortices transformed into creation fountains, and every inch in it overflowed with new possibilities.

It was here that Elena found a prophecy intertwined with her ancient texts. "'When the Heart of the Abyss is reborn, the world will enter a new era. All oppositions will become harmony, and all destruction will turn to creation.'"

Salina, sensing the transformations enveloping her, remarked, "Isn't this the answer we've been searching for? True balance isn't achieved through suppression but by permitting each force to discover its purpose."

Then, a great vision arose from the very bottom of the Abyss: ancient ruins, which had been sealed for ages, now started to rise-not as inanimate relics of the past-but pulsating with life as they turned into energy nodes full of life.

. . .

El quickly grasped the importance of the situation. "These ruins are more than mere historical artifacts. They embody living knowledge! They vibrate with the present energy system, opening up new possibilities."

Seline examined the ruins with great care. "You're right. They resemble seed banks, preserving the essence of ancient wisdom. And now, these seeds have at last discovered fertile ground to flourish."

What Monica picked up was really interesting. "These ruins are interacting with the Starseeds, creating a whole new frequency. It is like they collaborate to bring in this new energy paradigm.".

Victor did not say anything for a while. "Maybe this is what the ancients wanted to create; they left these ruins for us not to repeat their past but to inspire a new future.".

More and more miracles happened as the transformation of the Abyss continued to deepen, and energy-born creatures soon exhibited marvelous intellect while acting as active agents in the reconstruction of the Abyss.

. . .

Elena watched these beings with growing curiosity. "It is as if instinctively they know how the energies work. It is not knowledge that has been learned, but inbred into them.

Salina added, "Their very concept of light and darkness has already far surpassed our own. To them, they are but two sides of one and the same coin.

The shift in the Abyss began to leak into the world above. Rebuilding the city suddenly became immeasurably easier-irreparable wounds started to heal before one's very sight, renewed with a new life.

El, invoking the prophetic forces, looked even beyond. "This is just the beginning. When the Abyss begins to change course, so will the whole world begin anew."

Seline's Life Atlas was a thing of breathtaking beauty. "Every form of life will gain new possibilities, and each kind of energy will find its perfect expression.".

But Monica's would have the last word: "At this rate, the world is developing towards an unparalleled level of harmony and intricacy.".

Victor, perceiving the profound nature of these transformations, remarked, "We finally understand. The

Abyss was never an enemy to conquer but a partner waiting to awaken."

As the last rays of the sun wrapped the changing Abyss, it was no longer the place of fear and terror; it became a teeming world full of life and promise, a haven where life and death were in balance, creation and destruction living together-a tribute to the integration of old and new worlds.

Rebirth for the Abyss-and hence an admission to times past entwined with the birth of times to come: not in the celebration of power in suppression but in liberation. Every life had changed in one particular way on this journey; every rhythm of vitality carried its story of rebirth.

43

TRADITION OF PROTECTION

Also, with the Abyss reborn and reconstruction at its height, the most important challenge to all was the bringing into place of a new order of guardians. With the disappearance of the Eternal Ring and the sacrifice of Miller, the world needed this huge paradigm shift in how guardianship was conducted. It was not a question of transference of powers but a recasting of protection itself.

IN THE GREAT HALL OF THE SILVER STAR TEMPLE, the crystal-filled dome showed scars from battles of the past, allowing the sun to shine through the cracks and cast through the energy of the Starseed-a great dance of light and shadow. There in the centre of the hall lay the seven stone chairs of the former Guardians, all battered and smashed to pieces. The only one intact was the seat of Miller, the remaining energy he had left behind still emitting from it.

. . .

Eternal Time

El stood in front of Miller's chair; his fingers brushed the back of the chair as soothing, reassuring energy waves caressed them. Prophetic, with the insight of his power, he saw a lot of different futures, all converging upon one truth- the entire redesigning of the old system of guardianship.

"We can't repeat the mistakes of the past," he said, his voice hushed. "Single point of power too readily corrupted, too readily divided."

Seline opened her Life Atlas; shining threads of gold wove into a web suspended in mid-air. "Look. The new energy system that is arising appears to suggest something..."

"Yes," El said, his hand weaving toward the crisscrossing strands of energy. "Behold these nodes. Each is a point of focus and a point of release. There is no center, yet all is interconnected."

Monica's power armor hummed softly as it scanned in the energy waves. "This structure closely resembles a biological network: each node shows autonomy while working with the whole.

Victor emerged from the darkness, an unusual warmth infused into his voice. "The same sort of change is occurring within the shadow web. The frissons of shadow energy, so long isolated, now authentically reach out to touch.

Suddenly, a sharp cracking sound reverberated across the hall. All of them turned to see Elena clutching the Prophecy Crystal, which had cracked. Instead of shattering, however, a stream of gold light began to seep from the fissures.

"This is..." Elena whispered, her voice filled with wonder. "The renewal of prophecy! The crystal isn't shattering; it's reforming!"

Salina watched the phenomenon with interest. "It's not a mere reformation; it's changed into an utterly new mode of existence. See, the once static prophetic writings now flow like liquid light.

Suddenly, a soft humming issued from Miller's chair. A dimly radiant, yet warmly glowing radiation began to lift off it, taking upon itself the vague shape of a human body. Not an actual body-just a projection of pure energy.

"Children," Miller's voice boomed, both ethereal and unmistakably clear. "I expected your making this decision. The new guardianship system. it has to be based on understanding, not control.

. . .

El took a step forward. "Miller... you knew it all along?

The projection cocked its head to one side. "To some extent. But more relevantly, I had faith in you to follow your path. The sacrifice of the Book of Life was not an ending but a beginning to restore.

The Life Atlas of Seline shook terribly; its contours glimmered with life. "Wait... can you feel it? The energy of the Book of Life hasn't disappeared-it has been infused into the entire world!

Monica's system quickly showed her the incoming data. "Confirmed! Energy from the Book of Life is spreading into the Starseed network. It evolves into the very basis of the new guardianship system!

Victor was quiet for a moment, pensive. "So that's it... Miller sacrificed himself to stabilize the world and gave a working model for this kind of protection.

And little by little, Miller's projection clarified itself. "Yes, but this is just the beginning. The true guardianship system needs every one of you to elaborate on it, to perfect it. Remember, at no time has power been the objective — understanding is the bedrock.

. . .

And suddenly, without warning, Elena's Prophecy Crystal burst in a cascade of glittering lights that twinkled in the air. "The prophesies-they've changed from chains that bind the future to guideposts that light the way.

Salina watched as the shards of light took on forms that were altogether different. "Now let each one see their own prophecy. This is the true wisdom-a birthright given unto each."

As Miller's projection started to fade, he began speaking inside the hall: "The new guardianship system is already taking shape. It dwells no more in one spot, but thrives with the choices every living thing makes.

With those words still echoing, seven streaks of light suddenly flooded the center of the hall. Different from before, these columns of light did not burst forth from a single, bursting flow of energy. Instead, they were made up of millions of small points of light, gathered from the debris of the Starseed.

El walked up to one of the beams: "This is not a sign of power but a testimony to responsibility.

Seline nodded dreamily. "Each pillar is representative of one aspect of guardianship: prophecy, life, technology, balance, tradition, integration, and..."

. . .

"Wisdom," Monica kept on, "is the best thing that Miller gave us.

Victor looked upon the pillars pensively. "The amazing thing about them is that they're not set in stone. They'll change as the world does, just like life itself does.

Elena and Salina exchanged understanding smiles. "And it's our responsibility that this flexibility doesn't turn into chaos.

Suddenly, the pillars of light exploded, sending so many small pieces across the city; all fell into their own place, forming one big web in the energy field.

"Behold," El said with wonder in his voice. "It is now being born, the new order of guardianship no longer in this hall but over the whole world.

The Life Atlas belonged to Seline and was the largest to date. "Each life is part of this system, every decision weighing in upon the balance of the whole.

Monica's system made a final evaluation. "This

structure is much more robust compared to any centralized system. It can self-repair and evolve.

It sent ripples through the shadow network, and Victor felt them. "Above all, it is truly inclusive. Light and dark are no longer enemies, but each other's foil.

Miller's voice boomed out again. "The nature of caretaking. is to let each life live well. Go now, and live to carry out the burden of that knowledge.

As the last rays of sun slid below the horizon, the hall inside the Silver Star Temple entirely transformed. Cracks in what was once a shattered dome framed the breathtaking expanse of night stars; the seven stone chairs, which had been destroyed, began to dissolve in a blur of energy and merged seamlessly with the new network of guardianship.

This is the meaning of guardianship-not the transference of powers, but the rebirth of ideals; not substitution of authority, but continuation of responsibility. In this transcendent process everybody found his place and each form of power found its most authentic expression.

What had once been a title reserved for the elite few had developed into a shared responsibility worn by all living things alike. Most of all, this was the most cherished legacy which was left behind by Miller.

44

WAY OF THE LIGHT

The whole of Abyssal City shone in a morning light it had never been bathed in on this first dawn since the implementation of the new guardian system. It was not a light that blinded; rather, it was a soft-warm one, as if the world was enveloped by a golden haze.

He stood completely alone, with nothing but the remains of the very ancient Star-Gazing Tower, whose purpose was now changed and long since bereft of its prophetic power. He could see through its shattered remains to the remnants of Starseed, twinkling yet in the morning light, as if it were millions of fireflies at the break of day.

"Still troubled by the loss of your prophetic power?" Seline's voice came from behind him. The Life Atlas in her hands was no longer shining with those eye-piercing lights, but radiating a pure soft glow.

. . .

El shook his head, an amused quiver of his lips. "Quite the opposite. Unfettered from the tethers of the prophecy, for the first time, I see the present. See there..."

He nodded toward the eastern part of the city, where children played raucously amidst the ruins: some instinctively guiding bits of Starseed; most just enjoying the warmth of the sun. For a moment, none of them distinguished between the powerful and the powerless; pure, unadulterated joy.

Monica climbed the tower, her mechanical armor devoid of arms compared to the way it usually looked intimidating. "How very interesting. It seems the children who lost their unique abilities now fight so ingenious. But that's them looking at the world in the most simple, elementary manners.

Victor stepped out from the shadows, yet his entrance held no longer the dramatic flair it once possessed. "The shadow network has weakened, but I've observed that people are starting to perceive darkness in more instinctive ways. What used to invoke fear now acts as another lens through which they comprehend the world."

Just then, from the side of the temple, a tinkling sound was heard. Elena strode at the head of the formation, which by now included phalanxes of young priest apprentices carrying prophecy crystals that had dimmed; not even a speck of despair was etched on their faces, just curiosity and enthusiasm.

"What are they doing?" Seline asked, fascinated.

Salina went on, "Those children have found the magic in the fact that, while the crystals lost their prophetic powers, they capture the intricacies of starlight patterns perfectly. And with those, we are able to show an entirely new way of knowing.".

Suddenly, a strange pulse of energy caught the attention of everyone as a plant, previously beyond their imagination, emerged deep from the heart of the city. Its roots glowed softly, like a web of light around it, and its leaves revealed impressions of patterns, like veins of energy.

"The first Tree of Light," El whispered. "It does not need any special energy input. It grows and in turn gives energy to the life in and around it."

Monica's sensor gave a soft warning. "That's some wonderful life form. Not quite matter and not all energy, it's a completely new form. The most amazing thing is the way it balances light and dark energies on its own.".

. . .

Victor thought, "This perhaps is the true Path of Light-not relying upon overwhelming power, but letting life find its organic growth, finding the best path to thrive on its own.

Elena noticed something odd: "Look, everyone who comes along and touches the Tree of Light changes somehow. Not only in gaining powers, but they somehow change from within. They seem to be. lighter, more at peace.

Indeed, beneath the tree, people talked, shared tales of their lives, and offered assistance to one another. Free of the barriers of power that separated them, they found it easier to make friends. A Shadow Councilor was instructing children in how to recognize medicinal herbs, while a priest of the Silver Star Temple taught simple meditation techniques to anyone who wanted to learn.

"It is a wonder," Salina gasped, "when we rid ourselves of so-called 'higher powers' we start finding the easiest truths.".

The instant it reached the apex, the first sunrise shed light upon the Tree of Light, at which point the energy patterns inscribed into its trunk burst in radiance-not in blazing gold but as a soft almost ghostly light. Soon, a second and then a third Tree of Light emerged in other parts of the city.

. . .

They're finding where best to grow!" Seline exclaimed, "Like every tree was rooted in each and every place of an energy node.".

Monica studied this phenomenon: "There is something even more captivating with what these trees can do; they balance the energies, clean the air, and revitalize the soil. They cure war wounds in the most natural way possible.

Victor said, "And they do not reject shadow energy. Look over there-some trees are even thriving in the darker areas, able to capture just enough light for life to be continued.

Elena pored over the temple's ancient texts, her eyes glimmering with realization. "Of course! The ancient civilizations prophesied this day," she exclaimed. "They declared that the true Path of Light lies not in the heavens, but within every living heart. When we release our obsession with power, the world will effortlessly discover its balance."

Salina spoke in thought, "Miller must have foreseen all this; that's why he sacrificed himself.".

. . .

El nodded. "The power of the Book of Life never vanished. It continued living in a new form within the world. And these Trees of Light are the final proof.

And months went by, month after month, with different changes that unraveled silently. People learned about the world in simple terms around them, some how flowers grew, others how stars moved, and others how to understand the very basics of mechanical design.

Monica: "Technology now evolved in a much healthier way. Instead of seeking the ultimate power, people focused on improving the issue of quotidian life.".

Victor shared his epiphany. "While shadow energy has dissipated, the human understanding of darkness has spread. They have learned that darkness is an intricate part of everything in life.

With the sun down, the Trees of Light were glowing far more gently. Every one of their leaves shimmered faintly, casting a natural, soothing illumination over the city.

"Look," Seline said, pointing at the scene before them. "The pieces of Starseed fly over the treetops, as if weaving some sort of invisible net.

. . .

El smiled in silent contentment. "This is the true Path of Light, and it is not a straight road but is made up of different directions, which were freely chosen by life. Every choice is unique, yet it all leads to the same place in guidance harmony.

This is the very signature of the Path of Light, where all is sparkling, and nothing is illuminated by rough strength; every life sparkles, and all the sparks put together give the most brilliant and long-lived light.

As night fell, the glory of the Trees of Light was added to the stars above in a display beyond anything imaginable. Here, where there was no magic, the darkness was nonetheless set ablaze by the soft light of hope which filled the air.

45

THE BEGINNING OF RECONCILIATION

In the very center of the Abyssal City, something extraordinary was about to happen within its core square. Once a field of blood between rival factions, it had finally converted into a symbol of reconciliation. Shattered tiles still showed scars of battles that once took place, with small, green vines coming out of the cracks and giving off the impression of serenity and rebirth.

El rose onto the rickety platform, looking out as the immense variety of representatives finally began to show up: former members of the Resistance, residues of the Shadow Council, priests of the Silver Star Temple, and even the ancient consciousness stirred from the core of the Abyss-all here. And although lines of doubt still played upon their features, anticipation for the common future was ablaze so much brighter.

. . .

"It's incredible," Seline said in a breath, clutching her Life Atlas in her hand, taking account of the least stirrings of emotion in the crowd. While it lost the brilliance of its revelation, the Atlas did not stop showing the hidden truth behind a mask. "Look at their eyes, the hostility is gone-there's something new in them. understanding.

Monika's powered exosuit whirred softly, its scanner feeding her a comforting stream of information. "Group emotional oscillations are dampening. Hostility indices have dropped to a record low. And it's not suppression-the suppression is organic.".

Victor stepped into the light, his manner softer than it had been: "The most interesting thing is that these groups of people who were sworn enemies can now sit down and talk about rebuilding.

It was then that the impossible happened. A former ranking operative of the Shadow Council fell to one knee before the assembled Freedom Fighters and bowed his head. "For all that we have done in the past. I am sorry."

A silence befell the square as everyone held their breaths. This was a sight to behold. The Shadow Council was prideful, and very few had ever humbled themselves before anyone.

. . .

The representative of the Resistance, after some momentary resistance, went to his side and pulled him to his feet. "Let the past be in the past. It is how we erect our new home together that matters.

Suddenly, the prophecy crystal clutched in Elena's hands started glowing softly. "Look! It's vibrating to time with this reconciliation scene. It may have lost its prophetic powers, but it now appears to have turned sensitive enough to record true emotions.

Salina added, "It is not just documenting; it seems to be... enriching even the atmosphere of reconciliation."

Indeed, with due time, it became a very harmonious atmosphere in the square. Former sworn enemies started discussing their experiences and emotions among themselves. A long-standing misunderstanding and prejudice were resolved through emotional dialogue.

Suddenly at that moment, a unique power ripple welled from the ground. A few Trees of Light erupted out of the ground, weaving their roots in an intricate pattern to join the whole square in one glowing, living grid.

"This is no accident," El said perceptively, "The trees reflect longing in their hearts to be healed. It heals the hurts of this land in the most organic and natural way."

. . .

The instant it did, Monica's system went into scan mode about the phenomenon. "Confirmed! Life energy field undergoes qualitative change. Not a passive receptivity-herein lies an active choice. Every being present is doing this subconscious healing process.

Victor could feel the change in the shadows. "Even the energies of shadow have changed-so hostile, now teeming with soft and embracing essence.

And then, like a storm, the most overwhelming realization seized them-the Trees of Light were bearing fruit, fruits that none of them had ever seen. Their fruits shone softly, heart-shaped, softly pulsating with light.

Elena pored her eyes over her ancient texts. "These are. the Fruits of Reconciliation! According to legend, they only appear when the world is at true harmony.

Salina scrutinized the fruits with intent curiosity. "Each one appears to encapsulate a memory, a tale."

When the first fruit was ripe and finally fell, a miracle occurred. The fruit let itself be dissolved in thousands of sparks and dissolved into the crowd: Everybody experienced the memories of all the others, felt their pains, hopes, and struggles.

An elderly priest of the Silver Star sobbed unashamedly. "So... we all suffered the same without knowing that. Yet our perceptions were different, leading us down different paths.

A former Shadow Council warrior grasped the hand of a Resistance fighter beside him. "If we'd understood this earlier, maybe so many lives could have been spared."

El stood in the room, his eyes bright with tears, as the drama played out. "This is reconciliation-true, not forced compromise, but warm comprehension.

Selines eyes would hardly leave this breathtaking view. "Look to the roots of the Trees of Light..., they are combining the energies of the different groups-creating an entirely new balance.

Monica's system gave some astonishing information. "We are detecting a shift in mass consciousness. The change is much more stable than any imposed peace treaty.

Victor added, "What's most gratifying is that this reconciliation does not wipe out differences. It teaches us to appreciate them. Just as light cannot shine without shadow, every force has a value of its own.

As night fell, the square took on the most peaceful hour of the day. Spontaneously, people congregated under the Trees of Light, sharing food and making stories. New comprehension and closer bonding brought by each Fruit of Reconciliation continued to fall.

Elena and Salina exchanged warm smiles; the hope in their eyes reflected in each other. "This reconciliation was worth the wait," Elena said softly.

Reconciliation under such a premise is not born out of compulsion but out of understanding, not elimination of the past, but coming to terms with the scars that scar our lives. Every institution found its place on this journey, and every force found its due respect.

When the last tresses of twilight flung themselves over the horizon, the Abyssal City faced serenity. Above them in the firmament, a brilliant, star-filled sky mixed with the light of the Trees of Light to give witness to this historical moment of reconciliation.

This is not the end; this is but a new beginning. For true peace, much more is to be done by all of us, but now, at least a start has been made and hope planted.

. . .

THERE IT UNFOLDS BEFORE US, AN ENDLESS HIGHWAY. YET, even as the hearts of all of us still beat with tolerance and mercy, no gulf is too wide, no injury beyond redemption. This, indeed, is the most prized gift of reconciliation.

46

A NEW ORDER

After the reconciliation processes, the call for the establishment of the new order became the most pressing activity. The different representatives all gathered again in the Council Hall in the Abyssal City. What once was a symbol of the positions and status is now filled with the spirit of equality. Gone were those large imposing thrones that once lorded over the space but were replaced with a round council chamber. Each seat was in a circular manner and symbolizes equality and decision-making.

El paused as he stepped into the hall. Sunlight filtered through breaks in the dome and entwined itself with the energy of the Starseed, falling onto the floor in an intricate, beautiful latticework pattern of light and dark. And it was in continual movement, as if it were whispering secrets of infinite possibility.

. . .

"Hard to believe," Seline breathed, wonder lacing her tone. "Not so very long ago, this very spot was a battleground of power struggles.

Monica, then dressed in a new suit made for peacetime, peered out at the shifting energy fields her system had detected and said, "The energy field here is so harmonious. The energies of all life are instinctively synchronizing with one another.

The enormous Victor stepped out in the open, doing so without hurry, his movements slow. "Even more fantastic is the fact that shadow energy no longer should hide anywhere. It found its meaning-its integral part in this new world order.

It was then that something quite unexpected happened: those energy crystals, long symbolizing both power and status, suddenly began to crack on their own. Not complete breaks, but the shards floated gently in the air and rearranged themselves into a much more complicated energy matrix.

Elena comprehended what was happening the instant it did. "This is. the Web of All Beings! Ancient texts set it down as an energy structure manifesting only when true harmony is reached.

. . .

Salina said, "Each node is separate and part of the whole at the same time. Just what we need as a model for the new order."

A soft-spoken, but relentless, former member of the Shadow Council spoke up, "We once tried to have all the power to ourselves. Ironically, real strength is derived from common understanding and cooperation.

His words lit the fuse. Much to the surprise of many, what followed were not heated arguments but constructive discussions. Everybody listened to the opinion of the other and cooperated in determining the most favorable solution.

"Look toward the middle," El pointed out, "those Starseed fragments are responding to these conversations.

Indeed, the Starseed fragments began to configure themselves into a clear pattern, forming a three-dimensional organizational structure. The configuration was constantly shifting as if reflecting many different models of decision-making processes.

Monica's system rapidly evaluated the phenomenon before her. "This is an adaptive organizational frame-work. It dynamically changes to produce what is actually needed at the time, so it's always operating at maximum efficiency.

. . .

Victor watched with interest the shifting structure. "Most interesting, there's no permanent center. Power flows and decision making is collective."

Suddenly, several saplings of the Trees of Light emerged from the cracks in the council floor, at that point. The way they grew was absolutely amazing because their branches and leaves reflected the finest details in the web of energy.

Elena referred to an ancient text: "The Wisdom of Life! These trees burden the energy, but they can be the witnesses to this new order. They will record each milestone decision that would guarantee justice and transparency.

Salina realized another aspect of their significance. "These trees can sense emotional fluctuations. If discussions veer off course, they'll emit subtle energy waves to guide us back."

An elderly priest, adorned with the Silver Star, proposed an idea. "Rather than imposing strict rules, why not create a flexible consultation mechanism? In this manner, each group can engage in decision-making while staying accountable to the larger community."

The proposal received broad approval from all quarters. The representatives commenced a discussion on the practicalities of implementing such a system. Even when disagreements surfaced, they maintained their composure and patience, diligently working to forge a consensus.

Suddenly, the boughs of the Trees of Light carried a strange type of fruit. These fruits glowed softly, as if infused with the essence of the conversations being held.

These are Wisdom Fruits," Elena explained. "They store more than just information; the fruits distill the essence and give advice to the next generation.

Salina added, "What's most remarkable is that these fruits will update their contents over time, keeping it relevant to the needs around them as time goes on."

As the discussions went on, the framework of the new order became increasingly clear. It was not a rigid system but a living organism capable of self-regulation and self-improvement, adaptable to ever-changing circumstances.

El watched the collaboration occurring before him with a hopeful heart. "This is what true order looks like. Not a fragile peace upheld by force, but a deep harmony arising from understanding and consensus.

. . .

Seline was fascinated by something going on with the sets of energy fields. "Look, every time we reach an important consensus, it changes-the energy field of the city gets more stable.

Monika's system did a good forecast: "At this pace, definitely, the stability of this new order will most definitely be unparalleled by any system throughout history.

Victor was sensitive to the subtlety of the shifting shades. "What really matters is that this order is based on true insight. Every group finds its place in it.

And with the last proposal accepted, the Trees of Light exploded in a riot of brilliance, as the Wisdom Fruits ripened and rained down, dissolving into myriad lights that wove into the souls of one and all present. This was absolute surety for the new order: not laws etched upon cold stones, but a consensus lived in the hearts of every one.

A new order, not imposed from above by government, but built by the people themselves from the grass roots, not rigid edict but flexible principles; wherein every life is a creator and every act a forward step.

As night began to set in, a serene brilliance bathed the hall of the council; the branches of the Trees of Light swayed softly as if in blessing of the rising sun of this new era. This day did not reform the system but marked the civilization coming of age.

47

THE LIGHT OF HOPE

Scarce was the new order issued, ere, on the morrow, there shone an uncanny light over the City of the Pit. Not a blazing splendour, but a soft diffused glow which seemed to cling around the whole circle of the world with a thin veil of hope.

OTHER LESSON TYPES WERE HELD AMONGST RUINS-WHAT WAS left of the Observatory-where children had gathered. Seated in a circle, crouched around the base of the newly planted Tree of Light, while an elder spoke in circles around them-a rogue Shadow Councilor teaching the next generation the balance of light and darkness.

EL WATCHED FROM AFAR, QUIETLY OBSERVING THE WARM SCENE unfolding before his gaze. He had lost the Prophetic Power, but his eyes were clearer than they had ever been. "How interesting," he whispered, "that when we lose our lust for power, we find an almost infinite amount of lovely things to look at."

Seline joined him, her Life Map now dimmed from its old brilliance but capturing more of the subtler life energies. "Have you noticed?" she said. "The way these children are learning absolutely changed. They no longer strive towards strength due to ambition alone but study how everything relates to everything else.

Then everybody's attention was taken so surprisingly by a sudden discovery. An excited little girl pointed to the canopy of the Tree of Light: "Look! The starlight is dancing!"

Monica's mechanical armor sprang into action, swiftly analyzing the phenomenon before her. "Anomalous energy waves detected. It appears the Seeds of Starlight are responding to the children's pure curiosity."

Victor emerged from behind the shadow, soft and unobtrusive. "It's more than an answer," he said. "They're really showing them something. See those patterns..."

Indeed, the Seeds of Starlight danced through the air, weaving intricate patterns—sometimes resembling a delicate flower, other times a graceful bird, and at times manifesting into more elaborate energy formations. Each pattern appeared to contain profound truths, yet remained simple enough for even a child to grasp.

Elena was awestruck: "This is it-just like it was written in the ancient texts, the 'Words of Hope'! It was said that starlight will only enlighten when the world finally finds actual concord."

Salina added, "Each of these patterns is specific to the viewer and reflects precisely his questions and needs.".

The elder stopped his lesson and smiled kindly. "Children, what do you see?"

A boy exclaimed joyfully, "I see the light and shadow dancing together! They are not enemies!".

I see the roots of the Tree of Life!" the girl exclaimed. "And it's so nice down there, too!

The innocent wisdom spoken by each child echoed in their thoughts, right into the ears of grown-ups present there. This unsought give-and-take of learning and understanding was way more valued than enforced education.

. . .

It was then that a miracle happened: the Tree of Light started bearing another kind of fruit. The fruits were transparent in color, soft with lights pulsating inside.

"Fruits of Hope," she breathed. "They encapsulate the realizations of the moment and turn them into the seeds of wisdom.

Salina watched the fruits intently. "What sends me, though, is how they reach people who really need them, just like hope, which always seems to come at the right time."

One of them floated down gently into the elder's hands, and in that instant, the second his fingertips touched it, a long-buried memory sprang to life-a scene of his younger self, full with the wish to possess power. But this time, the memory did not hurt; this time, it made its appearance as a treasured lesson.

The old man sighed, "I see now, true hope lies not in possessing great power, but in using our experiences to help others.".

Seated around him, the children listened with rapt attention to his story this time, not about the struggle for power but about growth and understanding.

. . .

As El continued to watch this scene unfold, something suddenly clicked in his mind. "This is what legacy is all about-not in amassing power, but in sharing wisdom.

Seline's Life Map picked up a peculiar energy wave. "See," she said, "each time a new understanding occurs, the life energy of the city becomes more harmonious.

Monica's system supplied some remarkable data: "The collective consciousness field is undergoing a qualitative change. This spontaneous learning and understanding is preparation for a new civilization.

Victor, more sensitive now to the subtleties in the Shadow Network, said, "The most beautiful thing is this: such change isn't forced. Everyone is willfully turning to a better path.

As the sun reached its peak, a growing crowd had assembled at the Observatory. They came with food and water to share, and to share their stories, their experience. The Tree of Light spread its branches, shading all who were there.

Elena also registered a subtler shift: "The interactions between different groups seem so easy now. Without power differences, people are just more attracted to one another.

. . .

Salina added, "And everyone spreads hope in one's own way—through teaching, skill sharing, and helping out..."

As night descended, the air up at the Observatory finally condensed into a climax of magical wonder. Innumerable Starlight Seeds danced in the air and merged playfully with the riotous colors of the setting sun. The fruits hanging from the Tree of Light glowed softly and reflected a personal radiance upon every face.

He watched that heartwarming scene. "This is the light of hope-never the begetting of force, but the awakening of the soul.

Seline spoke softly, "Every life is a lamp. When we learn to light up one another, the world would never go dark.

The Light of Hope was to be that no one is to be controlled by something or another as their source of light, but rather an inner light-a continuum of every choice that one makes.

With the fall of night and the twinkling of the stars up above, the Tree of Light painted a brilliant picture. It was a new world of hope, wherein every life narrated its own story of light in an unusual manner.

48

THE CHANGE OF FATE

A miracle was happening in the ancient Hall of Fate, deep within the City of the Abyss: the ancient runes which chronicled the fate of the world in unyielding simplicity since time beyond time began to take form into an unholy self-changing now. As if space and time itself were remaking, a bright golden glow streamed inside the hall.

El stood alone, SME amidst the hall, with threads of destiny streaming around him. Unlike previously, those gold threads no longer clung to fixed paths but branched out and crossed over, reaching like so many living things. Dispossessed of his prophetic power, he could feel what had changed in importance.

Incredible, he breathed, his hand extended to touch one of the threads of fate. The river of fate hath many rivulets now, and endless.

. . .

Coming from the depths of the hall now appeared Seline. Her Life Map, though still dimmed, now revealed an even deeper transformation: "These threads of fate. they're trying to find further choices on their own. As if life itself finds paths into the unknown.

A wee Tree of Light had begun to sprout from the broken stone of the hall's floor, its roots dipping to touch the runes of fate, its branches arching up into the air in some wild lacework of energy.

A soft warning bell echoed from Monica's armor. "Anomalous energy detected. Fate runes are limning in resonance with the Tree of Light. No such combination has ever been recorded.

Victor appeared from some cleft in the ancient shadows, his voice full of amazement: "The Shadow Network discovers a completely new kind of energy. What was taken for granted, what was destined, is now undergoing such a sharp change.

Suddenly, the ceiling of this hall burst into this incredible brightness, where literally innumerable Seeds of Starlight were floating down from above, with some sort of guiding intent in the air as if to show the way.

. . .

Elena hastened into the hall, though her Crystal of Prophecy had long lost its foresight, it was now resonating strongly with these changes. "This is... the Awakening of Fate! There were ancient writings about this: when the world truly broke free from the fetters of fate, this would be the scene to appear.

Salina added, "It's not about breaking free; it's about breaking free into choice. Every life can now write its own story."

Suddenly, magnificent fruit began to appear upon the tree's boughs - crystalline orbs that glowed with an internal, trembling light, wherein threads of gold, representing fate, curved and meandered unblushingly.

Fruits of Destiny," Elena whispered. "They allow one glimpses of possibility, but they do not force a path.

While all of these fruits had astonished the group, an even more unimaginable event occurred next. The Pool of Fate right in the middle of the hall started to quiver even as innumerable fragments undulated their reflections on the water surface, showing glimpses of different times and spaces, and each image was full of life and hope.

The reflections caught Monica in no time. "These are

not prophecies but possibilities manifesting. Every option opens a new world line.

Victor mused, "The most amazing thing is that none of those options is mutually exclusive anymore; they're like tributaries into the sea, carrying us toward a better world.".

El strode to the Pool of Fate and peered into its undulations. "Behold? None of these visions speak of a thing being absolute good or bad, absolute victory or defeat. Each of the stories says something about life.

Seline's Life Map shouted back in surprise, "Hold on! A huge transformation is at work!

Indeed, the fate runes began their mesmerizing dance in the hall, remodeling themselves into an all-new pattern: from cold, stiff laws to blossoming, vivid energy paths. The roots of the Tree of Light connected with them easily, forming a living web of fate.

Elena found something in this ancient book: "'When fate ceases to be a shackle and becomes a guide on the path, the world shall finally obtain true freedom'".

Salina added, "This is the answer we've been seeking all

along. True fate is not merely about passively accepting destiny; it's about actively creating it."

The most unexpected of all the discoveries sent everyone gasping in one accord. From the Pool of Fate, swam a quite familiar figure as though it were the projection of Miller's consciousness out of his body.

"It seems you've finally understood," Miller said, his voice, though ethereal, imbued with warmth. "Fate has never been a fixed track. It has always been a network woven from countless choices. Now, this world has gained the freedom to choose."

El moved and asked, "So this is what was in your mind-to bargain your life for the freedom of the whole world?

Miller's image smiled faintly. "No, I just merely opened a door. The true architects of freedom are the choices made by every living thing.

As his voice faded away, the Pool of Fate suddenly erupted in a blinding flash of light. Tens of thousands of strands of fate rose into the air, forming a dazzling fabric that shimmered in every direction. Each thread represented a possible outcome, its path no longer isolated but crossing against others.

. . .

The new tapestry of fate, Seline breathed. Now, every man can find his way, his path inlaid within it.

The last word of Monica's system was: "At this rate, the development of the world no longer has to follow predetermined paths, as the realm of possibility expands exponentially.

Victor, however, more sensitive to changes around him, said, "What's most beautiful is that this freedom isn't a source of chaos—it's a driving force for creation."

Yet with the night, the breathtaking view was unfolded by the Hall of Fate: tons of threads of fates were swirling in the air, shining as one bright river of stars. The Tree of Light was gently swaying, its branches softly waving, and the Seeds of Starlight wove into it complicated patterns of hopes.

That was the great moment of destiny when the threads of fate snapped and left every soul free to choose for itself. It was then that the world took up its most beauteous aspect.

Nothing had been set in this New World; every avenue stood at the threshold of a new beginning, every step an opportunity to create something anew. Indeed, this was the rarest gift of all.

49

PURIFICATION OF THE SOUL

After the point of no return, a deep transformation began to flower unobtrusively within the hearts of every inhabitant in the City of the Abyss. The branches of the Tree of Light in the Purification Hall of the Silver Star Temple, which had, until now, been restrained by the dome, finally broke through, and on the ground below appeared an intricate pattern of light and shadow. The Seeds of Starlight dance across the canopy, each graceful dance imparting gentle ripples into the air.

El stood at the heart of the hall, his gaze sweeping over the assembled crowd. In this space, the barriers of status had all but vanished. Former foes and friends alike sat in serene silence, eyes shut tight, welcoming the profound transformations unfolding within their souls.

"Interesting," he murmured. "When we give up our need

to be in control, we can understand even the most profound truth about any living thing.

Seline stepped closer to him. Her Life Map, though no longer glowing with the former brilliance, vibrated with the faintest stirrings of the soul. "Can you feel it?" she asked. "The old wounds and obsessions are self-releasing.

It was then that one scene caught the attention of all: how a former member of the Shadow Council suddenly burst into tears-not sad ones, unshackling and purifying ones.

"I. I finally understand," he choked out, shaking, his voice trembling. "All that power I pursued couldn't protect anything; it fed my own fears."

Instantly, Monica's system detected the shift in the energy field. "Special soul waves detected. The cause is this spontaneous awakening.

Victor materialized out of the darkness, strangely quiet. "The Shadow Network evolves, too. Dark emotions are no longer just sources of pain, but a bedrock for growth.

The Tree of Light, as if echoing that change within the collective, began to softly glow. And the fruits also cascaded from it-gracefully-finding their way into the hands of those needing them.

Elena recognized the fruits before her. "These are the Fruits of the Soul," she said, "Legend has it that they only manifest when individuals genuinely release their attachments."

Salina continued, "Each fruit carries a different revelation, intricately designed to answer the deep-seated battles within every human being.

A young priestess of Silver Star squatted down to grab an adjacent fruit that fell on the ground. The moment her fingers touched it, the fruit degraded instantly into countless dots of light, condensing into her heart. A lightbulb of comprehension suddenly twinkled in her eyes: "So the goal of practicing is not to transcend others but to better understand life.

The energy in the hall started to shift ever so subtly as one by one, people experienced the soul purification. Where it had been heavy and weighed them down, it was now light and in harmony. Facial expressions softened; all were at peace.

Then, suddenly, from the very midst of the hall, flared a strange brilliance. Its source was a mystical Heart Mirror supposed to reveal the most truthful, honest rendering of a person's soul. But now, instead of showing just separate pictures, that mirror presented a group view-a tapestry so fine and intricate, fashioned from millions of souls.

El went to the mirror, lured by the riveting reflections that swirled inside. "Every soul is a starry night," he said. "If people learned to love the darkness along with the light inside themselves, they'd find the world a whole lot better.

Seline's Life Map showed the most magnificent pattern yet. "Look," she said. "The life energies of everyone here are in easiest harmony with each other. It is not a forced coming together-it's in harmony from inside.

Monica's system had some remarkable information: "A qualitative change of the collective consciousness field is occurring. More profound than any intentional effort to change is this shift.".

Victor felt the shift and added, "What's most remarkable is that everybody is retaining their individuality while meshing and integrating into the whole.

At this moment, branches of the Tree of Light unfolded with majesty, weaving a natural energy field around them. The Seeds of Starlight that floated started to align in a deliberate pattern to form a holy purification array.

Elena read from an ancient book, her eyes widening in surprise as she said, "This is the fabled Circle of the Soul! It doesn't change people, it shows them what they want.

A speechless Salina watched in wonder: "There, each man finds his place in the energy field, just like the orbiting of the stars.

Amazingly, with the increase in depth in purification, miraculous changes began to appear. These soothing energies released long-concealed emotions and pains left unsaid.

One older man, weeping, his voice quivering, stammered out, "No more hate. The hatred that I have carried so long in my heart, it was always a chain that I bound myself with.

A young warrior laid his weapon down. "Strength is not for harming others or proving myself. Strength is for protection and to build.

As night began to fall with the setting sun, the atmosphere within the Hall of Purification reached its poignant climax: the innumerable lights of the purified souls danced together in the air, weaving a magnificent river of stars. Each light symbolized a cleansed soul, and every flutter told its tale of redemption.

Mesmerized by the light in front of him, El finally understood what strength really meant: "Purification isn't about erasing anything; it's all about acceptance and comprehension."

Seline whispered, "When we stop fighting our hearts, that is the world in its finest form.".

It was the very essence of soul purification, a change from within, not imposed from without; an awakening to the realities of the present, not in renunciation of the immediate past. With it, the individual found his peace; with it, every soul was free.

In the evening, the stars seemed brighter than ever, as if the universe itself was rejoicing in this common rebirth. Refreshing like a light spring rain, this spirit of purification was pouring new life into each soul longing for renewal.

50

A NEW BEGINNING

At the height of the City of the Abyss, the remains of the Eternal Ring had transformed. A mighty Tree of Light towered upwards, stretching its sprawling branches up towards the sky, like so many columns supporting the heavens themselves. Its canopy stretched broadly across the city, interlacing, a dome of light and shade. For this place was to be consecrated, the restored testament of a people, the awakening of a world.

FIRST RAYS OF MORNING SUNLIGHT, FILTERING THROUGH breaks in the foliage, danced on the ground in a very intricate play of light and shadow. The El stood at the bottom of the tree, his attention caught by the crowd surrounding him-people from many factions, each holding their own stories, yet all connected by that one single spark of curiosity within their gaze.

. . .

"It's difficult to fathom," he murmured, "that after all we've endured, we've come back to the most fundamental of truths."

Seline joined him, her Life Map showing amazing coherence. "Look," she said. "Each of them is finding a place. It is not an imposed order-but one that has emerged of its own accord."

Monica called in, now in her newly redesigned mechanical suit with no offensive capabilities: "Energy readings indicate the life of the city is at an all-time high. And this was all done without the use of any superpowers.

Then Victor came in, bright and shining shadow, representative of the revolutionary difference now in his soul: "Surprising it is, but final balance between light and darkness was reached. It was not longer enemies, only different faces of the same medal.

Within the branches of the Tree of Light, dim rays of light started to shimmer, and from its canopy came countless Seeds of Starlight, all gently floating down and carrying with them an energy message.

Elena watched this in a daze. "These aren't normal Seeds of Starlight. They seem to carry a sort of guidance within them.

. . .

Salina said, "Like they're gifts from the new world, and every seed's a possibility.

A small girl stretched, reached, and picked one of the seeds. Her eyes shone like the stars as if she had unraveled some deep realization. "I see it!"-high with excitement-"It is the new direction of education, not only providing knowledge but letting everybody discover their genius!"

One elderly man caught his own seed and shared insight as such: "I now understand why history is preserved. It is not to dwell on painful times, but a lesson to be learned for the construction of a better future.

Suddenly, a crack had appeared in the trunk of the Tree of Light, from which some glistening fluid-a holy elixir, almost identical with the Water of Life-poured out. It soon started to drip on the ground and carry life with it into the surroundings.

"Water of Life," Elena said, instantly recognizing it. "The fabled essence believed to sustain all existence."

Where the Water of Life flowed, it seemed that withered flowers sprang anew, crumbling buildings began to mend themselves, and even the air was filled with renewed vitality.

And there it was, turbo-speeding into her head: "New forms of energy detected. Nothing is changed; everything becomes the best that there is to be seen.

According to Victor, "I think it is a mirror which reflects to each man's eye the fairest part of his own existence.".

Then something even more remarkable happened: the treetop canopy filled with millions of points of light, mapping the vast star map. It wasn't a constellation but showed an infinite array of possibilities in futures.

El watched the vision in a dispassionate intensity. "Each point of light is a possibility, and all of them lead toward harmony and creation.

The Life Map of Seline was revealing itself now in full detail for the first time. "A new network of life has been born," she says. "Each being part of it.

Then, out of nowhere, there was a voice-one that still echoed in the heart of everyone present. It was Miller's last whisper: "The new world began with an end, and this is not an ending-it is a start. The true test is not in the power you happen to be wielding, but in how you will use free will to create beauty.".

These words sent everybody's thoughts deep inside. Oh, yeah, this was truly a new start: Without the bondage of the extraordinary powers, each one of them should learn to create and live in the most simple and natural way.

Elena had once read in some very ancient text that "When the world returns to its essence, a new era shall begin. It shall not be the era of power, but of wisdom; not of control, but of creation.".

Salina it seems, watched the changes around her and said, "The prophecy came true, but it is even more wonderful than it described. Because this is what comes from all of us working together.".

By noon, it was at its fullest brilliance, wherein thousands of points of light danced in the air, interlacing into a magnificent tapestry of hope. Within that complex net, a place could be found by everybody, while creating his or her own story.

El gazed at the scene before him, a smile of relief blossoming on his face. "This is the answer we've been searching for all along. True strength doesn't lie in changing the world, but in transforming ourselves. True wisdom isn't about controlling fate; it's about crafting possibilities."

Seline said softly, "Every ending marks a new beginning, and this start is way more magnificent than we had ever imagined.

This encapsulated the new beginning: not resignation to destiny but creation teeming; not one way, many ways. Every life in this transmuted world was a creator, and every decision opened a new door.

As night started afresh, the Tree of Light shone brilliant in the dark, so proud with the myriads of stars dotting the sky, weaving up an awesome tapestry above. This was not an end but a beginning it was all about. At this moment of beginnings, each had hope and courage enough to move on their separate ways.

The new world started and remained only with the first chapter in the development of its story.

51

THE JOURNEY OF RENEWAL

It was only at the first dawn to follow the end of this cycle that the real process of reconstruction for the City of the Abyss began. As morning poured between rent clouds, wrapping shattered walls and ruins in tatters of gold, the seven Guardians sat down to deliberate the ambitious blueprint for rebuilding around a circular table within the newly completed Council Hall.

El leaned against the table, his hand dancing across the cracked marble surface. His Prophetic Power might have been diminished, but he could sense the memories etched into the stone. Every fissure seemed to tell the story of the city's agony and its rise anew.

"These cracks..." he murmured, his fingers gliding over a particularly deep fissure, "are not merely signs of destruction—they are the foundation upon which something new will be built."

. . .

Seline approached the table with her Life Map unfolded in her hands; threads of pale gold energy contoured the city, showing how parts that had been fractured were now alive with new vitality. "You see?" she asked. "It's not just reconstruction; it's growth.

Monica's powered armor hummed softly. "The energy field readings are very unusual," she said, calling up a holographic projection. "It looks like the areas devastated by the war are spontaneously reorganizing, as if. life itself is healing them.

Victor stepped forward into the light, his tone softer than usual. "The Shadow Network has felt it, too-the underground energy veins rewriting their web anew.

Just then, soft earthquakes rumbled across the hall's floorboards. The party stepped backward gingerly and watched in awe as a sprout of the Tree of Light sprouted triumphantly out of cracked tiles on the floors, its roots flowing like galaxies as they interwove the shattered stones into a mosaic of life.

"Always," Elena said, stepping into the great hall with a bunch of yellowed scrolls from the Silver Star Temple, "life finds the most incredible way of restoring itself. Ancient prophecy spoke about this day: when the city would awaken once and for all and would no longer require outside help to rebuild it.

Salina was staring intently at the tender sapling. "It does look like it is looking for an ideal place to grow," she said, pointing in the direction the roots spread. "Look, the roots deliberately avoid nodes of underground energy, yet still manage to stay in touch with them lightly.

Suddenly, everyone caught a different energy pulse. The surface of this round table wrinkled as if it was water. Countless Starlight Seeds rose upwards and wove into complex blueprints of architecture in mid-air.

"This is...." El gazed at the three-dimensional projections intently. "The original design of the ancient Abyssal City?"

The Life Map of Seline didn't hesitate but responded, "No, it's something deeper. These designs are the city as it would wish to be: an organic, self-healing, self-adapting creation."

Monica started to take a closer look into the projections. "This gives the energy systems beyond architectural theory that we know; in fact, it's a fully integrated regenerative cycle.

. . .

But extraordinarily," Victor said in a musing tone, "this just fits in so well with the underlying structure of the Shadow Network-the balance of light and darkness in it is such a nice balance.

As all were peering at the blueprint, a surprise occurred that made them gasp. A slim crack appeared along the edge of the table, and from within, a silvery liquid-like energy began to seep out. It wriggled its way onto the floor, and wherever it touched, broken material began to make a remake of itself.

Source of Life," Elena said, flipping one of the scrolls. "The fabled material which awakens the very essence of matter, it doesn't just repair the damage, it rejuvenates what is sleeping inside the materials.

Salina reached her hand out to touch the stream of silver. "It's warm... and it pulses like a heartbeat. It feels alive, like the lifeblood of a mother.

Suddenly, there came an excited commotion outside the hall. They rushed outside into an amazed sight: up and down the city, dozens of Trees of Light burst forth in blossoming arrays. The trunks intertwined with deep networks underground, and their branches laced across overhead in an endless canopy. Perhaps more astounding, the remains of war-shattered buildings showed gradual healing under the soothing presence of the trees.

. . .

"This isn't renovation," El breathed, staring out at the view in wonder. "It's the city finding its most natural shape.

Seline's Life Map showed dramatic changes. "Every tree is choosing where it needs to direct its energy first. They're not just growing anywhere-they're listening to the soul of the city.".

Monica's system warned, "Energy levels are surging! The vitality of the city reaches an unprecedented peak.".

Smiling faintly, Victor felt the shift course through the Shadow Network. "What's really warming is that this reconstruction doesn't erase the past, but rather, it turns scars into fertilizers. Every ruin gives birth to newer possibilities.

The heavens now opened in a rain of gold, with every drop a small Seed of Starlight, deep-planting in the relics of old. From the places they came in contact with the ground, crystalline vines grew upward explosively, up the fractured walls, weaving into intricate reliefs.

Elena watched the emerging patterns. "These designs... they speak to the story of the city. Every scar is kept, not in signs of destruction, but as symbolic of growth.

. . .

Salina pointed out another interesting thing: "You notice? All the plants that come anew do have healing properties. Some cleanse the air, others rejuvenate the soil, and some even calm one's mind..."

And with each passing day of reconstruction, more and more wonders emerged: areas that were long thought irretrievably lost blossomed, and former killing fields grew gardens. Most astounding of all was the organic manner in which it happened, as if the city itself had known all along how to heal its wounds.

By sunset, the reconstruction of the Abyssal City had attained a level of beauty never seen before. The Trees of Light bathed the surroundings in a gentle glow, their branches creating an atmosphere of tranquil illumination. As twilight descended, the starlight vines sparkled like a celestial river reflected upon the earth.

He had looked down upon the view of revival; happiness smiled in each wrinkle of his face: "This is how to rebuild, not by forcing it, but by provoking the awakening of life; not by erasing scars, but letting new hopes bloom from each scar.

It consummates all the essence of the way to reconstruction; in other words, the more sensitive one listens to the voice of the city and interprets the wisdom of living, the rebirth of the most beautiful kind already happened on its own. And then, each ruin becomes like a cradle for the new life, every wound emerged like a fountainhead of hope.

PART V

THE ETERNAL CHAPTER: THE RISE OF THE CITY OF HOPE

Where once the Abyssal City stood, it gave birth to this being that was the City of Hope. Almost living unto itself, its structure sprouts organically toward the needs of its denizens, the color of the streets changing by the mood of those traversing it. The light did not strongly glare but gently energized the heart.

It pulses with the lifeblood of the city, the Source of Creation, and even seems to hum in every nook and cranny, even carrying on the buildings' surface the signature in flowing patterns of energy: its heartbeat. A place of the most terrible battle became a garden, and within that garden, light and darkness were in harmony.

The Eternal Light wraps up the whole city around, not as a variably illuminating closure but as a promise of so many new tales yet to be minted. Everybody has turned storyteller for his or her fate, mapping new possibilities every day. In the very heart of the City of Hope, at the very center of the plaza, there stands a beautiful Tree of Light. Its branches and leaves reach over every nook and corner of this city, reflecting the new morning of this world.

A tale like this cannot have an end; for every ending, there should be a proposal of a fresh start-a rising with every falling of the curtain.

52

THE LORD OF THE ABYSS

Well, on the second dawn, which came after the grand cycle of the world was over, on the horizon of the Abyssal City appeared a strange halo. This was no ordinary morning light; rather, it was a spectacular scene-the perfect merge effect between the Starseed and the Abyssal Energy. It marked the beginning of a redefinition of the Lord of the Abyss.

Thrown by himself, El stood atop the Starwatch Tower, his eyes set upon the horizon to come. Morning light cascaded in a rainbow waterfall through the shattered dome of coloured glass, casting flecks of colour, mystical patterns on the floor below him. The power of prophecy might be long lost, but he could feel it-the weight of the air thick with change.

"Interesting," he said quietly, his fingers scraping

against the halo. "It would seem that the Abyss is trying to forge a completely new path.

A soft rustling of footsteps approached from behind. Seline climbed up onto the observation platform, her Life Pattern unfolding in the air, humming in soft harmony with the Abyssal energy. "Can you feel it? The Abyss has changed; it is no longer a chaotic vortex-it's nurturing something entirely new.

Suddenly, a low rumble emanated from the bottom of the Abyss. Everyone instinctively looked around and saw a great column of light rising upwards from the middle of the Abyss. It wasn't a surge of destructive energy, but rather a pulse of creation.

Monica's mechanical armor sprang into action, swiftly analyzing the phenomenon before her. "Detecting an unprecedented energy pattern," she declared. "The Abyssal Core is undergoing some sort of transformation. wait, these readings." Her voice carried a note of astonishment. "It's autonomously constructing a multidimensional energy matrix!"

Victor emerged from the darkness, his customary placid mask revealing a shade of astonishment. "The Shadow Network just called in with astonishing news. Those elder powers, long bound within the Abyss. they have started to cleanse themselves. This is something unprecedented in all of history.

In that instant, it turned into infinity, of thin strands of energy lacing themselves in mid-air in an infinite three-dimensional pattern: a huge network of runes, actually fusing the ancient signs of the Abyss with utterly new rules of energy.

Elena ran up onto the platform, her robe of pure silver blowing in the soft morning breeze. "Ancient books prophesied this moment in words like, 'When the Abyss finds its path, the world shall know true balance'.

Salina examined the runes closely. "This isn't just a reorganization of energies. this feels more like an awakening. The Abyss seeks another way to be.

But then came something even more amazing: The Abyssal Core suddenly burst into an enormous shining sphere of light, persistently radiating consciousness unlike a plain quality of energy.

"This is." El said, holding his breath, barely above a whisper, ".the consciousness of the Abyss awakening?"

. . .

Seline's Life Pattern immediately picked up the odd oscillations. "It's more than that, look at the energy flux. the Abyss is now acting above its function of a passively acting container; it's turning into an active source. It is trying to reestablish a link with the world.".

Monica's systems surged into overdrive as she processed the avalanche of data. "The energy matrix is taking shape in a way we've never encountered before. It's stable, yet astonishingly malleable. This challenges everything we believed we understood about energy dynamics.

Victor said, his sensitivity to the deep changes in the Shadow Network, "What's most amazing is that the Abyss seeks balance with the forces of light. It doesn't fight it or push it away anymore but instead seeks to rise to an altogether new plane of coexistence.

Instantly, in each of them, seven rays of radiating light issued forth, connected directly with each of them. Not hostile energy attacks, but gentle, communicative strands. And each contained something different in that light.

El looked into the set of infinite possibilities relating to the futures-not set paths, but fluid, envisioned choices. Seline saw life's secrets unfold far into the distance, a vision beyond the restrictions of her Life Pattern.

. . .

SUDDENLY, A FAMILIAR VOICE ECHOED IN THE MINDS OF ALL. IT was Miller's voice, though deeper and more profound than they recalled:

"The nature of the Lord of the Abyss is not truly to issue commands to powers but to regulate the currents of nature. At last, it has learned."

AS THE VOICE HAD UTTERED ITS LAST WORDS, THE transformation of the Abyssal Core began to reach its peak. The sphere of light started to rise before gently descending, but instead of returning to its previous position, it unfolded in mid-air, revealing a colossal energy platform.

MONICA'S SYSTEMS SCRAMBLED THROUGH THE STRUCTURE. "Adaptive energy exchange system-working principles: self-balancing, self-regulation in the flow of diverse forces."

VICTOR'S FACE WAS CONTEMPLATIVE. "IT'S LIKE A SAGACIOUS governor, and yet it is not mechanical-it's alive, full of consciousness."

ELENA EXCLAIMED, LYING AMIDST HER ANCIENT BOOKS ALL over, "That is what the ancients called the Heart of the Abyss: not a throne of rule but of exchange and creation.

INNUMERABLE MINUTE POINTS OF LIGHT SPRANG OUT ON THE platform each manifesting into a different form of energy.

They surged freely in the structure, mingled with one another, interacted-kept their individuality.

Salina's eyes widened with wonder. "Behold-at last, the Abyss has found its destiny. No more is it a chasm that sucks in energy, but now it has become a womb where possibilities are nurtured.

Suddenly, the platform burst into an extremely powerful turbulent-like wave of energy radiating outwards without restraint. This time, though, instead of scares, the wave embossed an unseen depth of enlightenment into all who were present at the event. For the first time, the Abyss had shown its power entirely calmly.

Wrapped in the change, El whispered, "I see now.the importance of the Lord of the Abyss isn't in holding the power but in understanding it, so at its will, it guides the energy toward the flow of harmony.".

As dusk descended, the Abyss revealed an extraordinary spectacle. The previously chaotic energy vortices had morphed into structured energy rivers, intricately weaving a radiant tapestry across the Abyss. Each river shimmered with its own distinct brilliance while maintaining a flawless harmony with the entirety.

. . .

The most informative about the change taking place was Seline's Life Pattern. "This is the real Lord of the Abyss- not a lord of power, but a lord of energy; not an enforcer of order, but a guardian of balance.

When the last streaks of the sun disappeared on the other side of the horizon, the Abyss lit up with tenderness and soothing warmth-a different kind of light: not painful or threatening but filled with warmth, which all life draws on. It was the final transformation of the Abyss: from an entity that once had threatened the world, it had turned into a wellspring of creation.

53

PRIESTESS OF LIGHT

The third dawn since the close of the great cycle saw the final transformation of the luminous power unfold before the Abyssal City. A solemn rite was about to take place in the newly restored central hall of the Silver Star Temple to decide upon the course of a new destiny. Holy light fell through the newly made crystal dome, intermingling with the essence of the Starseed, and danced along the floor with a magical grace.

Elena stood before the altar, her mastery of Holy Light now entirely transcending the old bounds. Her ancient ceremonial robes shone grave under the starlight to which their harsh splendor was now softened by a kinder force. The Tree of Light, sprouted from the ruins, softly danced around, carrying vital force into this moment.

"The moment finally has come," Elena said, her fingers tracing the soft glow of the ancient tome she was cradling, her voice full of emotion. "When light ceases to be a weapon against darkness, the truth is finally revealed."

Seline drew her gaze from her Life Pattern; a spark of insight flashed in her eyes. "The energy patterns have fundamentally shifted. Observe that light; it no longer projects in only one direction but is having a sort of conversation.

The temple walls glimmered suddenly, as if their surfaces heaved with ripples. A call from Victor-it had to come via the unintelligible Shadow Network. His figure materialized in one ray of light, an unimaginable blend of brightness and shadow. Nothing like that could have been envisioned before now. "An interesting find," he said dreamily. "Something special in the way the temple energy field is tuned. It seems to be trying to be in resonance with all forms of energy.

El's eyes narrowed. "It is no coincidence. The status of the Priestess of Light, too, faces a great transformation. In the same way that the Lord of the Abyss does, so too will she seek a new way of survival.

A holographic projection of Monica appeared beside the altar. Her data analysis system was running in real time with changes in the energy field. "The detected structure of energy is evolving to higher dimensions. The evolution doesn't involve an increase in power but a qualitative leap.

. . .

Instantly, a seven-colored light shone from within the altar, forming a great energy matrix without diffusing. Each beam came forth in its own certain manner from its own dimension of light and was in perfect harmony with its brothers. It was with the reception of these sorts of events that the viewers went into an astonished wonder.

Salina stepped forward with her twin attributes and heard the transformation in full. "Like the interplay of daybreak and twilight, light and darkness were not opposites, but just a different expression of one whole.

Then, even more breathtaking, something else came into view. From the middle altar of the temple exploded seven rays of lights, bursting through. This time, it was formed, not by one single strong energy source, but by millions of small Starseeds. Each of them shone in their light frequency, lacing into a breathtaking web of light.

The seven-colored light swirled, started to curve gracelessly and shaped a three-dimensional spiral while it went upward in the air, as it condensed into a new sign. It was not a mark but a key-a key with the power to unlock even higher dimensions.

Still clung to the fragments of his prophetic vision, El saw something incredible. "This sign. it is not just a mark.

It's a key. The key that can open the gate to other dimensions."

WITH EVERY WORD THAT HE UTTERED, THE SIGN STARTED TO hum. The entire length of the temple vibrated with that hum; the stiff walls wavy now, like ripples in the water. Ancient runes shone on the walls, not some unyielding law set in stone but dynamic crystals of perception.

ELENA FELT IT RIGHT DOWN TO HER MARROW. "THAT IS THE true source of the Priestess of Light-not to impose dogma, but to open up the possibility of dialogue; not to impose standards, but to provide a playing field for mutual understanding."

AND THEN, AN EVEN STRANGER PHENOMENON OCCURRED. THE dozens of Starseeds sprinkled throughout the city began radiating a light at a most unprecedented intensity. Their lights converged into a single towering column right up to the sky, powerful and a bridge from the world of matter to the spiritual world.

IT WAS THEN THAT A VOICE THEY ALL KNEW BOOMED INSIDE each mind-a last message from Miller, this time more profound, musical.

IT IS IN THE REVELATION OF EACH LIFE'S RADIANCE THAT IT IS not mere darkness that defines light. This is suddenly understood.

With his voice fading away, there was a deep sense of change within the temple. The old ceremonial robes broke their sternness and showed a softer and more tender nature. The altar, meant to be high above everything else and commanding respect, became a place of meeting and sharing.

Seline's Life Pattern showed remarkable changes in the flow of the life force. "All forms of life are now shining in their unique way, and it is the task of the Priestess of Light to guide them into their final blossoming.

As the last rays of sunlight poured through the crystalline dome, the final part of the ceremony began. The concept of the Priestess of Light had drastically changed. She was no longer just that symbol of authority; she had turned into the medium through which communication would take place. This was not an ending but more of a commencement. This was the moment when the nature of light had been redefined-not as something to fight the darkness, but as wisdom to understand everything.

When night finally wrapped the earth in its arms, even then it would not allow the temple to turn dark. The light of the Starseeds mingled with the rhythm of the shadows, and what came out was an outstanding harmony. This was not the killing of differences but the embracing of distinction, not the imposition of oneness, but the honoring of diversity. Thus, the new era had a real luminous beginning.

This, therefore, is the new chapter of the Priestess of Light, one in which attention is no longer focused on the opposition of forces but on what light itself is. All life can find its brilliance in this new chapter, and the respect due to every existence; a beginning to far more.

54

TREATY OF PEACE

Something was finally happening in the ancient hall of the council in the Abyssal City that had never taken place: a peace conference. Sunbeams streamed through the newly restored stained-glass dome and mingled with the shining light of the Starseeds, creating curious patterns on the floor, as if witnessing this moment in history.

THE ONCE TENSE COUNCIL CHAMBER WAS FILLED WITH ONE atmosphere of reconciliation around a round table that held representation from literally every single faction: the priests of the Silver Star Temple, survivors of the Shadow Council, leadership of civilian forces, and even primordially ancient consciousness awakened from the depths of the Abyss. Most incredible of all, a few Trees of Light had sprouted inside the hall; each of their branches interlaced with others, forming a natural screen of energy, gently yet powerfully protecting everything within.

. . .

El rose from the middle of the round table, his eyes scanning through the representatives' faces. Without the gift of prophecy, too, the bright light of wisdom and will shone in his eyes, firm and stronger than ever before. "Today," he started, his voice firm and unshakable, "we are here not to divide territories, but to break boundaries.

On his right was Seline; before her lay her Life Pattern, like a tapestry, reflecting the subtle web which spanned the globe. "All life has anticipated this," she said. "I can feel the vibration of it.

At this, one of the onetime elders of the Shadow Council rose. His black robes, still bearing the scuffs of battle, no longer held the edge in his glance that once was. "We. we have made too many mistakes," he said, shaking. "We thought control would bring about peace, yet it has only brought more devastation.

A young priest of the Silver Star Temple stood forward to speak when Elena leaned forward, her hand lightly touching his shoulder. "Let him finish," she whispered softly. "True peace requires listening to every voice.

Above the table, Monica's holographic projection sprang to life, recording this critical juncture of history in real time. "The energy field analysis indicates that mass feeling has stabilized and hostility levels are at an all-time low. It doesn't show that it has been bottled up but that there is a change of heart.

Through the light screen of shadow came Victor, his open face assuredly reflecting a feeling similar to one of trust. "The Shadow Network has verified the sincerity of these intents," he said. "It is not a superficial compromise but deep and profound.

Suddenly, crystalline leaves started falling delicately from boughs of the Trees of Light. Sparkling like precious stones, these were not signs of corruption but rather containers for the peace treaty. As each leaf alighted on the table in front of a delegate, unique writing appeared upon it.

"These are the Leaves of Life," Elena explained. "They record the most truthful of vows. No lie, no vow taken under duress, can ever mark its leaves.

Salina looked intently at the leaves. "Each one reflects the needs of its intended group, yet all point to the same goal—true peace."

The leaves begin to have words called out as if written upon them, and the most remarkable occurrence took place. Inside the council hall, a soft column of light started to rise. The light emanated not from one mighty power but a combination of unique energies that each delegate possessed.

In this light, El felt a great unity. "This is the Light of Peace. It never wipes out all differences, but what it cares about is every existence."

The projection of the world, as a three-dimensional image within the column of light, was alive-not some simple map, but alive with the flow and play of various forces at work. Energies that had once warred with one another found a way to live in harmony in this vision.

"Look there," Seline said, her finger pointing to a juncture of forces. "The energy of the Abyss is instinctively adapting itself to the surface energy. They found a way to coexist."

Monica's analytical system responded almost immediately. "A new energy pattern has been detected. This model self-regulates forces; therefore, no outside interference is necessary."

At that, one stood up from among the civilian forces. She was only a common healer, yet her eyes shone bright with understanding. "Peace must not be an agreement only amongst the powerful, but it has to do with the needs of every living being."

. . .

Her words light the fire of conversation, but for the first time, it wasn't debate; rather, deep listening occurred. Each voice was heard and valued in coming together in the search for optimum solution-finding. Thus, Leaves of Life began to work their magic, ever revealing new text, as if recording the very birth of peace.

Victor watched a subtle effect: "Do you see that? When true consensus is reached, the leaves start to glow softly; it's life itself confirming our vows."

Elena opened an ancient-looking tome: "Indeed, the sages said, 'True peace is not written on paper but etched into the heart'."

Then, suddenly, that hall was filled by an unexpected voice that came from one of those primordial consciousnesses in the bottom of the Abyss-a voice similar to a chorus among million whispers. "We saw empires rise and collapse, but such beauty never happened. When all life can be heard, true peace can take root."

The words brought a moment of silent reflection upon them, as if it were fitting for every word and its depth. The Starseeds started to float delicately in the air, painting a picture of serenity. This was not a dream but a truth actualized through mutual comprehension.

. . .

As the final terms of the treaty had been decided, all Leaves of Life shone softly in one gentle radiance. Lights from the leaves intertwined into a three-dimensional Web of Accord. Every node was a promise, every thread a bond.

He looked into the brilliant web. "This is the real peace treaty. A bond and not a chain of limitations, but one of understanding.".

Seline's Life Pattern unfolded the fullest view of the web. "Within this web is contained every life. Every force has been given due respect."

As Monica aptly puts it, "In place, this system would ensure that peace would no longer be fragile in balance but self-sustained harmony."

Victor said, perceiving the changes in the Shadow Network, "What's far more astounding is the fact that this peace is not based on suppression but on actual understanding.".

As the last rays of the sun had wandered into the Web of Accord, the light filled the hall of conciliation. The Leaves of Life were softly waltzing on gentle air, while the light of the Starseeds easily danced back into tune with the energy of the Abyss-witness to this momentous event.

This is the heart of the peace confluence-not the trading of interests but the resonance of hearts, not the balance of power but the uplifting of understanding. Under this new concord, every life will find its place, and every force will have room to grow.

But as the people began to leave, the Leaves of Life did not disappear in distance; they've turned to shining specks of starlight, seeding each heart present there. This peace was no longer a simple piece of paper; this was a promise branded into the core of each being.

That day meant more than a mere signature on a piece of paper-it marked the emergence into a new phase of civilization. Here began the road to real peace, which truly led into a brighter and more harmonious future.

55

THE ORIGIN OF CREATION

When the ink dried on the final signature and the night's sleep was finally over, a brilliant column of light burst into the morning sky from the center of the Abyssal City. It was an explosion, yet not of energy: a change of state. The feared Abyssal Core shook off its self-destructive nature and started rebirthing as a womb of life.

The entire energy grid of the city vibrated, as if that light beam went into the sky. Newly grown Trees of Light danced in a soft breeze; Starseeds sketched across the air with their trails on, even the Shadow Network-like ripples, as if waves of harmony stroked it. What happened was above and beyond all dimensions.

El, upon the newly built observation deck, stared out as the transformation unfolded before his eyes. The power of prophecy might have waxed and waned, but he could feel the weight of this moment deep in his heart. "Look," he said, pointing to the middle of the shining pillar, "the Abyss is no longer a vortex that consumes-its fostering infinite possibilities."

Seline's Life Pattern blossomed in the air, golden lines intertwining into a three-dimensional tapestry. "This energy pattern. it's unlike anything we've encountered before. Each stream of energy embodies the essence of creation, akin to seeds of life yearning for fertile soil."

In an unexpected turn of events, a discovery took everyone's breath away. At the core of the radiant column, a strange vortex materialized. Unlike the destructive vortices of yore, this one was weaving new manifestations of matter and energy.

Monica's systems were abuzz with delight. "Detected: energy conversion process-never-before-seen! Abyss is converting chaotic energy into creative energy, totally against the laws of energy conservation!"

From out of that bright shadow, Victor appeared, his face aglow with wonder. "The most amazing thing is, shadow energy is involved in this creation. The shadow is not only the symbol of destruction anymore; rather, it is emerging as an important ingredient of creation itself.".

. . .

A very miraculous phenomenon then happened: the vortex started crystallizing into intricate, luminous formations. Every crystal bore different creation properties: some could clean the environment, others enhance growth, while others would heal wounds.

Elena knew what those crystals were. "Creation Crystals! The ancient book talked about them-they only appear if the world has reached true concord and carry in themselves a germ of the creative force.

Salina continued, "And each crystal is different, as if the Source of Creation answers in this manner to the various needs of all forms of life."

The column of light suddenly pulsed rhythmically, sending waves of energy dancing, rippling outwards. No chaotic tremors, these were measured, harmonious beats. Each pulse released yet another wave of creative energy into the world.

Look! exclaimed Seline, pointing to various parts of the city. And this energy is stirring the dormant vitality: ruins morph into pulsar places and desolate land blooms with life.

Indeed, under the benevolence of the Source of Creation, the whole city had adapted to a brilliant change:

buildings that were destroyed during the war did not get rebuilt but flowered into new forms. Vines full of life crawled up the walls, stitching together breathtaking and useful natural patterns.

Monica's monitoring systems picked up those changes within that energy field. "These creative changes go way beyond that which manifests in physical form. The very fabric of space itself is changing. There are areas reflecting evidence of dimensional folding to create more living space."

Victor knew what deep changes were sweeping through the Shadow Network, and he said, "That's the amazing thing-the creative energy's reaching even down into the underground. The dark places aren't just metaphors of dissolution anymore; they're giving rise to weird life.".

And thereupon, the Source of Creation flung out its second wave. This time, the energy radiated outward in greater detail. Millions and millions of small sparkling lights swirled around, with accurate creative information.

El noticed something else: their uniqueness. "They are the seeds of creation, each bearing its own possibility."

Indeed, while these luminous points descended upon various places, each created a creative miracle, attuning themselves to the needs around. They wove energy fields that hastened the process of healing where the medical district was present, created networks that cleansed the air where residential neighborhoods were, and crafted matrices that downloaded knowledge where educational zones lay.

Seline's Life Pattern personified the very reason for such changes. "This is not a mindless creation-this is an intelligent response. The Source of Creation seems to perceive the most compelling need of each realm.".

Suddenly, another voice echoed, one that no one had expected to hear. From the bottom of the Abyss came the call again, but this time it was no longer chaotic; it held the wisdom of creation.

"Everything in life has a meaning. In finding and living that meaning lies the essence of creation."

Among the very ancient texts, Elena came upon one prophecy that quite literally rang deep inside her head. "This is what the sages called the 'Awakening of Creation.' When the Abyss finally truly understands the nature of creation, it will turn from an agent of destruction into a source of creation."

Salina watched the flow of energy closely. "The beauty about such transformation is that nowhere does it eradicate the existing parts; it builds on them, adding new possibilities."

The third and most powerful wave of energy poured over the standing city as they stood there in stunned wonder. In one instant, the Source of Creation seemed to reach out and turn some hidden mechanism. Streamers of light coalesced in the air, woven into an enormous and delicate webwork.

"This is the Web of Creation!" El exclaimed. "This is what connects past, present, and future together to allow the possibilities of creation to transcend the boundaries of time."

Under the power of this network, the city turned into a completely different organism. The dead ruins did not just get renovated but were reshaped as completely different forms. Buildings also started to become not resistant but adaptive, perceiving changes in structures. Further, the street turned to be dynamic social zones that stimulated communication and sparked creativity.

Monica's informational overload was nearing the saturation point of her system. "This level of creative development compared to anything so far seems overwhelming-heard of: It's as if another whole dimension has opened up.

. . .

Victor, keenly aware of the enormous shift occurring, observed, "But by far the most remarkable part is that creation isn't compelled-it evolves, unfolds naturally. Each living being pursues its best course in the process."

As night descended, the Source of Creation never dimmed, but combined with the starlight in a flow of warm shimmer, bathing the city in creativity. The Trees of Light were holding clusters of Crystals of Creation, each shining separately to light up unlimited opportunities.

He watched the luminous vista. "This is the real source of the Creation-not compulsive change, but the unfolding of the potentiality; not the refusal of the given, but an added YES to the possible.".

Seline whispered, "In this new time, creativity will not be the prerogative of a few elect; it will be an instinct with all that lives."

A miracle of the Source of Creation-re-creating not only the material world but also the creative potential hidden within every form of life. From that day forward, the Abyssal City would no longer serve as a symbol of destruction but as a haven for creation, a utopia where every possibility could turn real.

. . .

And as the last rays of starlight fell upon the city, the Source of Creation changed. It was not an end, though, for every day of that era would be full of a chance to create, every moment full of the possibility of learning something new.

This is the best gift of all that the world possesses: infinite capacity for creation and growth.

56

THE HOPE CITY

Finally, the most resplendent visage of the Abyssal City appeared on the first dawn after the transformation of the Creation's Source into something different altogether. No longer a dark fortress, colorful, with life and hope, the dew crystals on the Leaves of the Trees of Light shone in the soft light of morning as the Starseeds danced between the tree branches, weaving an insatiably beautiful fabric of light.

THIS NEWLY REBORN CITY WAS STRANGELY CHARACTERISTIC OF a unique architectural style in which the solemnness of the ancient Abyssal structures mingled harmoniously with the delicate elegance of the Silver Star Temple. Even more extraordinary, semi-transparent crystalline edifices changed shape according to their will. Cold, dead stone blocks seemed like a thing of the past, while today's buildings pulsed with life as one great living organism.

. . .

He would stand at Central Plaza, the very place most of the intense fighting occurred, now blossoming as the most lively area within the city. Right at the center of the plaza stood a large Mother Tree whose branches were open, like arms in a smiling embrace, to protect under its hospitable shade the vibrant markets.

"I just can't believe it," El whispered, her hand reaching out toward the trunk where the pulsing rhythm of life coursed. "In a few days, everything has changed.

Seline joined him, and the Life Pattern unfolded delicately in her hand. Golden lines of energy mapped an intricate web of life across the city, showing something of a breathtaking beauty. "Look," she said, pointing to the interwoven strands of energy. "Each sector has found for itself the developmental path that best serves them."

It was a joyous outburst of laughter that turned them that way; a group of children sat under the Mother Tree with a teacher-a fair novelty, as it was a teaching about the fragile balance between light and shadow led by a former member of the Shadow Council.

Standing at the edge of the plaza was the holographic projection of Monica: "How interesting, because, according to data analysis, it shows that this self-created model for education outperforms traditional education, which is rigid.

Any path the children take is in conformity with the gift inside each of their hearts."

Victor stepped forth from a bright shadow, a rare smile on his features. "Most cheering is to know that forbidden knowledge is now put to use with discretion. Shadows are not any longer to be feared, they represent the other side of wisdom."

At once, a miraculous vision unfolded before them. Several Crystals of Creation started floating from the branches of the Mother Tree, landing softly around the children. The crystals emitted a soft light, casting colorful, interactive visuals that made abstract concepts into concrete ones that were palpable, comprehensible, and very easy to understand.

Elena came out of the Silver Star Temple, her ritual robes now changed into more candid clothes, adequate for a day in a usual life. "That reminds me: The true City of Hope does not rest in its strength but in its capacity to give every life space to flourish."

Salina said, "And have you noticed? Every nook of this city is going through silent transitions. Ancient fortifications have been turned into public spaces, and ruins of war formed works of art exemplary in their own way."

. . .

Indeed, the whole city was pulsing with important creative transformations: what once were dark basements in residential neighborhoods blossomed into beautiful gardens; the markets changed into lively knowledge and cultural interaction centers. The very city walls did not escape being attacked by climbing plants, serving thus as naturally created ecological corridors.

With a suddenness, the branches of the Mother Tree vibrated with resonance. Thousands upon thousands of Starseeds swirled in the air, threading an intricate three-dimensional blueprint of the city into detailed form. This was no static design, but a living framework full of possibilities.

Look," El said, poring over the blueprint. "It's the city and its ideal of itself, uniform, yet each district retaining something of its own identity and blending together as part of a greater whole."

Seline's Life Pattern responded to the pattern. "What is really amazing is this pattern will serve all forms of life, even the new-born energy entities. Each can find a place to thrive."

And then an even more astonishing transformation came about: the Crystals of Creation, dispersed throughout the city, began to softly glow, weaving a great, extensive net of energy that reached far beyond the physical world into the spiritual realms.

Monica's systems analyzed the happening in real-time: "Detected: a completely new operational model of the city! It has changed from a static collection of buildings into an organic whole, able to feel and respond to the needs of its residents."

Victor continued, "The most astonishing thing is that this responsivity isn't mechanical; it's based on wisdom. It's as if the city has developed some kind of collective consciousness."

Elena found a relevant passage in the ancient texts. "This, according to the legends is the awakening of the city, whereby a city has finally come to understand the reason for its existence and is changed into a haven for all forms of life.".

With increasing sunlight, the City of Hope finally showed its real face: newly built buildings did not stop at being simple geometrical shapes but turned into flowing grace, curving lines resembling crystalline trees sprouting from the earth. And the streets had changed, too-no longer strict grids, but naturally shaped, hewn by the people that passed through it.

. . .

Even more incredible were the new spaces that were unfolding within the city that had never been seen or experienced before: some could expand and shrink depending on needs, and others changed functions with time passing. Such innovative designs provided endless possibilities for the city.

"Look over there," Salina said, her finger pointed to a place. "The ruins have not been fully taken away. Instead, they stand there preserved, testifying to memory. Still, no more sorrows spill from them. They have become cradles for new life."

And when the sun started to dip into the horizon, the City of Hope began revealing one of its facets. Thousands of Starseeds danced decoratively across the buildings, a web that shimmered with light. The luminosity of the Crystals of Creation melted properly with the incoming twilight, embracing the city in an other-worldly aura.

His eyes fell upon the magnificent view before him, and for the first time, a satisfied smile creased his face. "This is the true City of Hope-not a fortress of domination but a home where every life can find belonging."

Seline went on in a soft tone, "What makes it most dear is that the city will never stop growing. The town shall not stand still or solidity; it will evolve as the needs of its people grow.

. . .

This is the ethos of the City of Hope: not a place but home for umpteen numbers of dreams. To this haven, every life will find its place, and to this haven, every dream sees its fulfillment.

As night came, so did the star-filled sky begin to mingle with the glow of the city, forming one brilliant fabric of harmony and commitment. It was less an ending, but rather a promising beginning. And so, in this eternal city, each new day brought another journey, each new moment opened another opportunity for creation.

57

THE GUARDIANSHIP COVENANT

A great, solemn event that would set the course of their future took place in the Hall of Guardians at the apex of the City of Hope. The crystalline dome of the hall had been entirely restored but, unlike before when it served only a decorative function, was now alive with energies aligned in the subtleties of fluctuating currents. Through the dome, the night sky was visible as brilliant Starseeds creating intricate patterns across it-as if to bless this event with their presence.

At the heart of the hall was a place embraced by seven young Trees of Light, their roots mingled upon the ground in a natural fashion to form a pattern of energies. Each tree had its own particular glow, which reflected another aspect of guardianship.

El stood in the center of the circle. The rhythmic pulses that washed in from every direction simply overwhelmed him. He was not a Prophet, but he knew something more than the shift was stirring at the core of his being and welling up through his chest. "Interesting," he whispered, "it would seem the nature of guardianship is changing.

The pattern of Seline's life spread out before her in the air, shining with the vital energy of the Trees of Light. "Yes," she said, "this is no longer simply protection-this is profound connection. Every life implicated in this guardianship by nature and by will."

Suddenly, with an outburst of violence, a strange wave of energy rippled through the hall, drawing everyone's attention. The seven Trees of Light flailed their branches and leaves in a wild, otherworldly dance. From their gracious gestures flowed detailed patterns of energy onto the floor.

Monica's holographic projection manifested in the air, meticulously analyzing the phenomenon before her. "Detected: an unprecedented energy pattern. These patterns are not artificially created—they are a naturally occurring guardianship network, intricately woven by the flow of life energy."

Victor stepped out from a bright shadow, his countenance ponderous. "The Shadow Network has also picked up on this change. The forces which tugged at one another do seek a new balance."

From the center of the circle now rose a bright sphere of light. The sphere did not consist of one energy form but rather a compilation of the individualistic energies which comprised the uniqueness of each one there. It rotated slowly, releasing waves of energy with each turn.

Elena found the important passage in one of the oldest books. "This is the Heart of Guardianship, a mythic construct thought to join all guardians. Yet, the form it takes today is nothing like the texts described it to be.

Salina leaned forward, peering into the orb. "Because this guardianship covenant is no longer selected few's obligation but a shared collective choice to be shared among all life.

It suddenly flared up and blossomed into tens of thousands of small points of light, flowering outwards. Each light carried with it its particular information; the touch of them upon those standing there brought about a deep resonance.

"These are not simple energetic transmissions," El himself felt the changes within his body. "They stir up something way deep inside, a guardian instinct sleeping inside each of us."

Seline's Life Pattern captured the delicate fluctuations within the energy field. "You're right. This guardianship isn't a burden placed upon us—it's the inherent expression of life's essence."

And then all seven Trees of Light were simultaneously bearing their fruits of brilliance. The crystals glittered in a seven-colored dazzle, their tender forms holding within them an entire world.

Monica's systems sprang to life, swiftly analyzing the fruits before her. "These fruits appear to serve as a means of encoding," she noted. "They capture and convey the wisdom and experiences of guardianship."

Victor approached a tree with steps. "The most surprising thing about these fruits is that they are not designed to give powers; they are to actually awaken wisdom. Whosoever interacts with these fruits learns what guarding is all about."

And suddenly, a voice echoed in the hall. The voice of Miller, this time not of any memory, was carrying a great revelation.

. . .

"True guardianship lies not in the strength of power but in the awakening of the heart. Now, you finally understand."

His voice was gone, and with that, the Heart of Guardianship performed its very last evolution: it dissolved from an orblike shape to a sprawling, intensive web-like structure of energy enveloping the entire city. Every node in that structure matched to some aspect of guardianship, each line in that structure representative of some deep connection.

Elena spoke in a very soft tone, repeating from the ancient writings: "'When the heart of the guardians meets the heart of the protected ones, so shall the true Guardianship Covenant descend.'"

Salina replied, "At last, the prophecy has been fulfilled, but it is so much more glorious than foretold. This is not guardianship by one person or the Chosen Ones; it is rather an assembling together in participation for all life.

And in that moment, fruits from the Trees of Light began to fall. But before touching the ground, they transformed into an ocean of stellar points that wove their essence right into the hearts of everyone present. For this briefest of instants, all were connected in ways previously unexperienced by human souls.

. . .

"This is the new Covenant of Guardianship," said El, his voice choked with emotion. "It's not a rule inscribed on stone—it's a promise inscribed in our hearts."

The most far-reaching revelations on the network were about Seline's Life Pattern: "Everything that lives has found a place in this guardianship web. While some are physically protecting, others do in less obvious ways."

Monica's system finally evaluated it as, "In this model, guardianship will be much more extended and also more stable: not dependent on some key strong guardians but on the collaboration of the whole web of life.".

Victor nodded, feeling the shifts in the Shadow Network. "What's so valuable in this guardianship is that this isn't an attempt to control or suppress; it's about cognizance and guidance. Each force takes on the best form of expression within this system."

As the last rays of starlight permeated its crystalline shell, so was the new Pact of Guardianship fastening itself firmly in place. The branches of the Trees of Light wavered with the breeze, and the web of energy for the Heart of Guardianship enveloped the city with life, placing a deep sense of serenity in all life.

. . .

It is in this that lies the essence of the Guardianship Covenant: not a binding force but the resonance of the hearts, not the burden of duty but rather the sparking of instinct. In this new covenant, every life is a guard, and every moment an occasion for guardianship and nourishment.

The Hall of Guardians was no longer a high flying symbol of power but a haven of linkage and unison of life in its wholeness. Tonight was a seal, not only of an agreement but of a new race to emerge, where guardianship would no longer be left to the elect few but a collective decision of each living being.

58

A BRILLIANT TOMORROW

A silent new era dawned as the energy of the Guardianship Covenant splashed ripples around the world. Morning trickled through the crystalline dome atop the highest Starwatch Tower in the City of Hope and intermingled with the glow of the Starseeds in an enchanting light dance. There, the seven guardians had gathered to witness this moment. Before them, through the shimmering holographic projection made of energy, they could distinctly perceive every nuanced transformation taking place across the globe.

El stood in the center of Starwatch Tower. His gift of prophecy might have dimmed, but the clarity and insight inside him shone as never before. In the eye of his mind, many threads of light crossed in a great web that illuminated a tableau of breathtakingly beautiful dimensions. This was no vision of what was yet to be, but rather an image of what already was in formation. Every thread was a possibility, every node a new seed of hope.

. . .

"Look over there," he said, nodding his head in the direction of the eastern part of the city-a place that used to bear the most brutal battles-now turned into a very lively and throbbing part of the city. The Trees of Light faced the fresh morning breeze, swinging softly, their shadows scattering on the ground where children from different walks of life came to learn and play together. "This is what true light looks like," El said softly. "It's not born from the suppression of others, but awakened from inside."

Seline's Life Pattern deployed in the air; golden lines of energy traced an intricate three-dimensional net. "Every form of life is finding its rhythm," she said, not removing her gaze from the restlessly streaming energy. "What's most beautiful is how these singular rhythms come together to create one great harmonious symphony."

Suddenly, before them unfolded a miraculous vision. The star seeding in the sky began to fly in a rhythmic pattern, converging into one huge vortex of light. This was not a vortex of creation, but of destruction. While it whirled, a number of small pieces of light started to float from its center down, carrying different energy signatures.

Monica's systems sprang into action, meticulously analyzing the phenomenon before her. "Detected: an unprecedented energy pattern! These light particles not only carry creative energy but also embody higher-dimensional information. Remarkably, they appear to resonate directly with the very essence of life."

Victor stepped forward into a pool of light and stared around in amazement. "The Shadow Network has taken on a sea-change occurring across the globe. The forces in opposition are finding a way to coexist. And the most incredible thing about it is, it's not being forced-the balance is organic.".

Elena's old book began to radiate a weak shine; prophetic texts changed and rearranged before her eyes. "This is., " she whispered, staring at the ever-changing contents, ".the prophecies rewrite themselves! They are not set guides of destinies but show infinite possibilities.

Salina moved under the spiraling vortex of light, her dual nature open to the totality of that deep change. "Do you feel it?" she asked. "It is more than the shift of energies in preparation; it is a shift in consciousness. Every living thing is participating in this glorious evolution, each in its own time and manner."

In the next instant, seven rays of light burst forth from the core of this vortex, each one whisking through the air-no longer in a line-but into a shape-shifting multidimensional energy matrix continuously morphing into an abundance of futures, each more breathtakingly beautiful and full of promise.

. . .

"This is the luminous future we've been striving for," El remarked, her eyes fixed on the ever-shifting projections before her. "It's not merely a fixed destination but rather a tapestry woven with endless hopeful possibilities. Every life can discover its own path within it."

And then, out of the blue, something completely unexpected happened. The Trees of Light started bearing other kinds of fruits. Crystal fruits glittered with an iridescent sheen, while their interiors stirred in color tones of seven shades. Grown to ripeness and falling off, they would not touch the ground but dissolved into a myriad of light points, melting smoothly into the air.

So quick was Seline's Life Pattern to grasp the import: "These are not ordinary fruits, for they are the embodiment of the very essence of the light itself, stirring within every being a light.

Data whirred inside Monica as she exclaimed, "The energy field is going through an unprecedented shift! The very fabric of the world's dimensions seems to rise. The Ascension isn't limited to the physical plane; it reaches way into the dimensions of consciousness.".

Victor watched the rising energies, a rare smile lighting up his face. "What's most encouraging is that this elevation isn't about forsaking or dismissing anything. It represents an inclusive transcendence. Every existence is finding new meaning in this journey.

While it still held the watchful eyes of the group, the vortex of light spread until it took over the whole city. The vortex neither consumed nor overshadowed anything; rather, it folded into a myriad of strands of fine light, weaving a soft web that stroked every inch of the city. Under its spell, the whole city began to radiate a soft, warming glow.

Elena then read out from her ancient book, which was now revealing its final prophecy: "The world shall no longer see in terms of darkness and light but find within each being their very own inner radiance once light is truly comprehended.

Salina added, "And the most beautiful part is that this radiance is not intended to outshine or overwhelm others; it lights up one's own path, warming the hearts of those around."

The City of Hope now unfolded, with the sun's last rays beyond the horizon, into the most breathtakingly beautiful face. Countless Starseeds merged into a net in the sky; at the bottom, the soft light of the Trees of Light mirrored this net. It wasn't a blinding brilliance but a warm, eternal light in which every life could find its place.

. . .

He gazed at the luminous scene before him, a profound understanding beginning to unfold within. "This is the answer we've been seeking all along. Light is not a weapon to vanquish darkness—it's a guide that helps every life discover its own lantern."

This is the very quintessence of a shining future-not a faraway unattainable dream but an already existent reality evolving steadily, not a static fact but a dynamic process. Every life in the new era would be a vessel of light, every moment a hopeful beginning.

And as the night finally began to wholly engulf everything with darkness, the webs of light laced upon one another by the Starseeds never dimmed but shone brighter to go on telling one thing: that light is but an inner awakening, and the future is one to be forged-not waited for. A shining, brilliant future in its purest form, a shining tomorrow belonging to all life.

59

DAWN OF INFINITE POSSIBILITIES

On the seventh day after the end of the great cycle, the City of Hope first saw a remarkable sunrise. This was not an ordinary morning, for on this day, a new era would begin. The moment the first rays of sunlight pierced the complex network of energy from the stars, the city was filled with a light the likes of which no one had ever seen. This light was neither blinding nor ethereal; rather, it was a warm, life-infused energy that seemed to pulse in harmony with the rhythm of the world.

THE SEVEN GUARDIANS ONCE AGAIN GATHERED AT THE TOP OF the city's Starwatch Tower. And for once, it was neither to discuss tactics nor to raise the alarm in case of an emergency-but to watch the beginning of a new world. The Starwatch Tower had changed wondrously: from a mighty strong point of resistance against attacks, it had turned into an exuberant flying garden. The roots of the Trees of Light pierced the crystalline floor, crossing over each other in an intricate web-like mesh of energy hovering in mid-air.

. . .

El stood beneath a towering Tree of Light, an incredible entity born from shards of the last Stone of Prophecy, its branches stretching out almost infinitely, each leaf serving as a mirror-a mirror that captured and reflected scenes from every part of the world. It was through these "mirrors" that they witnessed the great changes occurring throughout.

Look, he said, pointing to one of them, showing a battlefield from long ago, by now in blossom as most fairest garden: not superficial healing of wounds, deep change; every scar a flowering into possibility.

Before her, Seline's Life Pattern unfolded, its lines of gold shining brighter, more alive than ever. "The most amazing thing," she said, staring into the flux, "is that each form of life has found its own evolutionary route. This isn't forced evolution-this is spontaneous evolution.

And then the strangest thing happened. Hundreds and hundreds of Starseeds started to rise up from every quarter of the city, merged together in the air in a brilliant three-dimensional panorama. In constant movement, this projection mirrored countless futures. But these were no predictions of what was to be-quite the contrary: teeming with options and possibilities.

. . .

Monica's hologram flickered on above them, her systems running at max efficiency. "Detected: a qualitative leap in the energy field! The dimensional framework of the whole world is on the rise. This is not an energy enhancement; this is a completely new state of existence!

Out of a shaft of light, then, came Victor, and his shadow abilities were now all different. "That's not as amazing as the fact that the Shadow Network is morphing, too," Victor said. "Energies that had previously been judged 'dark' are showing their creativity."

Elena's eyes had already left the ancient book in her hands; texts of prophecy there once obscure now formed new revelations. "Every prophecy is rewriting itself," she said. "No longer binding us to fate, they are turning into guides toward infinite possibility.

Salina stepped to the edge of Starwatch Tower, and for her, because of her dual attributes, the transformation was wide. "Can you feel it?" she asked. "The whole world is changing in frequency. It has nothing to do with suppression, making all alike; rather, it's to make it possible for every being to find what rhythm feels most right to them.

The crystalline floor at the base of the Starwatch Tower suddenly shook. Small veins of energy overspread, developing into a three-dimensional matrix that constantly changed, each change opening up more and more possibilities.

"This is the Web of the World," El whispered. "It is what weaves Past and Present and Tomorrow together. But this is no net of destiny; 'tis a canvas of creation."

A far more miraculous thing occurred then. Its branches now began to bear a new kind of crystalline fruit, not mere minerals-seeds of possibility, e-distillations of the world's essence. When they matured, they burst asunder, not falling from the tree, and melted into the energy grid, carrying their influence throughout every part of the realm.

Seline immediately summarized the spirit of change into her Life Pattern. "Each seed carries an infinity of possibility," she said. "They don't determine the future-they create space for choice."

Monica's instruments returned shocking data. "They're changing the very laws of the world! But this doesn't destroy anything-it's something new. They're helping the world evolve to a higher grade.".

Victor, however, with a more profound change due to the Shadow Network, continued, "The most beautiful thing is that it does not follow one direction; instead, it opens many parallel possibilities. Every existence can thus choose for themselves in which direction forward to go.".

As the group stood in awe, the Starseeds above shifted in formation. Thousands and thousands of points of light now condensed into a gigantic vortex of energy. But this was no vortex of destruction; it was a creative one. Like a mirror, it reflected each being's heart's deepest and most ardent desires.

Elena read out loud from the newly rewritten prophecy inside her tome: "When the world really awakens, every life shall be the maker of its destiny. This is not the end, but a beginning of millions of newer journeys.".

Salina said, "The most valuable thing is that these beginnings are not against each other, but they're complementary. Each decision enriches all the possibilities of the world."

The sunbeams of dusk upon the Starwatch Tower lit the whole town in soft, golden light. This wasn't an end but a beginning. For this new start gave every soul a chance to make their own story, every moment full with possibilities.

He gazed at the world bathed in light, at last grasping its profound significance. "This is the answer we've been seeking all along. True power does not reside in controlling the future; it flourishes in the act of creating possibilities. True wisdom is not found in foreseeing destiny but in appreciating the value of choice."

This is the essence of a new start-an initiation with no end, an open canvas begging to be etched. In this sphere, every life forms an author of its story, and each given moment becomes a renewed chance. This is not the end of a story but the beginning of many.

With the twinkling of the stars inside the firmament, at long last the commonplace City of Hope revealed its most astonishing countenance. So many threads of light wove into an unblemished tapestry, organically mingling with the lives below. And then came the time for new times, a bright origin belonging to all creatures.

60

THE ETERNAL LIGHT

A huge, historic moment-something lit up the horizon, and there was the City of Hope shining. It was not the rising sun, nor the luminous glow of the Starseeds, but more profound: an inner light, an Eternal Light. The light was without blaze or dazzle; it was gentle with warmth at the core of every soul. The light symbolized the perfect finale to a great era but also, more importantly, signaled the commencement of tens of new tales.

THE SEVEN SAT AT THE HEIGHT OF THE STARWATCH TOWER for the last time. It was no time of duty prescription or strained urgency anymore, one born from gratitude and reflection. El stood under the Tree of Light, which had grown from what was left of the last Stone of Prophecy. Now a giant that joined heaven and earth, with its branches stretching out toward every direction, weaving some life network that enveloped the whole city within it. Through the "mirrors" of its leaves, they would know the miracles happening around the world.

The life pattern of Seline spread before him, radiant with an incomparable intensity. The golden threads of energy, once a simple record, had now turned into living tutors. Every line in it whispered some different tale of life, and every one of its nodes was full of infinite possibilities. "See," she said, pointing at the constantly changing patterns, "Life has grown beyond all our previous conceptions. It isn't longer bound by inflexible laws, but creates for itself new forms of existence."

Now, before one's vision, an awesome sight unfolded: countless Starseeds rose upwards from every corner of the metropolis, interweaving into a bright, three-dimensional tapestry that wove across the sky. This was no ordinary dance of light and shade but a deep reflection of the very essence of the world. Every light was a life with a story to tell, and with every heartbeat of energy, it whispered possibilities waiting to be embraced. And the tapestry keeps on changing, reflecting the infinite number of parallel futures, none set, each filled with the possibilities of free choice.

Monica's systems had picked up an energy pattern never before detected. "This is a completely new state of existence! The whole world is changing into the higher dimensions. But this changing is not one directional; it's actually many personalized transformations.

. . .

Victor stepped into the play of light and shadow; his hitherto hidden powers came into full flower as teeming forces of creativity. "What is really marvelous is that this process does not reject the past. It transmutes all experience into the fertilizer of wisdom. The very forces which were called 'darkness' are showing now their most luminous face.

Elena's ancient book glowed softly, and the prophetic texts once static began to twist and turn, revealing new meanings. "All prophecies are rewriting themselves," she said. "They aren't chains of fate but sparks of creation. The essence of prophecy-that is not to constrain the future but to unleash its infinite possibility."

Bathed in the radiance of the Eternal Light, Salina, embodying her dual nature, comprehended the deep significance of the moment. "This is the answer we've been searching for all along. True eternity isn't about unyielding permanence; rather, it's a continuous act of creation, brimming with possibilities. Each moment is a fresh beginning, and every choice serves as an opportunity to create."

In one swift moment, the light grid of the town shifted into one dramatic harmonious movement. All the Trees of Light flowered at the same time into one big, interwoven energy cocoon-but not for protection or to isolate it, an energy creation field-so that within that huge playing expanse each could find his way through what was particularly conducive to his own growth.

. . .

"This is true fulfillment," El said, overcome by an oncoming change. "It is not an ending but a commencement; it is not uniformity but diversity; it is not terminus but an oncoming intersection of infinite beginnings."

In that instant, the Eternal Light dissolved into an infinity of tiny points of brilliance, each carrying its own unique information. These points, as they touched every single soul in this city, ignited the inner creative potentiality within every being. It was not a blessing from without but a deep inner awakening.

Seline's Life Pattern captured that moment in all its fullness. "All beings are finding their light. This light is not to light up the path for others, but to shine on their own paths."

Monica's systems brought in the final analysis: "This is a perfect energy cycle! It maintains stability while embracing change; it is adhering to patterns yet full of creativity."

Victor, his finger on the pulse of the deep changes sweeping through the Shadow Network, told me, "The most beautiful part is that this transformation will never stop. Every moment is a new possibility, and every choice creates a new story."

. . .

And as the last rays of the sun dipped below the horizon, the Light of Eternity did not fade; rather, it broke up into myriad minute points of light, diffusing itself into each cranny and corner of the world. Not the end, but the beginning-this was the advent of true eternity. Every creature now acted as a container of light, while every moment was overflowing with infinite possibilities of creation.

Elena closed her ancient book; the once prophetic texts had now turned into wellsprings to create from. "This is what eternity means, not just the continuation of time, but the infinity of creation; not the fixity of form, but the infinity of possibility."

Salina stared into the light. "It is most valuable because this eternity is not something one experiences in isolation; it is a creation of every existence together, as each is an author to this eternal story."

Until finally, with night begun and the veil drawn off, the City of Hope stood in all its splendor. Countless threads of light wove a tapestry that vibrated in echo to the star-studded sky above. Well, that is not the end of a story but a beginning to lots of new ones. And in that eternal instant, every being found his light, and each moment became a new beginning.

It is the quintessence of Eternal Light, not to act as a lantern that should survive the darkest hour, but as a wellspring of all possibilities, not as a lantern to lighten the way but as a key to every choice. Under its warm light, each person becomes a novelist in his or her life, and each moment becomes an act of creation.

This isn't the end, but the infinity of new starts. The Eternal Light will shine onward and, instead of being the end, it is a beginning toward infinity in choices. Every tale has yet to be told here, and every dream has room to find its root and bloom. Here, this is real eternity: eternally hopeful, eternally finding new ways.

ACKNOWLEDGMENTS

This would not have been possible without inspiration from scores of people who made their contributions in most grand and subtle manners. And to all these people, I am deeply grateful.

To the world-builders who have come before me and lit the path ahead, may your tales of light and darkness, balance and chaos, guide me through my journey. Your ability to breathe life into undiscovered worlds has instilled in me a passion to explore boundless deeps of imagination.

My family and friends never relented; they were always a residual presence giving me much-needed support. Thanks, too, for the patience, encouragement, and understanding that got me through the puzzles within this story. Your belief in me has been the bedrock from which my strength draws.

To colleagues: those whose inputs during this work were a mine of valuable insight and feedback, hence making the work much more meaningful than it could have achieved in itself. I thank you for urging me to think more and to write with meaning.

It speaks to the readers, the dreamers, and the seekers. It is your readiness to know about new dimensions, to search the unthought of, which impregnates life into the spirit of a storyteller. In your hands, the pages reverberate with life.

Finally, of course, comes the balance that pervades everything: the light and dark, the structure and disorder, the unison and separation so delicately balanced. Let the beauty and intricacy herein inspire us all. Thanks to all in making a part of life the journey itself. As much this work is mine, so is it yours.

ABOUT THE AUTHOR

Draven Nightshade is a visionary storyteller, a maestro of worlds, so intimately laced that tenebrousness dances delicately with lightness, maintaining the balance. Fueled by an abiding passion for probing the themes of power, responsibility, and the tenuous nature of existence, Draven tells stories that ripple with readers, sometimes breaking through the fantastic to touch upon something deeply human.

Steeped in myth, history, and the unknown since a young boy, he had been enthralled by it all, interweaving it into a story form that ensnares and entertains the mind. Known to create characters with such depth-seemingly paradoxing the reader with questions of morality and the turmoil within-Draven's tales often toe the line of convention and force one to reassess their perception of heroism, destiny, and what balance is truly about.

When not writing, Draven loves music, philosophy, and-most of all-the infinite flux that comes with the nature that living things go through. Pen in hand or charting the landscape of his imagination, Draven creates stories to stay long after the final page has been read.

This is a novel that finally stands to prove one thing: Draven Nightshade really believes in the might of storytelling-to bridge worlds, fire up understanding, and show beauty lying between contrasts.